FEARLESS

TIA LOUISE

This book is a work of fiction. Names, characters, places, and incidents are products of the author's imagination or are used fictitiously. Any resemblance to actual events or locales or persons, living or dead, is entirely coincidental.

Fearless
Copyright © TLM Productions LLC, 2022
Printed in the United States of America.

Cover design by Lori Jackson Design.

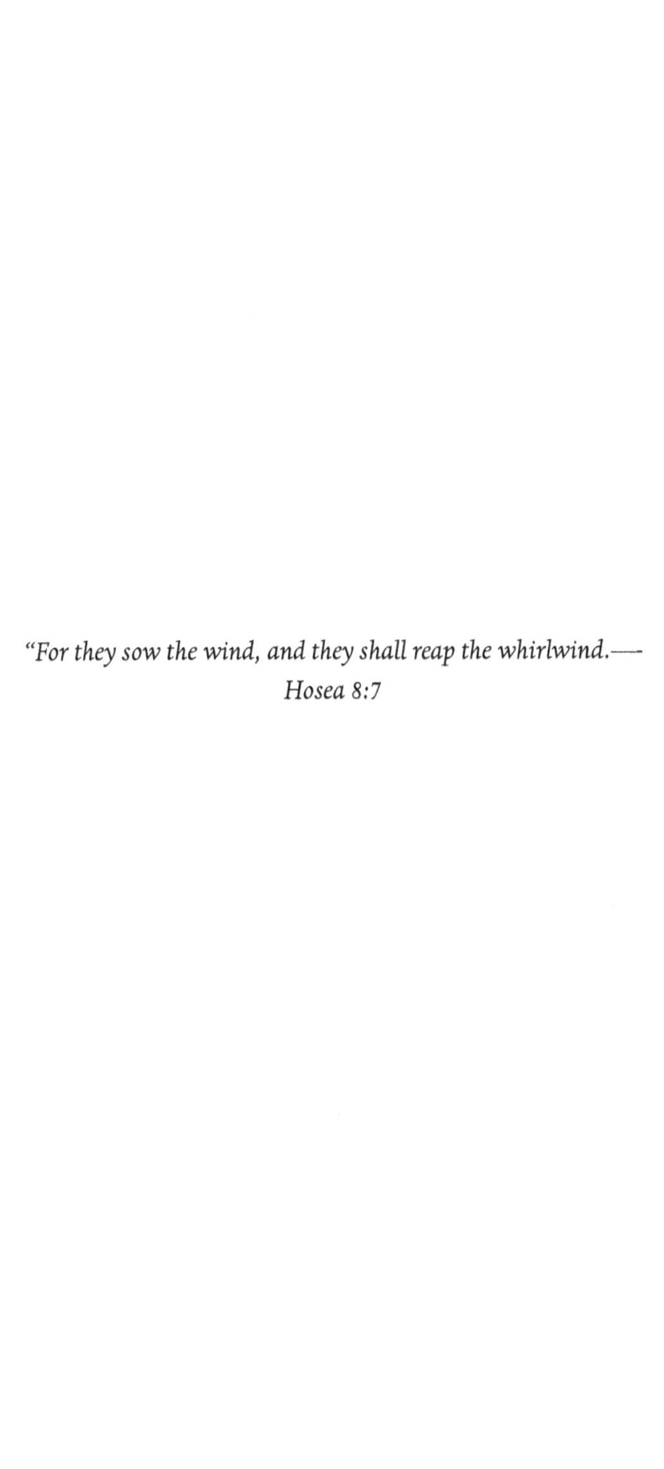

"For they sow the wind, and they shall reap the whirlwind.—-
Hosea 8:7

“God gave us roses so we’d have memories in December.”
—Variation on JM Barrie

PROLOGUE
Blake

"**G**O BACK TO THE PARTY." THE MAN'S VOICE IS QUIETLY menacing, black eyes glittering in the reflection of the green lawyer's lamp. "Don't make me remind you what happens when you get in my way."

The tiny, silver scar tingles above my left eyebrow, and my heart beats like a rabbit trying to escape my ribcage. I'm way out of my league with Victor Petrova, but I never back down from a bully.

I'm more accustomed to standing up to bored, mean-girl bullies. You know the ones, with too much money and no imagination. This guy is on another level. He's the embezzling accountant who's sleeping with my mother, hurting my sister, and rumored to be connected to the mob type of bully.

But I'm the only one who will face him.

The last time I stood up to him, I ended up in the emergency department, and I confess, my confidence took a hit.

Squaring my shoulders, I defy him. "It's not a party, it's a wake, and my father's estate is most definitely my business, especially with my mother being... how she is."

Victor's thin lips curl, exposing large teeth behind a groomed mustache. "How is your mother, Blake?"

Exactly how you want her—blind to your bullshit. I don't say it out loud.

"She hasn't been well since my father died. I'm the oldest, so if she's incapable of doing business—"

"She hired me to handle your father's business. You're only sixteen. Now stop being a little shit and run along. Don't worry, I won't touch your weekly allowance."

"The way you don't touch my sister?"

His eyes flash, and my pulse jumps. But he immediately controls his expression, leaning back with a slimy grin. "Jealous?"

Bile floods my throat. "Hana's only thirteen. If I find out what she said is true... it'll be worse for you if I can prove it."

He shoves the brown folder forward and stands abruptly, rounding my father's desk too fast. "Hana is an addict, and everyone knows it. Hurling accusations will only land you on the wrong side of what's happening here."

"My sister likes to party, but she's not a liar. Too bad for you, pedophilia went out with the seventies."

His meaty fist clenches, and a shudder races down my body. "You'll shut your stupid mouth, or I'll shut it for you."

Setting my jaw, I hold my eyes open, my posture straight, my tone steady. "I hope you *are* stupid enough to hit me again. It'll be the last bit of evidence I need to get you out of our lives for good."

He stops just short of where I stand, unclenching his fist long enough to grasp my upper arm and jerk me hard enough to leave a bruise. "If you know what's good for your mother, for your sister, and for you, you won't ever threaten me again."

My feet skitter across the Persian rug as he drags me to the door and tosses me out of the room. A hall table breaks my fall with a loud crash, another bruise, and the heavy wooden door slams shut. The metallic sound of a key turning in the lock seals the deal.

"Shit," I hiss through gritted teeth.

After my father was found dead in his chair at the club two weeks ago, my mother gave that rat Victor Petrova the keys to the kingdom. The doctors said it was a heart attack, even though Charles van Hamilton had no history of cardio-vascular disease.

Poor Mamá delayed her annual ski trip to St. Moritz by a week to play the role of the grieving widow, and she's been in her room popping pills and fake-crying her way through bot-tles of champagne with her idiot friends ever since.

No comfort for her two daughters, not that she ever has been. Not that dear ole Dad ever was either. He liked to say it took more than forty hours a week to support our privileged lifestyle, but it was bullshit.

The van Hamiltons have more money than God, and Hana and I both have trust funds that will keep us wealthy well into retirement when we each turn twenty-one, should we choose to work. Dad only cared for us to look good in public and not embarrass him.

Done and done. *But behind closed doors…*

It's my turn to make a fist, and I bang it against the deep green marble tabletop. Victor will ruin us, and I don't have any allies in New York—at least, none who can help me with some-one like him. I scrub my fingers against my forehead, threading them into my raven hair trying to think of something, *anything* to get him out of our lives.

"Blake, is that you?" The deep voice startles me, and I turn so fast, a miniature knight in actual chain mail on a matching horse falls off the table.

The man steps forward quickly and catches it, putting his

body in direct proximity to mine, filling my nose with the rich scent of sage and citrus. It floods my brain with memories, and as he stands straighter, my throat grows tighter.

Hutchence Winston is a blast from my father's discarded past, a face I haven't seen in years. A face that is now a grown man's, towering over me with dark hair curling at his temples. He's dressed in a proper suit for a wake, and his broad shoulders and muscular arms strain beneath the expensive fabric. My knees actually weaken.

I've known a lot of men, and I'm not easily impressed. Still, he's always had this effect on me, since we were kids. For a moment, I almost forget I have a very real problem.

Key word: *Almost*.

Clearing my throat, I slide my hands down, straightening the sheer black overlay on the short, ivory-silk dress I'm wearing.

"Hutch." I hold out a hand to shake. "What are you doing here? I thought the Winstons dropped off my father's friends list years ago."

The truth is, the Winstons and the van Hamiltons have a prickly history, going back to the founding of Hamiltown, our namesake village near the South Carolina coast.

It's a long story for another day.

Hutch's dark brow lowers over his stunning pale green eyes made more stunning by his suntanned olive skin. A short beard covers his cheeks, accentuating his full lips, and he curls his perfect nose at me.

"I'm not here for you or your father." There's the annoyed tone I remember. "I was visiting my dad while on my leave, and your uncle asked me to check on you. I assured him you were fine, but he insisted I come here in person."

"And here you are." Crossing my arms, I do my best to pretend I don't give a shit. "You know, I've never understood your relationship with my great uncle."

"Doesn't surprise me. Have you ever had a real friendship in your life?"

That stings, and I blink quickly to stop the burn in my eyes. *Bastard.*

"Shows what you know." Shaking my long hair back, I force a smile. "I guess you think being in the army makes you some kind of hero now?"

"I'm an officer in the Marine Corps. I don't know about *hero*, but it's a worthwhile occupation."

He says it like another challenge, as if to ask what I'm doing with my life that's so great, and it gives me an idea.

Stepping forward, I place my hand on his solid forearm, lowering my voice. "I'm sorry. I was rude. It's been a difficult week."

The corner of his left eye twitches. Hutch has known me too long to fall for any sweet act, but if I'm going to get his help, perhaps I can use the unspoken tension between us to my advantage.

My touch doesn't put him at ease, but his voice gentles. "I'm sure it's been a hard time. Your uncle was worried you might need assistance… somehow."

"You're so kind."

"I'm not kind. I don't want to be here, and I'm sure you have handlers."

"You've always known everything." I do my best to flirt, sliding my fingers along his Armani suit. "You pretend I'm the snob, but I think you're far more snobbish than I am."

"I don't play games, Blake." He catches my hand from rising to his shoulder, and the muscle in his jaw moves. "I've fulfilled my obligation. You look fine to me."

"You look pretty fine to me, too." Holding his hand, I pull it behind my back so my body presses to his, my small, teenage breasts flatten against his solid chest. His eyes flare, and I rise on my toes to speak in his ear, allowing my lips to brush his skin. "A little southern comfort would be nice."

I'm willing to kiss him if it'll do the trick, but when I meet his gaze again, fire is in his eyes. I can't tell if he's turned on or furious—or both. He yanks his hand out of mine and grips my shoulders, moving my body away from his.

"You're drunk if you think I'd blow my reputation that way."

"So you're thinking about it?" My voice is sultry, and I can't tell. *Is he?*

"You're high."

The door behind him flies open, and we both look up to see Victor glaring at us. His gaze melts into a slimy grin, and his eyes glide from my flushed cheeks down to my breasts, barely hidden beneath the thin fabric.

"I didn't think you'd still be here. Were you waiting for an escort to your bedroom?"

My skin literally crawls at the insinuation, and Hutch looks ready to explode.

"I'm taking care of her," he growls, clutching my upper arm and hauling me down the hall, away from the rat.

We're on the other side of the house before he slows, looking up and around the passage. "Is your room even on this floor?"

"You're hurting me." My complaint earns me a short jerk.

"Then stop acting like a child." His jaw is tight, and I'm pissed he's so fucking hot.

Hutch Winston activated my sex drive three years ago. I was thirteen and he was eighteen, and Dad brought Hana and me to visit Uncle Hugh in Hamiltown for the Fourth of July celebration. Hutch stood on that pier in his swim trunks, a mountain of mouthwatering muscles, and I ovulated for the first time. He seems to have improved with age.

Releasing my arm, he's still seething. "Go to your room."

"You're not my dad."

In a blink, he grips my arm again, anger rippling off him in hot waves. An uninvited thought sneaks through my brain, *I wonder what it's like when his restraint slips…*

"You're out of control. I'm going to speak to your mother, then I'm leaving." He pauses a moment, dropping his square chin and exhaling. "Sorry for your loss."

He leaves abruptly, and I collapse against the door. Hutch Winston is a force of nature, and I fucking blew it. So much for getting his help, not that I've ever laid the groundwork to ask him for it.

Scrubbing my fingers against my forehead, I search for a solution. I should've just thrown myself in his arms and started crying or done something damsel in distress-like. I should have told him my fears about Victor.

Like that would've gone any better.

Hutch wouldn't buy my tears any more than he'd fall for my teen seduction. Still, he might have listened to my story. My shoulders fall, and I open the door to my massive bedroom. It's too late for post-mortems. If I'm going to get Victor away from my mother and protect Hana, I have to do it myself.

I'm just getting ready for bed when my phone rings, and I look down to see my mother is FaceTiming me. I accept the call, and I can tell by her eyes she's tipsy.

Correction, she's drunk.

"Blake van Hamilton, you are to pack your things at once." Her eyelids flutter as she sweeps her arm dramatically. "I've just secured a spot for you at Bishop of the Holy Family. You're leaving on the ten o'clock train."

My jaw drops, and my entire room shifts to the side. "What the hell? What are you talking about?"

"You'd better rein in that tongue, young lady. It's a Catholic boarding school, all girls. Just what you need to improve your attitude."

A tiny explosion goes off in my brain. Am I old enough to have a stroke? These are not my mother's words. My mother doesn't think about me enough to say these words to me.

"No!" I blurt, cringing at how childish I sound. "What about my schoolwork? Hana? I can't leave."

"The sisters have assured me they can work out your schedule. Roman will be down to collect your things in two hours. End of discussion."

I feel like I'm drowning in a vat of molasses, struggling to find my bearings through thick sludge. How could this happen? What the fuck would wake her from her champagne stupor long enough to even come up with such a plan? Should I run? Hide out at Debbie's until she finally leaves for St. Moritz?

I'm trying to decide when my eyes land on his, lurking in the background, stony green staring back at me through my mother's computer screen.

Bastard.

Hutch did this.

It's only a moment before my screen goes black, and I start to scream. That meddling, arrogant, know-it-all *bastard*. He's playing right into their hands.

I'm being shipped to a boarding-school prison, where I can't help anyone. He's ruining everything, and at sixteen, I'm powerless to change it.

Fisting the sides of my hair, I squeeze my eyes shut and internally lose my shit. It's the only place I've ever been allowed. I grab a pillow off my bed and throw it across the room, then I charge after it and kick it all the way back to my bed.

Grinding my jaw I go to the window and watch as he leaves in his car. He's done his damage. Hutch Winston is going to regret this.

I won't be sixteen forever, and I'll never forgive him for what he's done.

CHAPTER 1

Hutch

Present day

"I CAN'T KIDNAP THEM, HUGH. YOU HAVE TO GIVE ME A REASON to bring them here." I'm sweating my ass off in Hugh van Hamilton's lavish greenhouse inside his six-thousand-square-foot, sprawling estate.

It's one of the oldest homes in Hamiltown (Yes, *Hamiltown*), and it's situated at the end of a quarter-mile-long driveway canopied by arching live oak trees.

The van Hamiltons founded this borough around the turn of the last century, and their massive family estate and the wizened man growing old inside it are all that's left of their lurid legacy.

Almost.

His two spoiled nieces, daughters of his dead nephew, are alive and well in New York City, and from what I've heard, neither of those Park Avenue princesses is interested in returning to their hometown in the swamplands near the coast of South Carolina.

At eighty, Hugh is five-ten and a hundred twenty pounds

soaking wet. His gray hair is neatly smoothed away from his face, and he's wearing khakis and a button-down shirt with a light blue bow tie. His beige felt Stetson is neatly arranged beside his glasses on a nearby table.

He's a relic of the days when men took casual attire seriously; when appearance mattered more than anything. When transgressions were hidden from view, and family secrets were swept under the rug or shoved into the closet or ignored.

I am not of those days.

My family, the Winstons, were town founders as well, but we didn't fight for prestige. My father was obsessed with Wall Street, and when I was young, he moved to an apartment on the Upper East Side of New York City where he still lives almost year-round.

My mother was a "Hamil-townie." She raised my two younger siblings and me here in this "wholesome" village, in a nice house I now own, and until the day she died, she taught us to value hard work and honesty.

We have as much money and "culture" as the van Hamiltons, but I was never part of the spoiled, silver-spoon crowd. The one time I visited my father in the big city, I wasn't impressed— not with his flirty female assistant nor with the kids my age and younger. They struck me as desperately bored, filling the void with meaningless sex and mindless parties, or pulling the wings off butterflies.

They were either entirely corrupt or thoughtlessly cruel.

I disliked them intensely, except for her. She was different. Still, I can't imagine Blake wanting to be here.

"Sorry for the heat." Hugh tugs the crocheted shawl tighter around his arms, on top of his tailored three-piece suit. "Ever since my last round of chemo, I've had a hard time maintaining any body heat."

He's practically a skeleton, and it hurts me to see him this way. This man has become like a surrogate father to me through the years. He's not perfect, but who is these days? I help him as much as I can, and he's given me advice the two times I asked for it.

So, I try to lighten the mood. "Next time I'll wear shorts and carry a Yeti full of hard seltzer."

"Heavens." He chuckles, shaking his head, and affection warms my heart. "Don't insult me."

"Judging from this favor, I'm trying to figure out what kind of pied piper you think I am."

"Blake will come home because I asked her to." He shakes his head and adds quietly, "Hana will do whatever her sister tells her to do."

The last time I saw Blake, she was a striking sixteen-year-old with long, dark hair and fierce, silvery blue eyes. She didn't starve herself to fit some WASPy stereotype, unlike her pale, younger sister Hana. Blake was independent, beautiful, tough, and when I saw the way her mother's accountant looked at her, a man twenty years her senior, my vision went red.

I went to her mother, who immediately shipped her off to a Catholic boarding school I recommended. It was the best move to keep her safe, but I know she hated me for it. I saw her eyes right before her mother ended the call. She would've killed me if she'd been in the room.

"She won't be happy to see me." My tone is somber.

Hugh arches an eyebrow at me. "I didn't think you cared if people were happy to see you."

"I don't, but I also don't go looking for trouble."

"Sometimes you have to manage a little trouble to get what you need."

"She's the type of trouble I *don't* need. If you don't give me a reason, she'll slam the door in my face."

"It's better if I don't tell you my reasons, but trust me. They need to leave the city, at least for a little while. Ignorance is protection."

His words make the skin on my neck tighten. Hugh has known me since I was a teenager, since before I retired from the Marines and became a private investigator, and the last time he wouldn't give me a reason, I was staring at a dead body in the trunk of his chauffeur's car.

As a PI, I'm not required to report my clients to law enforcement, but I do my best not to take on more than I can handle. "That's not how the law sees it."

"It's how the people who matter see it." He walks over to a mahogany bar trolley waiting at the glass wall. "Can I offer you a drink? I can't have alcohol anymore, but I can watch you enjoy it."

"I'm not much of a day drinker, thanks."

"By the book. Good man." He nods, turning from the trolly. "I have to say, I wasn't sure about the beard, but it suits you. It adds to your *persona*."

I automatically scratch the scruff on my cheek, unsure if he's giving me a compliment or a dig. I'm not sloppy. I'm not a suit guy, but my black jeans and boots, navy Henley and Carhart jacket are appropriate for my work.

"Blake and I haven't spoken in seven years. Does she even consider this place her home? She's never lived here."

"I sent her a letter. It's possible you might not need to do anything at all, but if a week goes by… Don't give it a week. If she doesn't come here in a few days, I need you to follow up. My grandniece is a smart girl, but she thinks she can control her world, and she can't."

I know the truth of that statement.

Stepping over to a potted tree, I lift an enormous, dark-green leaf. It looks fake, it's so shiny, and as I lean closer to get a better look, a bead of sweat tickles along my hairline. I take a handkerchief from my back pocket and wipe it away as I return to where Hugh stands beside a table.

He's using tiny scissors to trim what looks like a miniature oak tree, and he glances up to see me sweating through my shirt. "Norris will bring you ice water if you prefer."

"What I'd prefer is a straight answer. The last time you withheld information, I overlooked a dead body in your trunk. You still haven't explained that one."

"I told you it was self-defense. My security guard handled it."

"Yeah, that's what you told me."

Only problem was the dead man appeared to be eastern European, and he had no identification. When I ran his prints, nothing came back, which as a former Marine, leads me to believe he was a spook, or a foreign spy. I've been waiting for the other shoe to drop ever since.

Hugh places the small pruning shears on the table. "I trust you, Hutch. You're a straight shooter, and you know when to sit on things." His bushy gray brows furrow so the two become one. "I need you to protect my nieces. You're the law. You can do that."

"I'm not the law." I exhale a chuckle. "I'm only a detective, and your nieces are grown women. This isn't a police state."

He dismisses my argument. "People listen to you, Hutch. You're a natural leader, and they trust your judgment."

All traces of laughter leave my tone. "I'm not so sure I deserve that."

"Which makes me trust you even more." He puts a hand on my shoulder, and we start walking towards the door. "Everyone makes mistakes, but I know you've lived a decent life. I've witnessed it firsthand. If you have to go to them, tell Blake I asked you to do this. Tell her it's my final wish. Hana will follow."

My brow furrows. "Your final wish?"

His tone immediately lightens. "As in the last thing I'll ask of them. Don't be morbid, my friend."

"I'd say the same to you, but I'll tell you. I can't commit to this. I've got Pepper now, and I don't know what the hell I'm doing there. I don't have time for more females to worry about.

"Pepper… that's your sister's child? What is she, eleven?" He gives me a wink and taps the side of his nose. "She'll be fine, just let her be a kid."

Nodding, I can't argue. Jenny's daughter is a lot like her, although it doesn't give me much comfort. My sister always had a reckless streak. She was an adrenaline junkie, and I don't know if Pepper's going to turn out like her or like me. I'm not afraid of anything, but I know my limits.

The old man seems to read my mind. "What happened to your sister was a tragedy. Sometimes the best of us are lost through no fault of our own."

"Maybe." I'll never believe Judy deserved what happened to her, and losing my sister hurt like hell.

"Will you help me, Hutch?" Pleading gray eyes meet mine. "Protect my nieces. They're all I have left in this world."

I swallow the growl in my throat, and with a heavy exhale, I nod. "I'll be sure they get here, and I'll keep them safe while they are here. That's as much as I can do."

He reaches out and braces my shoulder. "Thank you. I'll never forget what you did for me."

My lips tighten. "One of these days, we're going to sit down and hash out what happened."

"One day." He nods, thin lips tightening grimly. "Now you'd better get going. I sent Blake a letter a few days ago. Hopefully it will be enough."

"She loves you. If you asked her to come here, I'm sure she will." God, I hope I'm right. If I have to go to New York and try to bring her here, it will not go well.

"Just promise me you'll be sure she does."

The urgency in his tone puzzles me. He's hiding some-thing again, and I don't like it. "You let me know if you need my help. With anything."

"Don't I always?"

Unfortunately, the answer is no.

CHAPTER 2

Blake

"**W**HAT THE HELL?" I FREEZE IN PLACE OUTSIDE THE SMALL black limo dropping my sister Hana and me at our Manhattan apartment building.

It's not yet two a.m., but I wasn't having fun tonight. The anonymous note about Hana being in some porno left on my table at the Vogue soured my stomach, and after that, all I wanted was to track her down and go home.

Done.

Secondary objective is to get her inside and lock up the doors until she sobers up, and we can sort out what the hell she's done now and how to fix it. Only the scene unfolding on our front steps changes everything.

Dark rain mists over my arms and hair, making the rainbow strobe of police lights and emergency vehicles more vivid. It's like we're still at the club.

Hana bumps into me from behind as she exits the vehicle and snorts a giggle. "Whoops! Sorry, Blake."

She hasn't even noticed the garish display right in front of us. A small crowd is starting to form, which means whatever it is just happened.

Two police officers hold up their hands as the media appear quickly, jumping out of vans or racing up on foot to take pictures or whip out cameras. Another officer is stretching yellow tape to block everyone out.

That's when my eyes land on three large cops dressed in all-black uniforms surrounding a dark lump on the wet concrete. A thick strawberry-blonde braid catches the light, and my chest collapses. It's a young woman, arms and legs spread and bent in odd angles, but the thing I see, that I don't want to recognize, is the thing making it difficult for me to breathe.

Emergency workers are doing their best to cover everything, but I recognize the brightly patterned, gold and black Versace robe. I'd know it anywhere, because she bought it last summer when we were together in Miami. She said it was in memory of a great designer gunned down before his time on the steps of his beautiful mansion.

"Debbie?" My voice cracks as I recognize my friend.

Her body is broken. She's lying on the cold, wet ground, face down in the gutter, on the steps of our beautiful building.

"What the fuck?" Trip is out of the car, and he pushes past me, skidding to a stop at the police line, where an officer stops him and pushes him back.

Cold seeps into my bones as I watch a uniformed woman continue to spread a tarp over my friend's body.

I think I might faint.

"I don't understand… What's happening?" Hana's voice pulls me back, and I spin around to get her away from the grizzly scene in front of us.

She doesn't need to see this. Hell, I don't need to see it. I don't want to remember Debbie this way, dead on the cold concrete in her gold satin robe, dark red liquid seeping from her mouth and nose.

"Oh!" My ankle almost turns in my stilettos, but I grab my sister's arms tighter to stay upright. "What was that?"

Looking back, I recognize the fluffy white Louboutin slipper with her initials stitched in black cursive across the band. Bile rises in my throat, and I leave it there. I don't look back. I don't imagine how it flew off her foot as she fell to her death.

What happened? Why? It doesn't make any sense.

"What is that?" My younger sister's voice is loose, and she grips my arms as I lead her around the scene to the front door, trying to divert her attention. "Is that Debbie's slipper?"

The side is marred with dirty water. "Just leave it. It's part of the crime scene now."

"What do you mean?" Hana looks from me to the growing mob of spectators.

More police cars arrive and an ambulance, although I can tell from the slump of Trip's shoulders they only need the coroner.

Flashes strobe in the night—the paparazzi are here, or what's left of them these days. Even a news van is pulling up on the scene. I guess some people still watch television. The old people who live in our building, the same ones who'll lose their shit over a spoiled debutant attracting so much attention by dying.

"I don't understand. Why is it a crime scene?" My sister looks from me to Trip as he slowly approaches, following us into the building.

"It's illegal to kill yourself in Manhattan." Trip's voice is mirthless, almost sarcastic, and I decide I need to be upstairs, in our apartment, drink in hand. *Stat.*

You don't sleep when someone you love dies.

I'm going on twenty-four hours, eyes wide open.

Hana is on the couch with gold facial strips under her red-rimmed eyes. "I don't believe it. It had to be an accident.

She just bought a closet full of designer dresses during fashion week. We were talking about all the parties we would attend at Cannes."

"*Debbie Does Death*?" Trip lifts the newspaper from our breakfast cart. "Seriously?"

He unfolds the black and white print and turns it so I can read the headline plastered above three columns and an unflattering photo of our dead friend at a bar looking very rough.

Assholes. It's so fucking unfair.

"I guess that passes for clever these days." We're not allowed to complain about how we're treated in the media, right?

Our life of privilege is blanket permission to judge whatever goes on behind closed doors, especially to us girls. We're always labeled as out of control or crazy or hysterical.

Debbie was my closest friend. She was the only friend who kept in touch with me the two years I was stuck in prison at Bishop of the Holy Family. She was my roommate at Columbia, and she helped me find modeling gigs so I didn't have to ask my mother for money before my trust fund matured.

Now she's dead.

My stomach cramps, and I skip the omelets, sausage, assorted breads, and fruit waiting for us along with coffee and juice and head straight for the bar. I take the Mamont vodka out of the small refrigerator and pour two fingers, neat.

"Would you pour one for me, Blake?" My sister holds out her hand, and my eyes narrow.

"Me, too." Trip lifts his chin, and I clamp my teeth over the snarky response on the tip of my tongue.

I'm not Trip's bar wench, and I don't think my sister should be drinking first thing in the morning. Still, we've all had a shock. We're all suffering, and I'm the oldest. I pour them each a lowball vodka and try to figure out what the hell we do now.

Pressure tightens my temples and an ache twists between my shoulder blades. With Debbie gone, I have nothing in this town except my sister, as if Hana can be thought of as a functioning adult. I know she has her reasons, but we've got to make a change.

I'm adrift in a sea of soulless children, and it hurts, deep at the base of my ribcage, radiating through my stomach. I'm not sure I can pretend I'm strong enough this time. My nails are scratching on the bottom of the barrel.

"Has anyone told her mother?" I hand them their drinks and walk back to the bar to retrieve mine.

"Does anyone know where her mother is?" Trip snarks, and my eyebrow arches. "Anyway, I'm sure the authorities will find her. We can just let that play out as it will. I'm in no mood to tangle with Belinda Desayda-Rice right now."

"Not since you slept with her?" Hana pushes a deep-red, manicured toe into his side, and he brushes her away.

"That was a year ago."

His presence annoys me. "Shouldn't you check on your own mother?"

"God, no. The last thing Cheryl needs is me poking my head in the middle of her latest threesome."

Trip has lived on our couch for the last several months since he got kicked out of his Upper East Side apartment. He's not the best influence on Hana, dabbling in drugs and gambling. I can ignore him, but my sister is always getting sucked into his schemes, and it's cost me several times to keep it off the radar.

I'm about ready to order him to leave when my second unwelcome visitor bursts through the door.

"O, em, gee, Blake! Did she really throw herself off the balcony in nothing but her Louboutin slippers?" Natasha sweeps in, with her royal-blue Yeezy puffer coat wrapped around her shoulders like a cape.

"No." I'm not letting that rumor take hold. "She was wearing her Versace robe."

"Debbie was always such a drama queen." Rainey, Natasha's underage minion, scratches at my frayed nerves.

"I'm going to my room." Hana stands, vodka in hand, and curls her nose at the two females. "It's stuffy in here."

"Perhaps you should try coffee for breakfast," Natasha quips before turning her eyes on me. "How are you holding up, B?"

Exhaustion radiates in my bones, and I just want to be away from the city, away from these remoras. They attached themselves to my sister while I was in Connecticut, and I haven't been able to get rid of them.

"I'm not great. None of it makes sense. I'm having a hard time believing it."

"Do you think the rumor mill is right? Do you think—"

"No." I shake my head, remembering my sister's plaintive cry. *Who would want to kill Debbie?* "I know Debbie. She wasn't mixed up in anything shady."

"But how well do we truly know anyone anymore?"

I don't like thinking that way. Debbie and I had been friends since forever, and while she was a playgirl, she was always in control.

Speaking of which, "Where's Greg?"

Trip was Debbie's plaything, but Greg was her actual boyfriend, at least that's what they told everyone. He has yet to make an appearance.

Natasha waves her hand, plucking a strawberry off the breakfast cart. "Oh, you know Grisha. He's not one for big family gatherings."

"It's not a family gathering. It's a wake." A bitter memory of a similar, horrible night flickers through my mind.

Of course Greg isn't here. Like Trip, he doesn't act like normal people, and it's because he's into shady dealings, always too smooth, always paying with cash.

Debbie was worried the last few days. She was always

looking over her shoulder. *If I say anything about the traffic in Milan or about the traffic anywhere, it's a signal I need help.* She'd had too much to drink the night she said it to me, and I dismissed it as nonsense while giving her a hug and reassuring her I'd always be there to help her.

I didn't help her last night. *Oh, God, she wasn't mixed up in anything shady, was she?*

I think back to the anonymous note left on my table at the bar. It was a QR code for a file server. I didn't look, but it claimed to be a porn film starring Hana, and someone named *Papi-O* wanted twenty thousand dollars to keep it off the Internet.

Could the two events somehow be related? Shaking my head, I rub my fingers over my eyes. My sleep-deprived brain can't connect the dots, and I'm probably just being paranoid.

"Will they even have a funeral?" Trip polishes off his vodka and lies back on the sofa as if he'll nap. "Their family tradition is cremation."

"Is that a tradition?" Rainy snorts a laugh.

"If they do, it'll be at the family vault. How many people can even fit in the space?" Natasha is still picking off the breakfast cart.

Their voices are sandpaper on my skin. Their callous remarks are too cruel, too unfeeling. My breath grows shallow, and I can't seem to inhale all the way. *Am I having a panic attack?* Shaking my head, I can't do that. I have to keep it together.

Hana was right. It's stuffy from the cheap perfume and the hot air coming from people's shitty mouths. I've had enough of their insincere concern—or total lack of concern. I need fresh air. I need to get out of this apartment.

Crossing the room, I pause at the small table in the foyer. A stack of mail waits to be opened, and right on top is a monogram I recognize. It's the initials of a man I value as much as the father I lost seven years ago.

Taking the linen envelope from the stack, I slide my finger along the seam. He never calls. He doesn't pressure me. He only suggests. Gently.

Dearest Blake,

On the occasion of my eightieth birthday, my greatest gift would be to have you and Hana come for a visit to our family home in Hamiltown. I've prepared rooms for you. You only need to arrive. Included are two train tickets and passage from the station to the house.

All my love,
Hugh

I study the elegant script on the crisp sheet of folded paper. Sure enough, paper tickets are tucked inside, like something out of an old movie.

Lifting my chin, I scan the room of high-fashion vampires with too much money, too much time, and no souls. "Why don't you all go home?"

Trip arches an eyebrow, "Are you channeling Bette Davis?"

Natasha makes a pouty face. "I'm sure you're tired, B." She nudges Trip in the ribs. "We'll take this party down the hall. Shower and join us when you and Hana are ready."

I tilt my head as if I'll nod, but I don't. We won't be joining any of them.

Trip leaves his empty tumbler on the table, pausing as he passes to kiss my cheek. "You'll let me know if you need anything?"

He's annoyed, but I couldn't care less.

He annoys me. "I don't need anything."

My tone is dismissive, and he turns, wrapping his arms around Natasha and Rainey's waists. "Come, girls. Time for an Irish wake."

The door closes, and I carry the letter down the long, mahogany hall to my sister's door. What I said to Trip isn't true. I do need something badly. I need to be away from this place. I need something real, fresh air, peace.

With a soft knock, I step into Hana's plush, white bedroom. She's lying on the bed, and I go to her, sitting beside her and smoothing her long, spiral curls away from her face. Her eyes are closed, and the empty tumbler is on her nightstand.

"Why did she do it?" Hana's small voice breaks, and I blink against the heat stinging my eyes.

I don't know the answer to her question. I can't fix this, and I don't want her getting any ideas.

Clearing my throat, I speak softly. "Uncle Hugh invited us to visit the family estate in Hamiltown. He's turning eighty, and I think it would be the perfect escape from what's happening here, don't you?"

I hold the letter where she can see it, and her brow furrows. She squints at it then turns away without even reading. "Whatever you think, B."

Like always. "I'll wake you in a few hours. We can be on the train by lunch."

She's not responding, but the decision is made.

We're getting the fuck out of here.

CHAPTER 3

Hutch

THIS IS MY FAULT.

The van Hamilton mansion is eerily quiet. Not a portrait is tilted, not a corner of a rug is upturned. I follow the butler across the parquet floors out to the small greenhouse, where I last saw Hugh. The small bonsai tree is still where he left it, tiny pruning shears on the table beside it.

I lift the tool, but it's too small to do any real damage. "The last time you saw him was when he went to bed last night?"

Norris flusters like a gray-haired, overheated penguin in his uniform. "He has to take his pills. He needs his medicine. How can I give him his medicine if he's not here?"

My lips tighten as I survey the area, remembering our conversation. He all but told me this was coming, and I didn't take him seriously, or I accepted his clumsy cover, when I know damn well Hugh van Hamilton doesn't say anything he doesn't mean.

He said coming home would be the last thing he'd ask of Blake and Hana.

Keep them safe was the last thing he asked of me.

My fist flexes. *Dammit*, how could I have let this happen?

"Oh, Mr. Winston, we've got to find him." Norris is making me uneasy, so I wave him off and head to the back entrance.

The four-car garage is also quiet, clean, with no signs of struggle or forced entry. An Audi sedan is parked beside a black, Lincoln Town Car. Beside it is an unused Bentley, and in the fourth space is an overused golf cart.

My partner Oscar rises to his full, six-foot-four height from where he'd been crouching behind the limo. His skin is covered in ink from his neck to his waist, down to both wrists. The tattoos cover some pretty gnarly burn scars.

"What's the good news?"

Pale-blue wolf eyes meet mine, and he shakes his dark head. "Nothing."

He's not much for conversation, but I need more than that.

A growl rumbles low in my throat. "Dammit, Scar. There's gotta be something. No one disappears without leaving some clue behind."

"Looks like Hugh did." He's not being cocky.

Scar Lourde doesn't like "no clue" cases. He's the best tracker in the world, and he prides himself on being able to find anyone or anything. When we first met overseas, he was a contractor with the Marines. We found spies, bombs, hijackers, hidden bunkers, suicide bombers… He saved my ass more than once, and he's practically psychic when it comes to finding evidence.

When he dropped by Hamiltown for a visit five years ago, I all but begged him to join my fledgling private investigation firm. I'd retired from service, and we were just getting established. I was the leader, the muscle, and my brother was the brains. Scar was exactly what we needed, and now I can't imagine doing our work without him.

"We've got to keep looking." I remember my last conversation with Hugh. "This isn't some random stranger."

"You'd search as hard for a random stranger." Scar's deep voice is quiet, and I concede.

"I'll search harder for Hugh."

"There's no struggle, no forced entry. His car didn't leave the garage…"

"So it's a kidnapping?"

"Or he wandered off."

Our eyes meet for a beat, and I shake my head. "He's ill, but he doesn't have dementia."

"And he wasn't kidnapped." My younger brother Dirk walks up to where we're standing.

My father always called him Duke because of his ability to fit seamlessly into both worlds. He's equally comfortable sipping Ono champagne cocktails on the Upper East Side as he is eating bologna sandwiches in Slim Harold's in Hamiltown.

But he's primarily a computer genius—hell, he's a fucking genius period. I'm lucky if I can get his ass out of bed before noon, but it's because he's up all night tracking bad guys across the dark web.

"If it were a kidnapping, there'd be a ransom note or at the very least someone taking responsibility. I checked all the downstairs windows, the surrounding drive, the lawns, and I did find one thing—two, actually."

"What?" Oscar straightnes, and my shoulders tense.

"I found these. Car let them out five minutes ago."

He steps to the side like he's a game-show host, revealing two females with confused expressions, holding suitcases.

It's actually two very beautiful women, one I remember well, only the last time I saw her, she was a sixteen-year-old troublemaker, a firebrand too attractive for her age, and especially for our five-year age difference.

"What's happening here?" Blake's voice is slightly lower

since I last heard it, still she's coolly elegant in her tailored brown blazer over an ivory shirt and dark jeans.

Her silky, brunette hair is smoothed over one shoulder in a wavy ponytail, and when her striking silver eyes meet mine, they narrow. My stomach tightens, and my jaw grinds.

I don't have time for that involuntary response.

"Surprise!" The pale blonde next to her exhales a soft laugh then she covers her mouth quickly, staring at the ground as if she's embarrassed we're all looking at her.

Hana hasn't changed at all. She sounds high. Her dark blue eyes seem too big for her face, and spiral white-blonde curls hang loose down her back, swaying as she wobbles on her stilettos. The filmy, floral dress she's wearing does little to cover her too-thin body.

"Why are you here?" Blake's sharp tone demands our attention, and I'm not in the mood.

Too much is going wrong today, and I'm tired from spending all afternoon searching this house. Now the sun's going down, and we have nothing.

"Norris called us. Your uncle wasn't in his bed this morning, and he didn't come back by noon. He's not in the best of health, so we came immediately to investigate the situation."

"Why is it your business if my uncle isn't in his bed?" Blake's brow arches, and I see she's only gotten stronger over the years.

Clearing my throat, I ease up, not wanting to fight. "I'm a private investigator. As I said, Norris called me, but even if he hadn't, your uncle is a close friend of mine. I'd have come regardless."

"A private investigator." Her full lips press together, and she pulls an envelope out of her pocket. "Then I guess you should see this. It came in the mail a few days ago."

I take it, quickly unfolding the thick paper and scanning

the words. He said he'd sent her a letter. *Protect my nieces*, he said to me.

"I don't know why he doesn't just call or text like a normal person," Blake grumbles as I think. "Anyway, he asked us to come home for his birthday. Why would he do that if he were planning to leave?"

I nod, returning the note to her. "I don't have an answer to that question, at least not yet."

"Well, doesn't this note at least prove he planned to be here?"

"It would appear that way." My jaw sets, and I'm not so sure what her uncle planned—or what he suspected.

I know he was worried enough to get them here, worried enough to involve me in their protection.

A throat clears behind me, and I look back to see my brother tilting his head towards the door, and I know what it means. Too many people are in the house, and we're in danger of corrupting or even damaging evidence.

"Let me take this. You're coming to my place." Stepping forward I place my hand over Blake's on the handle of her suitcase.

She immediately recoils. "Excuse me? I'm not going anywhere with you. This is our family home. We're staying here."

Defiance sparkles in her eyes, and the tension that has always existed between us fires in the front of my brain. I've always known how smart she is—it's also her biggest weakness. She thinks she's the smartest person in the room, and it makes her vulnerable. She's not strong enough for this.

"The mansion is a crime scene. We don't know what happened to your uncle or who might be watching the place. Perhaps whoever did this knew you were coming."

"No one knew we were coming. I only decided this morning."

I nod, making a mental note. "Still, it's not safe here. We

don't know enough, and there's plenty of room at my house. My niece lives with me. I have a housekeeper. You'll be perfectly safe and comfortable there."

Hana lifts the side of her dress and does a wobbly little turn before Scar steps forward quickly and gently catches her arm, taking her suitcase.

"Thank you." Her voice is like tissue paper, high and just above a whisper. She places a slender, pale hand on his muscled, inked forearm and looks up into his darkness. It's like watching a biker with a kitten, but I don't have time for distractions.

"I'm not staying with you." Blake's shoulders are set, and I knew it would be this way. "We'll find a hotel or a bed and breakfast."

"You won't find any of that here." Dirk chuckles. "Hamiltown is not exactly a booming metropolis."

"Exactly." I take her suitcase from her hand. "It's not a discussion. You're staying at my place. I have an entire upstairs floor where the two of you can set up, undisturbed. You won't have to see anyone if you don't want to."

Her eyes widen, and you'd think I'd offered a golden turd on a silver platter. "I'd rather go back to New York than stay at your house."

"But you're not." I start walking to my black Silverado, and Scar falls in behind me. "I'm keeping my eye on you until we understand what we're dealing with here."

"I didn't ask for that." I hear her steps hustling up behind me, and I stop, turning to face her.

Inhaling deeply, my shoulders broaden, and I'm done arguing. "No, you didn't, but your uncle did. Now come on."

Confusion lines her brow, but I'm done. Tossing her bag in the back of my truck, Scar does the same with Hana's before holding her hand and helping her climb into the backseat.

I hear my brother consoling Blake behind us. "I'd offer to let you stay at my place, but I've only got one big room."

Oscar doesn't say a word, but his eyes never leave Hana. He watches her like she's something he's never seen before, like a Viking entranced by a mermaid.

I don't have time for anymore discussion, and I'm fucking hungry. "Let's go."

Blake's chin juts forward with the clench of her teeth, and it shouldn't be so attractive. She takes a casual step past me, and I catch her waist to help her into the back of my truck.

It makes her hesitate, and she flashes those eyes at me. "Tell me, Hutch Winston, do you always handle people like trained monkeys?"

"Yes." My tone is flat. "I get away with it, too."

"Aren't you lucky?"

"No. I'm pretty fucking tired and hungry."

"Then we should go back to New York. We didn't ask to come here."

"And I didn't ask you to come here, so don't make my life more stressful."

"I'm not interested in your life, Mr. Winston."

"And I'm not interested yours, Ms. van Hamilton, but I made a promise to your uncle, and I intend to keep it. You two are going to stay with me. For whatever reason, criminals love returning to the scene of the crime."

Her gray eyes widen. "You really think someone's going to come here?"

"I'm really not taking a chance, and I'm definitely not leaving two sitting ducks as bait. Now, let's go."

All her fight disappears, which should give me pause.

"I'll do it for Hana."

Her Achilles heel. She'll do anything for her sister. I'm not so sure it's a good thing, but I'm not looking too closely at my feelings at this moment. What matters is finding Hugh and making the person who did this pay.

CHAPTER 4
Blake

HE'S TOO BIG.

He's too big and too attractive, and let's not forget how he destroyed my life, destroyed Hana's life, sent me to a fucking all-girls boarding school where I couldn't stop Victor from skimming thousands of dollars off my father's estate.

Also, I hate him.

Now I'm installed on the second floor of his oversized farm-style home, tucked away on one of the older streets in Hamiltown, but I don't want to go back to New York. I want to stay and find out what happened to my uncle, not to mention, I have to figure out what to do about this blackmail situation.

My lips part, and I consider asking Hana what she remembers about *Licking Lady Liberty*, possibly the most idiotic name for a porn film. It's pointless even to ask, she never remembers anything the next day.

Exhaling a heavy sigh, I sit up on the soft double bed across from the one holding Hana's suitcase as she unpacks it. I've already unpacked and changed into black palazzo pants and a scoop neck top. My sister is still in the same floral dress, and the scent of cooking drifts up from below.

A soft knock on the door precedes the voice of Lurlene Jones, Hutch's housekeeper. She reminds me of a golden hen, short and round, and the mother we never had. She bundled us up here and instructed us to make ourselves at home and let her know if we needed anything.

"Dinner's ready if you'd like to come down." Her smile is warm. "Roast beef and mashed sweet potatoes with fresh sweet corn. It's pretty good if I do say so myself."

Hana blinks at me curiously, and I shrug. "We'll be right down."

"We will?" My sister watches me like I'm someone she doesn't know. "I thought we were staying here under protest."

"We are, but we don't have to starve." Not that I'm sure I'll be able to eat with the knots in my stomach.

"I'm fine staying up here if that's what you want."

I also know she'd get her supper from a bottle if I let her. Maybe this trip isn't going the way I envisioned it, but I still have her out of the city, away from her usual crowd. Maybe I can use this time to get her closer to healthy.

"We're going. Come on." She follows me out the door and down the short hall to the staircase.

Hutch's home is true vintage with polished oak furniture and pale plaster walls. Portraits hang on wires hooked in the crown molding, and chandeliers are anchored by elaborate ceiling medallions in the middle of each room.

Our footsteps are muffled by antique Persian rugs covering dark wood floors. It's exactly what you'd picture in your mind if you thought of nineteenth-century southern architecture.

A wide, white porch wraps around the exterior, and it has pointed arches and huge windows looking out on massive live oak trees in the front yard.

The trees comfort me with their trunks as wide as cars and

their black limbs swinging low to the ground. It reminds me of being a little girl and visiting Uncle Hugh with my father. Hamiltown dates back to the turn of the twentieth century, and these trees date back to the dawn of time. They remind me it's possible to survive anything.

Entering the bright yellow dining room, I pause when I see our host standing at the opposite head of the table with a little girl looking up at him. Her head is just above his waist, and her light brown hair is styled in two braids on each side of her head.

She's wearing knee-length white pants with elastic in the legs, gathered above her striped white athletic socks, and a bright red jersey with *Stinky's Snow Cones* in white lettering over a giant number eight.

I'm pretty sure it's a softball uniform, and she's frowning up at Hutch. "But Coach Perkins asked specifically for *you* to throw the opening pitch at our first game. He wants you."

"I've got a lot going on right now, Pep. There are plenty of other people in town he can ask." Hutch puts his hand on her shoulder, making her look even smaller, and she crosses her arms, pouting fiercely.

"Uncle Dirk said you'd say no. He said I'd have a better chance of getting the devil to eat one of Stinky's snow cones than getting you to do it."

Hutch's dark brow furrows. "Dirk told you that?"

"You're not going to let him be right, Uncle Hutch, are you?"

"No, but I'm definitely having a chat with him."

"So I'll put you down for the opener! Woo!" She pumps small fists over her head in a little victory move then holds out a hand. "Give me your phone."

His frown relaxes, and he slides the device from his inside coat pocket.

She takes it and holds it up to him. "Face, please."

A hint of a grin teases at his lips, and it does melty things to my insides. His sweetness with this girl, the way he allows her to order him around is so unexpected.

She starts tapping on his phone, and he scoops her up by the waist, looking over her shoulder. "What are you doing now?"

"Put me down, ya brute!" Her legs in those striped athletic socks swing as he sways her side to side.

"I'm not a brute, I'm your uncle. What are you doing with my phone?"

"I set up a series of reminders so you don't forget." A few more taps, and she gives it back to him.

He's still smiling when the chair beside me falls forward against the table with a sharp crack, causing us all to jump.

"Oh, I'm sorry. I didn't mean to…" Hana rushes forward to catch it.

Hutch and the girl turn to face us, and his smile quickly melts into a neutral expression. Mine does the same.

Wait, was I just smiling?

"Blake, Hana," Hutch gestures to the little girl, who's blinking at us with big brown eyes. "This is my niece Pepper. She was my sister Judy's child. Or is."

"Judy was my mom." Pepper marches over to where we're standing and holds out her hand. "She got real sick last year, so God needed her to become an angel. Now she watches over me from heaven."

My brow rises at her matter-of-fact tone, and Hana squats in front of her. "I like your name. My dad died when I was about your age… I think. I was thirteen."

"I'm eleven." Pepper nods. "But I understand your mistake. Everyone says I'm mature for my age."

"You're lucky. I've never been mature for my age."

I bite my lip, genuinely impressed by this child's ability to both boss Hutch Winston around and get my reclusive sister to be so self-aware—and then say it out loud.

"Let's take our seats." Hutch motions to the table. "Lurlene planned a big meal tonight. I think she expected to have leftovers."

Hana glances at me as she carefully pulls out a chair on the other side of Pepper, away from Hutch at the head of the table. Pepper climbs into her chair, and I'm left staring at the empty seat at Hutch's right.

Straightening my shoulders, I walk around the long table and take the chair beside him.

He hesitates before sitting. "Lurlene also made iced tea, but I have red wine if you prefer."

"Tea is fine," I answer quickly, not wanting to give Hana an opening.

He lifts a white pitcher and pours four glasses then takes his seat. I'm curious why he's not having something stronger.

Lifting the lid on a large, white platter reveals dark brown, sliced roast in gravy surrounded by cooked carrots and onions. Pepper takes another bowl that holds red-orange mashed sweet potatoes, and the boiled corn is the last to make the rounds. Rolls are in a wicker basket wrapped in a red and white checkered napkin.

The clanking of utensils against china is the only sound for several minutes as we all serve ourselves. When we're done and the dishes return to the center of the table, Pepper is the first to dig in.

I taste a small forkful of the sweet potato mash, and as soon as it touches my tongue, a burst of buttery, savory goodness fills my mouth. I'm embarrassed when my stomach makes a noise, and I quickly take another, bigger bite, noticing my sister doing the same.

"I can't remember the last time we sat down to a real family meal." Hana's never been comfortable with silence.

"Really?" Pepper frowns, talking with her mouth full. "What do you do?"

Hana takes another bite of the creamy sweet potatoes and shrugs. "I usually order takeout or grab a falafel off a food truck. This is really good."

"What about your mom? Doesn't she have dinner with you?"

"Pepper." Hutch's low voice contains a gentle scold, and she glances at him unsure.

"It's okay." Hana waves her hand, sipping her iced tea then quickly covering her mouth. "Mm—that's sweet!"

"Ms. Lurlene makes the best sweet tea." Pepper bounces in her seat, grabbing her glass and taking a large gulp. "I help her. She uses two cups of sugar for a pitcher of brewed tea."

"I'll remember that." Hana nods. "My mother drinks champagne for dinner."

Pepper pauses, confused. "How does that work?"

"It doesn't." I cut in quickly, shooting Hana a stern look.

My sister quickly lowers her forkful of meat and puts her hands in her lap, looking down.

Pepper hops up on her knees, reaching for a pink cupcake from the center of the table. "It's okay. I always get in trouble when I talk too. Cupcake?"

She holds it out to Hana, who gives her a little smile, taking it. "Thanks."

Pepper grabs another, and while the two share cupcakes, I turn to Hutch.

"Lurlene made all this?" He nods, chewing a bite of roast. "I'm sorry if she's having to do more work with us here. Tomorrow, I can try to find us a place to stay—"

"No! She's excited you're here!" Pepper answers before Hutch even takes a breath. "She said it's about time Uncle Hutch had a woman in the house, and she kept smiling and adding stuff to the grocery list."

My eyes widen, and Hutch's voice rises in volume. "Blake

and Hana are staying with us for a case. It's strictly business. Nothing more."

Pepper's eyebrows rise, and she finishes her last bite of cake, swaying side to side in her chair. "I don't know where Lurlene gets her info, but that's not how it sounds…"

"Pepper, enough." Hutch's tone is fierce, and he gives me a glance I have never seen on that broody face before. Is he apologetic? "Time for bed. Take your plate to the kitchen."

So he does have a weakness. Hana is sitting quietly now, and I've eaten as much as I can, completely finishing my luscious sweet potatoes.

Placing my napkin beside my plate, I stand. "Thank you for this delicious dinner, and for the lovely accommodations."

"It's the least I can do." Hutch's tone is all business again as he stands. "I'll tell Lurlene you enjoyed dinner—and clear up any confusion about why you're here."

I hesitate, trying to decide if I should tell him it's not that big of a deal. Ultimately, I see Hana waiting and give him a nod. "Good night."

"Let me know if you need anything."

We won't, I decide silently.

We're back in our room, and Hana is lying on the double bed across from mine. The French doors along the balcony are open, and the sound of crickets is deafening. The musty scent of damp trees drifts in on the humid breeze, and it all mixes together, taking me back to a time so long ago when I was very young, before the trouble started.

Hutch was different tonight at dinner. His shield was lowered, and he seemed almost human. I haven't forgotten what an arrogant bully he can be, and I haven't forgotten my vow to make him pay for ruining my life, for enabling the damage that took place after I was shipped off to boarding school.

At the same time, seeing him tonight with Pepper got to me. He revealed a side I didn't know existed.

"Pepper's cute." Hana holds a satin pillow, and I glance at her lying on her back, tracing her finger along the stitching. "I used to want a little sister."

"She's got a lot of personality." I lift the quilt on my bed, frowning at how thin it is in the cool night air drifting around us. "Are you cold?"

"Not really. You could close the doors."

I like them open, the sounds, the scents… "I'll find us some thicker blankets. Be right back."

I've washed my face and changed into gray sleep shorts and a black tank. My long hair is pulled up in a ponytail on the top of my head, and my feet are bare on the soft wood floors and even softer rugs.

I check closet after closet on our floor with no luck. The lights are off downstairs, so I decide to slip down and try to find a blanket in the living room. I'm sure I saw one on the ivory sofa.

Creeping softly across the living room, I'm disappointed to find nothing. This is ridiculous. He has to have more blankets somewhere in this house. Inspecting my outfit, I decide I'm decent, and he said to let him know if I needed anything.

"Hutch?" I call softly, tapping on the heavy wooden door.

Pepper has school tomorrow, so I don't want to disturb the house. I don't get an answer, so I place my hand on the doorknob, and the door gently falls open a crack. Peeking my head around the barrier, I see his wood-paneled room is bathed in yellow light from a bedside lamp.

My eyes catch on the small statue of a knight in real chain mail on a horse. It reminds me of a similar statue that once belonged to my dad, and I file the thought away.

A navy comforter is on his king-sized bed, but no blankets. Surely he has some hidden somewhere. I just need him to show me where.

"Hutch?" I call again, tiptoeing farther into the room.

I'm all the way in when the sound of water streaming meets my ears. My lips part when I realize he's in the shower, and my heart beats faster when I see the bathroom door is open.

I should go back to my room or wait in the living room. Yes, that would be the right thing to do. I've made up my mind to do just that when a low groan freezes me in place.

"Fuck, yeah…" Another groan, and my jaw drops.

I creep forward, unable to stop myself. Is a woman in the shower with him? And if one is, why am I unreasonably furious about it? Hutch Winston doesn't belong to me.

Another, deeper moan sends me closer, and my hand touches the bathroom door. It opens a bit more, giving me a full view of Hutch in the shower, completely nude, and alone.

His head is bowed, dark hair falling over his temples, as his biceps flex and his fist pumps vigorously between his legs. He's leaning forward, bracing the wall with his hand, and his back is a lined wall of tense muscle.

My lips fall open as I watch, as wetness floods my core, and I'm breathing faster. Deep red and black tattoos I didn't know he had ripple on his back and arms. He's pumping faster, solid muscles flexing as water traces every line in his perfect body down to his tight, sculpted ass.

I'm hypnotized by the sight, and hot all over.

"Fuck," he groans again, and his hips start to rock.

Oh, God, I can't breathe. I imagine those hips rocking at my back, pumping into me.

His fist moves faster, and every muscle in his body flexes beautifully as he breaks, groaning seductively, milking his cock.

His chin lifts, eyes squeezed shut, and with a satisfied moan, he exhales the word that stops my heart. "Blake…"

He said my name.

I'm gasping through parted lips, and his head turns. His eyes lock with mine, and I'm a deer in headlights. I can't move as he straightens and turns to face me, water running down the lines of muscle in his torso, his cock long and thick between his legs.

Blinking out of my daze, I spin on my toes and walk fast to the door. I've just reached it when his palm flattens against the wood, slamming it closed, caging me with my back to the door, facing him.

"What are you doing in here?" His voice is low and husky.

My gaze is downcast, noticing the towel loose around his waist, the lines in his stomach disappearing into it, the bulge in the center. Water drips from his hair onto my cheeks, and he catches my chin, forcing me to meet his stormy green eyes.

"I'm sorry…" My voice is breathless.

We're both breathing fast, and without a warning, his mouth crashes against mine, soft lips forcing mine apart, and fresh water fills my mouth as our tongues curl together.

I exhale a whimper, kissing him back, gripping his broad shoulders as his hand slides up my bare thigh, lifting my leg to his waist. Pressing his hips against me, I can feel the hardness of his erection through the towel, through my thin cotton shorts, and my knees liquify. I want it…

Wait, what am I doing?

His face lifts, breaking our kiss with a wet gasp, and I stagger back, opening the door and dashing through it, running all the way to my bedroom in the darkness.

CHAPTER 5

Hutch

WHEN SHE LEFT THE DINING ROOM AFTER DINNER, I COULDN'T stop thinking about her, about us and our history.

She's too beautiful.

She's spoiled and entitled.

She's pretty and pretty wild, and don't forget she's five years younger than me. A party girl, which I do *not* find attractive.

Only it's a lie, I *do* find her attractive.

She's on my mind too much, and now she's in my house, which is a major irritant.

I couldn't stop thinking about her undressing one short flight of stairs above me. I couldn't stop picturing her sliding those pants over her curvy hips—was she wearing a thong? Nothing at all? Removing her shirt and her bra, were her nipples hard?

I needed to regain my focus on finding my lost friend. Instead, I was standing in my bedroom with a hard-on. Since when was I *that* guy?

Rubbing my hand along the back of my neck, I knew the

answer. I'd been that guy since we were teenagers, and I saw her in that bikini at the lake, gazing at me like she'd never seen a man before.

At eighteen, I was no stranger to female attention. I knew the effect I had on women, but it had never been an issue for me. I was focused on my goals: going to college, becoming a Marine, getting my private investigator's license.

That day, for whatever reason, her wide-eyed gaze full of hunger and lust unearthed something primal in me. I turned away fast, surprised and a lot shaken. How could a girl her age make me feel desire? It had never happened before.

I jumped in the lake and swam away.

Hell, I stayed *far* away until I could clear my head, until she was gone.

Fast forward three years, and she'd only grown more attractive. Sixteen was still too young, and she was a fucking temptress. She clutched me with hungry eyes in that dim-lit hallway.

Desire painted her cheeks pink, and her nipples pointed beneath the thin material of her black and white dress.

When her pillow lips parted, my dick grew hard, and I had a searing fantasy of her on her knees… It made me fucking furious. It would ruin everything.

I'd done my best to avoid her, but her father had died. Hugh asked me for a favor, again, and I was curious. I wanted to know if she still had that strange power over me. Short answer, she did, and when that asshole Victor opened the door and looked at her like a shark on blood, he's lucky I didn't grab him by the neck.

I knew I had to stay away from her, but I wasn't about to leave her there for some other guy to touch. I was a bastard, but I did what I did. I had her mother send her to the nuns.

Now she's in my house, and it's all still here. My possessiveness is primitive and demanding.

Why would Hugh do this to me? And where the fuck is he?

Stripping off my clothes, I needed to shower, to get this tightness off my skin, this arousal out of my dick.

Standing under the warm water, I closed my eyes and saw her again looking up at me with silver eyes, curious but restrained. My hand slid down to grasp my cock, and I remembered her breasts pressed to my chest.

I've never tasted her full, pink lips. I'd like to taste all of her, turn her around and slide my cock deep into her hot, luscious body.

Picturing her dark head pressed against my shoulder as my hands explored all of her, the heat between her thighs, her wetness, the soft swell of her full breasts, her hardened nipples. How would she sound when I made her come?

My hand moved faster, pumping my erection as orgasm raced up my inner thighs, climbing higher into my balls, tightening my muscles. Energy surged through my veins, blanking my mind as I dropped my head back and exploded, exhaling her name with a groan.

I slid my hand from base to tip while warm jets washed the evidence of my lust down the drain, as my orgasm subsided. I had my release, but it wasn't the same.

It will never be the same as sinking into her tight, wet core, having her on my lap or taking her from behind. Is it even a possibility?

Blinking my eyes open, I catch a glimpse of a dark figure in my peripheral, and I turn my head. She's standing in my bathroom in tiny shorts that show off her shapely legs, a black tank top that barely covers her round breasts, and her hair is up in a ponytail.

Her cheeks are flushed, and she's breathing fast. It's like that day so long ago when we had our first look at each other. *Forbidden fruit.*

"I'm sorry!" Her voice is high, and she spins around, walking away quickly.

I don't know what possesses me, but I can't let her go. I grab the towel, tying it around my waist and stopping her before she escapes my room.

"What are you doing here?" Even I can hear the raw craving in my voice.

She won't meet my eyes, but she's flushed, chest rising and falling rapidly. Her soft lips part, and I do the most out of character thing. I let go.

Leaning down, I cover her mouth with mine, forcing her lips apart as my tongue invades to find hers. A whimper scrapes from her throat, and I'm instantly hard again. She grips my shoulders, kissing me back, curling her tongue with mine, and I reach down to lift her soft thigh, wrapping it over my hip. I want to sink my cock inside her. Would she let me?

Breaking away, I meet her heated gaze. She's gorgeous with her lips swollen and pink from my kisses, her breasts flattened against my chest. Her expression is hungry, but instead of reaching for more, she pulls away from me.

I release her at once, and she hurries out the door, leaving me dripping wet in a towel, watching her calves flex as she climbs the stairs in her bare feet, not looking back.

Closing the door, I rest my head against it, horny and frustrated and pissed at myself. What have I done? I'm supposed to be protecting her, not trying to fuck her.

I have to fix this.

Several minutes later, dressed in gray sweats and a dark green henley, I climb the stairs to the second floor. If the lights are off, I'll leave it until tomorrow. If not, I'll apologize and ask why she was in my bedroom. She must have needed something, and I'm sure it wasn't the manhandling I gave her.

Yellow light glows beneath the door, and I tap softly,

hesitating. Perhaps I've done enough for one night. No one answers, and I'm almost relieved as I turn to go downstairs.

I've taken one step when the door opens, and her soft voice stops me. "What do you want?"

Something I should not touch, I think to myself before turning to face her.

She's wearing a thick robe over her tank and short shorts and her high ponytail is now down at the nape of her neck. It makes no difference how much she shows or hides. She's a grown woman, and she's irresistible to me.

Clearing my throat, I return to where she's standing outside the door, holding it closed. "I came to apologize. I wasn't myself just now."

Her silver eyes narrow. "That's too bad. You were more human just now than you've ever been as long as I've known you."

I'm not sure if she's teasing me or being serious. She's not smiling, so I stay the course. "Anyway, I hope you'll forgive me. Was there something you needed?"

"Blankets. Hana and I were chilly, and the thin quilts on these beds aren't cutting it."

Nodding, I motion for her to follow me to the end of the hall where a narrow closet is located. "I think everything is in here."

Sure enough when I open the door, a chenille blanket falls on my head. "Pepper," I grumble, taking the blanket and folding it properly, putting it on the shelf where it belongs.

A sniff behind me tells me she's laughing, and my shoulders relax. "My niece is a true eleven-year-old, always half-doing shit."

"She's adorable." Blake walks to where I stand in front of the closet. "How long have you had her?"

"Judy died... almost eighteen months ago." Funny how

the pinch in my chest never gets softer when I remember my sister. "Ovarian cancer. We had time to prepare, but…"

"I'm so sorry." She puts her hand on my arm, and I almost forget she's a jaded New York party girl.

Standing in the hall of my old family home with her this way is messing with my head. I'm serious, focused on my work, and having her here is way too distracting.

Lowering my arm, I move away. "If that's all you need, I'll head down and let you rest."

"Actually…" She steps forward and returns the blankets to the closet. "Hana is asleep, and I have questions. Can we talk now or are you tired?"

"It's only ten. We shut things down early because Pepper has school, but I'm usually up for a few more hours."

"Is there somewhere we can go?"

I lead her down the stairs and out one of the doors lining the large living room to the wrap-around porch. It's a cool night, but not too cold for me to need a coat.

I glance at her thick robe and arch an eyebrow. "Do you need a jacket?"

"I'm good." Her hand is at the neck of her robe, and she holds it closed as she looks out into the dark night.

Purple wisteria is blooming, clusters of petals like grapes dropping from the eaves in a curtain. The landscapers installed lights to illuminate the massive live oaks at night. It all gives the place an almost mystical appearance.

"I remember this so well," she sighs.

Going to the porch railing, I sit with my back to a column. "What's on your mind?"

Gray-blue eyes meet mine, and she blinks a few times as if she's choosing her words. "Do you have any idea what happened to my uncle? Any leads? When's the last time you talked to him?"

Unease tightens my stomach. "I saw him yesterday.

Something was on his mind, but he didn't tell me what." I hate giving clients bad news, but I decide to be straight with her. "I don't have a clue. He asked me to be sure you and Hana came here. He wanted you out of the city, and he asked me to protect you."

Her slim brows furrow. "He didn't say why?"

"No. All I know is he was worried about your safety."

"Not much to go on." She puts her hands on the rail near where I'm standing.

"I've been going through his recent contacts." I hesitate, wondering if she'll return the favor and be straight with me. "How much do you know about Victor Petrova?"

Taking a step back, her eyes flare before she smiles. "What did he tell you?"

"Not as much as you just did."

Her smile is tight with anger. "I thought you didn't like playing games."

"I don't. This is all too real, and you have to trust me if I'm going to honor your uncle's request. I need the whole story."

"Maybe I don't want your protection."

"Maybe that's not your call to make."

She starts for the door, but I step between her and escape. Her jaw sets, and that defiance fires in her eyes. It burns hot in my stomach.

"I'm not interested in kissing you, Mr. Winston. I don't even particularly like you."

Dropping my chin, I exhale a laugh. "Is that so? Why don't you like me?"

"You're an overbearing jerk who tries to run other people's lives."

"Is this about your little trip to boarding school? You were spiraling, Blake. Anyone who cared would see it."

"You interfered in a situation that was none of your business."

I want to say she is my business, but I don't. "I helped you."

"Are you trying to pretend you cared? Someone who cared would have asked me what I was going through, how it felt to have my father die and my family retreat to their own personal vices. You simply ordered my mother to send me away, and she was all too ready to get me out of her hair."

"Your mother drinks her lunch from a bottle and was ready to give me a lap dance while I was standing up."

"What does that have to do with me?" She's standing right in front of me hurt and anger blazing in her eyes, and fuck it, I want to kiss her again.

Now that I've tasted her, I can't get enough. I want to wrap my arms around her and tell her I'll take care of her, lean on me. Instead, I fall back on my training.

I take a beat and inhale, exhale.

Studying her angry face, the lines in her forehead, I notice a thin, white scar above her left eyebrow. "What happened there?"

"Victor Petrova happened. Thanks to you, my father's estate lost thousands before he was exposed, not to mention the abuse he inflicted on my sister."

"He was embezzling money from your family's estate?" Stepping to the side, I rub my hand over my chin. That would explain a lot about Hugh's behavior lately.

"When I threatened to expose him, he slapped me across the room into the fireplace. I came to and discovered he was long gone, and my mother couldn't be bothered."

"He did that to you?" Fury clouds my vision. "Where is he now?"

"Nobody knows. He got what he wanted from us and disappeared back into the hole he crawled out of."

"I'll find him, and I'll make sure he gets what he deserves." *If I don't kill him first.*

Her eyebrow arches. "Now you're a hero? At my mother's apartment, you refused that title."

"I've learned life is a little more nuanced than I once thought."

"Nuanced? How does a homicide detective accommodate nuance in the search for justice? It sounds like letting people off with a warning."

"Nuance and justice are not opposites. I'm a private investigator with a focus on homicide, there's a difference. I have a victim, and it's up to me to find the perp and bring him or her to justice."

"So you're the Dark Knight? He ended up not being so heroic, didn't he?"

"I don't know about fictional characters. I live in the real world, and it's time you did the same."

She pulls her robe tighter and attempts to pass me. "Why didn't you help me?"

Reaching out, I stop her by the shoulders. "I helped you the only way I could in the middle of active duty. I got you out of a bad situation."

"You left Hana alone and exposed." She pulls away from my grasp, turning her back to me. "As a Marine, you should know not to leave a man behind."

"My choice was helping you."

"I didn't ask for your help."

"Didn't you?" That night is vivid in my memory. "I remember you getting very close and personal."

She shakes her head. "You were offended. Or disgusted."

"I was twenty-one, and you were sixteen. I was smart."

"What are you now?" Her chin lifts, and she looks up at me.

My eyes slide from her full lips down her neck to her full breasts. The beautiful girl is now a gorgeous woman, and I want her so much. Only, there's too much anger between us. I don't like it, so I give her space.

"Now I'm tired. We should get some sleep. We've got a lot of work to do tomorrow."

CHAPTER 6
Blake

"Remember when we would slide down it?" Hana stands at the foot of the grand staircase in Uncle Hugh's estate, our family home, running her hand down the wide railing.

"You were the only one small enough to slide down the banister. It hurt my hoo-hoo."

Dirk gave us permission to come today and look for clues. After a fitful night of not sleeping, fighting all my twisted emotions, I finally drifted off at dawn. Hana always sleeps until noon, but it was a first for me. Dirk was at the house when I ventured downstairs in search of coffee, and he assured me the place had been swept by their team.

Actually, he encouraged me to come here and see if I could find anything unusual, missing, or new—anything I didn't recognize. Norris led me to this office.

"If I can get you anything, Miss Blake, or if you have any questions, please ask." The old butler had been so distraught. "We need to get your uncle back."

"I agree." I smiled, giving his hand a squeeze, and he left us alone.

Now I'm hesitating at the door while my sister lifts her old-school Canon EOS camera to her eye and snaps a photo of the grand entryway. "Are you planning to document the house?"

"For starters." Rapid clicks fill the silence. "It's amazing."

I look up at the tall ceiling surrounded by the large, rectangular, second-floor balcony. Uncle Hugh's home is more like a castle with dark, polished-wood paneling and ornate brass fixtures. It reminds me of something out of a classic Hollywood film, where the women wore beaded gowns all day and the men wore suits and fedoras.

"Is that a kitten?" Hana takes off towards the back hall, and I exhale a sigh, going into my uncle's pristine office.

Everything that happened between Hutch and me last night presses on my mind. I've hated him so much and so long for what he did, for meddling in something that didn't involve him, only to find out now his motive was personal.

All I saw was the threat from Victor to my family.

All he saw was the threat from Victor to me.

He did what he did to keep me safe. He never considered I would never choose my own safety over Hana's. Or perhaps if he did, he didn't care, and I don't know what to do with that. I never believed he felt more than annoyance towards me.

Speaking of annoying new information, a text from a blocked number appeared on my phone this morning. Apparently, the anonymous note was all theatrics. This dickhead knows my contact info, and he's gotten bolder.

Skipping town will only set the clock forward. Fifty thousand, one week, or the video goes viral. -Papi-O

The price is going up.

I stared at the screen for a long time trying to decide what to do. If I'm going to play ball and keep this shit under wraps, I'll have to reply. At the same time, I haven't looked at this alleged porn film. It could be a hoax. Anonymous notes, blocked numbers, and ridiculous names do not inspire a lot of confidence.

Hutch claims he's here to protect us, but if I show it to him, it'll confirm all the bad things he thinks about my sister. No, I'd rather save him as a last resort if I can't sort this out myself.

Fifty grand is more than my monthly allowance, but if I make a partial payment, it's possible I can keep this guy appeased.

My brow is furrowed as I take a book off my uncle's desk. It's a ledger with names and amounts in it, like a list of payments for services, but it doesn't make any sense. Sidorov, Alexeyev, Ivanov… Why was my uncle dealing with eastern Europeans?

"Hey, girl, what's the good news?" Dirk interrupts my thoughts, and I glance up to see him standing in the doorway with that giant, scary, tattooed guy behind him.

"Not much." I hand him the book. "Have you seen this?"

He takes it, scanning the names and numbers quickly. "It looks like a basic accounting ledger. Do you know more about it?"

"I have no idea about anything anymore, but it's odd that all the names are foreign. Is there an eastern European community in Hamiltown?"

The big guy steps forward, and his brow furrows as he looks at the page. He doesn't speak.

"I'll ask Hutch if he knows anything about this." Dirk squints one eye up at me. "If you don't mind?"

Shrugging, I hold out my hands. "Go for it. I hadn't seen my uncle in years, so I'm sure Hutch knows more than I do about his business dealings."

Hana bursts through a different door, chasing a bouncy orange tabby cat. Her cheeks are pink, and her blonde curls are slightly frizzled around her face.

She looks better than she has in a long time. "Is it okay if I run down to the stables? I want to photograph the horses."

I look from her to our guards—I'm pretty sure Hutch told them to keep an eye on us, Mr. "I promised to protect you."

Big and Tatted clears his throat, and Dirk gives him a nod. "Scar can walk down with her. Just to be sure everything's okay."

"I don't think we've met." Crossing the room, I hold out my hand. I appreciate Dirk's offer, but I still look out for Hana. "I'm Blake van Hamilton. Hana is my little sister."

"Oh, sorry." Dirk steps to the side. "Blake, this is Oscar Lourde. He's our tracker, bounty hunter, go-to scary guy. Nobody's getting past him."

My eyes go from Dirk to the tall, muscled man covered in ink. His long hair is tied up in a samurai bun, and a messy beard covers his cheeks. He watches Hana with a lowered brow and wolf eyes... and something more I'm not sure I like.

"Is he mute?" I tilt my head to the side, trying to catch his attention.

Oscar turns his gaze on me, and it chills me to the bone. I want to believe Hutch wouldn't work with anyone dangerous, but I don't feel entirely safe around this guy.

"I can speak." Scar's voice is deep and raspy. "When there's something to say."

"Okay, then." Chewing my lip, I glance at a smiling Dirk. "My sister's a photographer. She's also, a bit... How do I say it?"

"Special." Scar's heavy boots scuff on the floor. "I've got her."

With that he leaves us alone in my uncle's office. As soon as he's out of sight, I turn wide eyes on the younger Winston brother. "He's safe, right?"

Dirk presses his lips together, shaking his dark head. "No way, he's a badass with some serious baggage. He's scary as fuck, but he won't hurt your sister."

Exhaling heavily, I go to my uncle's chair and drop into it. "What's going on around here, Dirk?"

"I have no idea, but we're going to find out. I'll start with the names in this book. I'm pretty good at finding things on the dark web. If your uncle was mixed up in something shady, I'll find it. There's always a trail."

"So you're still a computer genius?"

Dirk was always handsome, not as tall and bulky as his brother, but lean and muscular. Smart and sexy—if that's your type. Apparently my type is arrogant, bossy jarheads who slam you against the door and kiss your face off. I shift in my chair just thinking about it.

"Yep, and now I'm trying to use my skills for good." Dirk winks, giving me that dimpled grin that makes all the girls swoon. "What's new with you? Still modeling?"

"God, no, I only did that to pay the bills." I stand and walk around my uncle's office, looking up at the bookshelves. "I'm not tall enough, and I don't have the right body type for modeling. I'm too curvy." Looking over my shoulder, I wonder if I have another secret admirer. "I'm surprised you even knew I did that."

"I wouldn't have known, but I found my brother's spank bank one afternoon looking for a computer manual."

Heat rushes to my face, and I turn away before I blow my tough girl façade. "Whatever."

"So what's your story? It's been a while since you visited Hamiltown. Catch me up."

Dirk is only two years older than me, and when we were younger, we were friends. "Well, I finished at Columbia, got my degree in psychology."

"What?" He pretends to be surprised. "Why psychology? I thought you'd go into fashion merchandising or something like that."

"I don't know. It interested me. I guess I thought it might

help me understand people better." My mind drifts to all the people I don't understand in my life, from my mother to Hana to Debbie…

"Did it work?"

"Nope." We share a light laugh. "What about you? You came back here to work with your brother, the asshole? I thought you'd follow your father to Wall Street. You always had the brains for it."

"I've got the brains, but I also have a soul." He shrugs. "I'm not into hookers and blow. Besides, Hutch isn't so bad. He's stubborn and hates admitting he could be wrong. But he will, and it's interesting work."

"Interesting?" It's my turn to show disbelief. "What in the world ever happens in Hamiltown?"

"You'd be surprised. Last week we caught a guy flashing old ladies."

"No!" I cry, placing my hand on my chest. "Not in wholesome Hamiltown!"

"Come to find out, he was autistic." He makes a thoughtful face. "He still has to keep his pecker in his pants, though."

Snorting a laugh, I shake my head. "Why aren't the cops dealing with these things?"

"You know how it is. Everyone calls Hutch. He's their guy. They get what they need, and nobody gets a record or goes to jail. He's the original neighborhood cop."

"But he's not a cop." I hold up a finger. "He's a private investigator."

"Try peddling that crap around here." Dirk gives me a wink. "How's your mom?"

"Same as always, doing her best to spend all her money. Shopping in Milan and Paris, skiing in St. Moritz. When she feels guilty, she works on the spring charity gala."

"Reminds me of Pop. He only ever cared about his shit.

Sometimes I wonder why he even had kids. Then I remember my mom."

"Your dad should've hooked up with my mom."

"Who's to say he didn't?"

I feel like we should open a bottle of rye and make an afternoon of reminiscing and comparing notes, but I remember the reason we're here.

"So what are we going to do about Uncle Hugh?" I exhale softly, my chest heavy. "Where is he, Dirk? Do you think he's been hurt?"

"I don't think so. My guess is he might be hiding out somewhere."

"But he asked us to come home. Why would he do that if he was running away?"

He nods. "That's where my theory falls flat. I don't know, but I can tell you Hutch won't sleep until he finds him. That man is like a father to him."

I'm comforted by his words, and I believe they're true.

"What's happening here?" The low voice jump-starts my heart, and I turn quickly to see the devil himself standing in the doorway in loose jeans and a black tee stretched taut over his muscles.

Hutch looks different to me today, and when his green eyes rise slowly from my waist over my breasts to my eyes, it's like a caress that stokes the fire smoldering in my belly.

"Got something for you." Dirk hands over the book.

Hutch opens it and quickly scans the pages. His dark brow lowers, and he glances at me briefly before passing it back to his brother. "See if any of this corresponds to a direct investment company called RDIF Kazan."

"RDIF Kazan." Dirk nods and heads out the door, leaving me alone with the brute.

Crossing my arms, I study him. "Do you know what that's about?"

"Last night, you told me Victor Petrova had embezzled from your father's estate, and it finally started making sense. I think your uncle was watching this investment fund, following the money to see if it led back to Victor."

My arms drop along with my jaw. "You think he was trying to recover what was stolen from us?"

"Maybe. It would fit with the numbers, the theft. Your uncle liked to do things on his own. He would say 'ignorance is safety.'"

"Do you think…" A knot grips my throat, and I take a breath. "Do you think they killed him?"

"I don't know. I hope not."

A sob hiccups in my chest, and Hutch closes the space between us, crushing me in his embrace. I grip his arm, surrounded by sage and citrus and the warmth of his body.

"I can't lose another person I love." My voice is small, and pain like knives stabs my stomach.

I feel pressure at the top of my head, and I hear him inhale deeply before answering. "I won't stop until I find him, and I won't let anyone get away with hurting him. That's my promise to you."

Closing my eyes, I nod, doing my best to collect myself. Clearing my throat, I step back and wipe my eyes with my fingertips. "I'll help you. I think that must be why he wanted us here."

"I know why he wanted you here."

I look around the office, unsure if we know anything. "Why?"

"I told you. He wanted me to keep you safe, and most of these guys are located in New York City. It was the worst place you and Hana could be if something went down. They could use you as leverage."

"So what now?"

"Now it's our turn to follow the money, and the good news is we're some badass mother fuckers."

My lips press into a tentative smile. "That's something."

He slides his hand along my arm. "It's more than that. Now let's find your uncle."

CHAPTER 7

Hutch

"**Y**OU WERE RIGHT." DIRK TURNS HIS LAPTOP SCREEN WHERE I can see it, sliding a finger down each of the names in the ledger. "They're all partners in the investment group."

"Track them down. I want to know where all of them were the night Hugh disappeared."

"You think these guys do their own dirty work?"

"Probably not, but we'll start at the top and work our way down."

It's after dinner, and Hana and Pepper are in the living room playing Mancala. The noise of glass beads tapping on wood mixes with their soft squeals and laughter.

Scar stands with his back to the archway watching them, and Blake said goodnight, going upstairs to shower. I've done my best not to imagine that scene since she left us, her naked body under the spray.

"Feels like a real breakthrough." Dirk shakes his head. "But I can't believe it would be this easy."

"One of us needs to go to New York." I look from my brother to our silent partner in the doorway.

Seconds tick past, and Dirk exhales a laugh. "I guess you mean me, since I'm the only one not completely whipped around here."

"It's not like that. Hugh asked me to keep an eye on his nieces."

"Which Scar and I are fully capable of doing."

Standing to my full height, I look down at my little brother. "I also have another commitment. It seems you told Pepper she had a snowball's chance in hell of getting me to throw the first pitch at her softball game?"

Dirk holds up both hands. "Hang on, that's not what I said."

"It's pretty close."

"Fine." He shakes his head. "I'll go to New York. A visit to dear old Dad might be the perfect excuse for poking around a shady Russian investment group."

"Hell, he probably does business with them."

"Nice." Dirk slides his laptop into a slim case and punches Scar's shoulder. "You ready?"

The big guy pulls his lip ring between his teeth and nods, glancing back once more to the girls sitting on the floor. Hana's in white sweatpants and a red cropped sweatshirt that looks like it's been washed too many times.

When she sees them leaving, she hops up, and the shirt rises to show off a tiny gold hoop piercing her navel. I've never seen a wolf salivate... til now.

"Pepper, time for bed." I step to the door, giving the low order.

Pepper runs to me, and I catch her in a jump. Hana lingers behind a moment, watching us do our usual, loud grunts as we squeeze each other good night.

"Night, Uncle Duke!" Pepper cries over my shoulder, and Dirk gives her a high five.

Then he punches Scar's shoulder again. "Come on, bro. Looks like I'm pulling an all-nighter."

"Goodnight, Hana." Scar's voice is smooth, almost civilized, and Hana's cheeks lift with the ghost of a smile.

"Remember to think about those photos." She walks slowly to where he's standing. She's so delicate next to him. "It'll be fun. Not nearly as painful as all those tattoos."

He looks down. "I don't do photos."

Her voice is soft but unexpectedly strong. "Try something new."

He straightens, and follows my brother out the door without another word. Hana watches him go before walking slowly to the stairs, not looking back.

I'm not sure if I'm happy or annoyed by this development. From what I know, she's an addict and a loose cannon, and the last thing I need is my best tracker distracted by whatever bad shit follows her around. I need his head in the game.

Still, if he's keeping his eye on her, that's one less person I have to worry about.

Exhaling deeply, I look up the stairs. And I'm a fucking hypocrite to talk about being distracted. Blake has my brain all twisted, but at least she'll cooperate with me. In her way.

Turning I head to my bedroom, thinking about our next steps. My mind hasn't shut off since the day Hugh disappeared. Hell, it's been running like a computer in the background since the night I discovered that dead body in his trunk.

I feel more certain than ever this shit is connected. The question is *how*.

Stripping down, I step into the shower. Tonight I'm not as tense thinking about her, and I hope some of these pieces will come together under the hot spray.

My hair's wet, and I'm standing at the desk in my bedroom in only my gray sweatpants. As I expected, halfway through my shower, I got an idea and needed to sketch it out. I've drawn a triangle on a blank sheet of paper. Petrova, the RDIF, and the van Hamilton estate are at each point with Hugh in the center. My bet is on money laundering, and Hugh was building a case.

Snatching up my phone, I text Dirk what I'm thinking and what I know from my conversation with Blake last night. He agrees it appears to be about Victor and the embezzled funds.

Is it possible Hugh went to New York to confront them himself? Dirk's question pulls me up short.

No. He was in too poor health for that. Still, we haven't found his cell phone, either online or in the house, which leads me to believe he didn't want to be tracked. *It would be my last guess. But keep your eyes open.*

I put my phone down feeling good, like we're making progress, when I hear a light tap on the door.

"Hutch?" Blake's soft voice stirs in my stomach, creating a warm brew.

I cross the room and open it to see her standing in those gray short shorts again. She's in that black tank with her hair up on her head, and her eyes blink quickly from my bare chest to the bulge in my sweats and quickly up to my eyes.

She's flustered and fucking gorgeous.

"What's up?" I give her a half grin, and she blinks to the side.

"I'm sorry, I didn't mean to interrupt… whatever you're doing in here."

I imagine she's thinking about what I was doing last night—and now I am too.

"I was just texting with Dirk. It's possible we've had a breakthrough. He's headed to New York to chase it down."

Hopeful eyes return to mine. "That's good news, yes?"

"It's a solid lead." Stepping back, I cross my arms over my bare chest. "What can I do for you?"

Her full lips press together, and her eyes trace my arms before blinking away. "I wanted to thank you for today, at the house. I didn't mean to break down on you like that."

Sliding my arms down, I gentle my tone. "A lot's happened. It's natural to feel overwhelmed."

"Still, I'm sorry if I made you uncomfortable."

This girl, always acting so strong, always pushing me away. I want to pull her close again, inhale her sweet scent. "You never make me uncomfortable."

She clears her throat, shaking her head. "Well, that's all. Thank you, and it won't happen again."

She steps back, starting to go, but I reach out to catch her hand. "Hang on."

She pauses, looking at the place we're joined, and I release her.

"I know you're angry about what happened in the past, but you can't hate me forever."

"I can try." Our eyes meet, and she's so damn sexy doing her best to stay mad with her nipples peaked and her cheeks flushed in her bare feet with those cute red toenails. "You're still the townie jarhead who traveled a thousand miles to ruin my life."

"Easy now." My chest tightens. "It wasn't like that. I couldn't finish my tour without knowing you were safe and out of that fucking place."

"Then you can't judge my sister for how she is now. I wasn't there to protect her."

I don't know if she's right. That damn silver scar on her

head is proof positive she isn't strong enough for the rat's nest we've uncovered. I only know one thing right now.

"I'm not going to retread old ground, Blake. I did what I did for you. Maybe it wasn't perfect, and I'll own that. I want to make this right."

Her lips tighten and she steps closer. "You still think you can charge in and fix everyone's problems like some knight in shining armor no one called?"

"I stopped thinking that a long time ago."

"So, the stubborn bully has changed his ways?"

"I'm not a bully. I'm also not some Upper East Side asshole you can toy with."

"You don't know me at all if that's what you think."

My brow furrows. We're not shouting. Our voices aren't even raised, but she's standing in front of me, breathing fast. My will to fight begins to fade.

She traces her finger along the tattoo covering my shoulder. It's a red and black shield that reads *Veritas*. Truth.

Silver-blue eyes meet mine. "You're not a knight, but you have a shield?"

"It's my job—to find the truth, see that justice is done."

"I'd think you were a square if I didn't know you better." Her eyes glide down my bare chest, to my waist and lower, and her eyebrow arches. "Were you having a repeat of last night in the shower?"

I reach past her to push the door closed, then I put my hands on her shoulders and lean down to run my nose along the top of her ear, into her hair.

She smells like the fragrant roses that grow along the fence in the back garden, and watching her melt under my touch has my dick an iron rod in my gray sweats.

"No." My voice is deep. "Tonight I want the real thing."

"Give me your hand." I do as she says, and she takes it, lifting it to her lips. "So big... Like all of you."

Then she places it on her breast. I feel her tight nipple pressing against my palm, a mouthwatering handful. "Show me what you want."

Our eyes meet moments before our mouths. Warmth sealing together, a volcano is in my chest on the verge of eruption. I press her back to the door as our lips part and our tongues curl. It's been a long time coming, and I have no reason to resist her.

I lift her legs, wrapping them around my waist, and her arms loop around my neck. Our mouths chase each other's as I rock my hips against her core. Her thighs squeeze, and she rides me, little noises escaping her throat on each lift.

My brain is on fire, but I manage to break the kiss, catch my breath before completely devouring her. Looking down, my primal urges roar to life at the sight of her scuffed, pink lips, and her dark, hungry eyes. Still, I have to be sure.

"Are we doing this?" I sound like an animal.

"Weren't we always?" Her eyes hold mine, and I have my answer.

We were always going to be here, whether it was tonight or some other night.

I move my hand under her butt, curling my fingers and memorizing the feel of it in my hand. Hugh sent me a copy of her magazine spread two years ago, claiming he was so proud, he was buying a copy for everyone. I'm pretty sure that wasn't true.

Not that I'm complaining. She was hot as fuck, a pinup with mouthwatering curves for days. Her hair and swimsuit were wet, and the top of her bikini barely covered her round breasts. The string bottoms cut into her ass in a way that got me off, and I dreamed of touching her, sliding my tongue along every inch of her body. Now it's happening.

Releasing her legs, I lower her to her feet, and her hands go to my waist. Her fingers push at the waistband of my gray sweatpants, and I reach down to shove them off my hips.

Stepping out, I kick them away, and my erection points right at her.

Her full bottom lip disappears under her teeth, and she reaches down to grip my shaft, sliding her hand up and down my hardness. I wince, fighting back a groan. A drop of precum is on the tip, and it smooths her strokes. I'm ready to rip her clothes off and fuck her hard, but it's our first time.

She's a grown woman now. Her body is mine to claim, and I intend for this night to be memorable for us both.

CHAPTER 8
Blake

HE'S HUGE. EVERYWHERE.

Stretching higher, I kiss him, tangling our tongues as my hand continues slowly pumping his iron cock. His muscles are tense, and the barely restrained power of him has wetness flooding my core.

Breaking away with a low groan, he lifts my tank over my head before covering my peaked nipples with large hands.

"I've wanted to touch you for so long." His hot breath coats my skin, and I rise on my toes as my eyes close. "I'm going to taste every part of you and fuck you hard."

"Yes…" I manage to exhale.

He turns my back to his chest, lifting my breasts with both hands and twisting my nipples between his fingers. The sensation floods my lower belly with lust so strong my back arches.

"Oh, God, I'm going to come." My orgasm starts to flutter, and he stops.

"Not so fast." His cocky grin is at my ear, and I turn my head to bite his jaw.

"Asshole," I tease, and his hand slides over my stomach.

"You'll thank me when I make you see stars."

No doubt. When I stood in the doorway, I nearly swooned at the sight of him shirtless, muscles flexing in those gray sweatpants that did nothing to hide his fucking donkey dick.

I had to push back at him and that damn, satisfied smile. I couldn't be *that* easy, but my fight only turns him on more, which turns me on more, which brings us to this place.

I've had a one-track mind since I saw him in the shower and he kissed my face off last night. Now I'm pressed against his body, and his large hand slides down my bare stomach.

"Are you ready for me?" His fingers pass my waistband, spreading my body and finding my clit.

"Oh, yes," I exhale as they circle, then whimper as his thick digits move lower, pushing deep into my saturated core.

"So fucking wet." His beard scratches my neck, and he pulls my skin between his teeth.

I'm so close to coming, my knees tremble, when all at once, the floor disappears. He sweeps me into his arms and carries me to the bed, dropping me onto my back on the mattress before stripping off my shorts and my thong at the same time.

A whisper of cool air touches me briefly before his face is between my legs, large arms spreading my thighs as he drags his tongue slowly up the seam of my core, beard scuffing my hypersensitive skin.

Screaming a moan, I arch hard against the bed, and he stops, moving up and over me to cover my mouth with his. My taste is on his tongue, and he kisses me long and sloppy before lifting his chin to meet my eyes.

"Be quiet, or you'll wake Pepper." His green eyes are hotly amused, and I grab his face to kiss him again.

Our mouths slide against each other, and it's like the most decadent, forbidden fruit. How long has this fantasy been growing in the back of my mind? As much as I want to hate him for his arrogance, I've never been able to deny my body's need for his.

His narrow waist is between my thighs, and as our legs slide together, his rigid cock presses against my stomach. I want him inside me so much it hurts.

"Fuck me, Hutch." My voice is ragged, and his eyes darken.

Leaning to the side, I hear him dig in his nightstand drawer before pulling out a condom. The square packet is beside me on the bed, and he rises to his knees, looking down on me.

"Can you be quiet?" It's a stern demand, like he might spank me if I don't, and a thrill races to my toes.

"What if I say no?"

He blinks slowly, and the muscle in his jaw moves. "Here." He puts a pillow in my hand, and guides it to my face. "Use this."

I'm about to hit him with another sassy comeback, but his mouth is on my pussy again, and I grip the pillow to my face as fiery hot deliciousness sizzles in my belly. He traces his tongue over my clit, moving it quickly around and around, hungry and relentless.

His lips close fully over my most sensitive parts, and he sucks, once, twice, and I break with a scream fisting the pillow as my hips jerk and my legs tremble.

My pussy flutters wildly as he quickly rolls on the condom. When I feel his tip nudging my entrance, entering slowly, another burst of spasms grips my core. I bite the pillow to drown my voice as he drives fully inside, burying his fat cock all the way to the hilt.

"Jesus!" I gasp, and cool air hits my face.

He throws the pillow to the floor. "I want to see you take me."

"It's too big," I gasp, arching my back.

Large hands caress my ass, fingers sliding down to trace my inner thighs. "Relax, baby. You got this."

Slowly, he begins to rock, sliding in and out, and my lips part. "Oh, God…" I gasp, repeating the words as my back arches.

I rock my hips around the sensation of utter fullness as my body changes, molding to him completely.

"Oh, yeah." His voice is hot, urgent. His eyes squeeze shut, and a bead of sweat runs down his temple as his hips rock. "So fucking tight…"

My fingernails cut into his forearms as he picks up speed, driving into me faster. The friction is incredible, and my hips rise off the bed to meet him. My third orgasm is coming fast, and when my lips part, he covers them with his, consuming my scream in his kisses.

He pumps into me hard and strong as my orgasm breaks, and I moan loudly into his mouth. He keeps going, on and on, before holding. Large muscles flex beneath my fingers, and his cock jerks deep inside me, filling the condom.

Our lips slide against each other's as he groans. We're shooting through the stars together, holding each other in a release a decade in the making.

Hutch's strong arms are around my waist, and he holds my back to his chest, skin against skin. I trace my finger along the lines of muscle in his forearm. It's nice, but I wiggle around to face him in the bed.

For a little while we drifted in and out of sleep, and now it's after midnight. The full moon shines so brightly through the window, it's like a misty, black-and-white day.

Propping my head on my hand, I study his perfect face, square jaw, full lips painted silver in the moonlight. The house is so quiet.

He lifts a lock of my dark hair, curling it around his finger, and I have to ask, "What are you thinking?"

He blinks slowly, as the corner of his mouth rises. "You're in my bed."

"Are you sorry?"

"No."

I trace my finger along the edge of the black and red tattoo on his shoulder. "I thought you hated me. You were always so angry… Until last night."

"I've never hated you." Our eyes meet, and his are dark. "You were a temptation I had to avoid. Fucking jailbait."

His confession tickles my stomach. "I'm not that much younger than you."

"Enough to matter." He slides his hand along my waist, and heat follows its path. "I waited a long time for this."

I slant my eyes at him. "Dirk said you had my magazine spread."

The muscle in his jaw moves attractively. "Dirk has a big mouth."

Rolling onto my back, I scrub my hand over my forehead. "It was embarrassing. I am *not* fashion-model material." My face heats as I remember how it went. "The photographer said he'd never shot a girl my size before."

He props on his elbow, moving my hand away. "A healthy, gorgeous girl with sexy curves?"

"I'm pretty sure he meant I was fat."

"Fuck that guy. You looked good. *Really* good."

That old embarrassment melts in the warmth rising in my chest. "You've always looked really good to me."

Leaning down, he seals his lips over mine gently, sliding our tongues together, and lighting my insides. His spicy, fresh scent surrounds me. Salt is on my tongue, and I thread my fingers in his soft hair. His rough hand slides down, over my hip, then between my legs.

His lips move into my hair. "Are you sore?"

"No." I pull his shoulder so he's on top of me, resting his weight on his elbows. I lift my knees and wrap them around his waist. "Fill me up."

A quick kiss and he retrieves a fresh condom from the nightstand before rolling it on and resuming his position. Our mouths meet, tongues entwine, and a bubble of anticipation grows in my stomach. One long thrust, and my chin lifts with a moan.

His body holds me down with his delicious weight, and I close my eyes, riding the waves of pleasure taking me higher. As my orgasm filters through my pelvis, I savor this release. I let it consume me, blocking out any fears and doubts.

The bubble bursts, filling me with shimmering pleasure, and he comes with a deep groan, finishing inside me.

It's a curious bliss, this gorgeous mountain of a man wanting me, praising me, filling me. It's an appealing escape from the shit show I'm hiding from back home—a suggestion there might be something different waiting for me in this place I've always avoided.

But I have so much to sort through first, and I don't want to think about it now.

Tomorrow will be here soon enough.

CHAPTER 9
Blake

Too soon. The thought drifts through my mind as dawn slowly brightens Hutch's master bedroom.

My eyes open, and I look around the masculine suite. It's all dark woods, navy fabrics, and straight edges. I'm wrapped in a warm cocoon on one side of his king-sized bed, and I hear the whisper of his breathing across from me.

Sliding quietly out of bed, I tiptoe to where my gray sleep shorts and black tank lie in a heap just inside the door. Last night feels like a different world to me now. I'm shaken and disoriented, like did that actually happen?

I steal a glance at Hutch, gorgeous with the blanket draped low across his waist. One arm is over his head, and he's a Michaelangelo lying in repose with the yellow light of dawn highlighting his sculpted physique.

Biting my lip, I slip through the door without waking him.

The second floor is silent and dark, but when I enter our room, I'm surprised to see my sister up and fully dressed in jeans and riding boots. A red and cream plaid flannel shirt is open over her gray tee, and her hair is in a low ponytail.

She takes one look at me and continues gathering her things.

"Where are you going?" I ask softly.

"I'm heading over to Uncle Hugh's to take some pictures. Dawn is really beautiful at the stables."

Hesitating, I look to my bed then back at her. "I'll go with you."

"Hurry up. It's a short window of time."

We're out the door in less than five minutes, in the golf cart I recognize from my uncle's garage, driving to the estate in the misty morning.

"How did you get this golf cart?"

She shrugs. "Scar said he'd bring it over for me last night."

I look behind the seat to see her canvas bag is packed. She appears ready for a day of work.

"Did I fall asleep for a hundred years?"

Hana shoves a spiral curl behind her ear and gives me a quick glance before returning her eyes to the road. "I think coming here was a good thing. The city is so toxic. Don't you love the air? I don't remember it being this way when we visited before."

I want to say it was probably because she was always high— or because she appears to be sparking a little romance with Hutch's silent and scary partner.

Instead I simply agree. "It's nice."

I've got enough going on in my brain with everything that's happened to me in the last twenty-four hours.

She slows the cart and stops at the front door. "Hop out. Unless you want to go with me to the stables?"

"No, I'll stay here." I look up at the grand entrance. "I'll make us some coffee and breakfast if I can find anything. I'm sure Norris can help me. Come back when you're finished."

Her eyes have a distant look, and she nods. "I'll be back in a half hour."

I watch her silently cruise away, a mix of relief and anxiety swirling in my chest. Will her new interest in life continue if we return to the city? Should she stay here? Rubbing my forehead, I put my hand on the door before I realize I don't have a key. I have my phone, but I knock, waiting to see if Norris will answer.

He does in a burgundy silk damask robe. "Miss Blake! I wouldn't have expected you at this hour. My goodness, I'm not even dressed. Are you alone? Do you require coffee? Tea?"

This old man has been with my uncle since I was a child, and I hate to see him so stressed and anxious. Placing my hand on his forearm, I give it a squeeze.

"Coffee would be great, but don't worry. I'll make my own if you'll show me around the kitchen. Hana is taking pictures in the stables, so she'll be a few minutes. Is there anything I could make for breakfast?"

"Of course, Miss. I have eggs, batter for pancakes, waffles, scones—"

"Eggs would be perfect. And toast? Bacon?" He nods, and I put my hand in the crook of his arm. "Lead me to the kitchen, and I'll do inventory."

Norris excuses himself, and I pour a cup of coffee. I tell him to take his time, while I walk through the house, thankful for a bit of alone time to sort out my thoughts.

Dropping onto a plush velvet sofa in the living room, I think back over the last twelve hours. I slept with Hutch, several times, and it was very, very good. A charge radiates through my belly, and I put my hands over my face. What am I doing?

I can't start something with him. We have nothing in common. All we have is ridiculously hot chemistry. He's firmly established here in Hamiltown, and my life is entirely in New York…

A life I hate.

Still, my friends are there…

Or are they?

Besides Hana, Debbie was my only real friend in the city, and a weight presses down painfully in my chest when I think about what happened to her. Coming here, finding Uncle Hugh missing, I realize I haven't even searched for the latest on her case.

Taking out my phone, I do a quick Google search that tells me… Police haven't released any details. With a sigh, I consider texting Trip. The very idea makes my skin uncomfortably tight. I don't want to talk to him.

I could ask Hutch to help me—and take a chance of giving him even more reasons to judge my sister, my lifestyle, and my so-called friends.

Hutch Winston and I are very different people. We don't share the same world view.

Or do we?

Being in this place, seeing Hana here, I feel like my life in New York doesn't reflect who I really am and what I want, at least not anymore. I do want peace—it's why I jumped on my uncle's invitation to come here so fast.

Pushing off the couch, I take my coffee mug to the kitchen. There's really no point in devoting so much time and emotional energy on this when I don't even know how Hutch feels. If he's not serious, all the mental gymnastics could be a colossal waste of time.

I'm feeling pretty silly and childish when I notice Norris hurrying to the front door. My brow furrows, and I don't remember hearing the doorbell ring or anyone knocking.

When he opens it, my stomach drops. Two men I do not want to see saunter in like they own the place.

"How's it going, chap?" Trip slaps Norris on the shoulder

like they're old pals when they've never even met. "We're looking for Blake and Hana."

"Trip?" I'm frowning as I close the distance between us. "What the hell?"

"Blake! And a kind hello to you, too." Trip arches an eyebrow at me, and my lips tighten.

"Sorry, you caught me off-guard." I hold out my hand, and he takes it, stepping forward to kiss my cheek. "How are you doing? What are you doing in Hamiltown?'

"Coming to see you, of course." He sets his Hartman luggage on the landing, and Norris moves it to the side. "New York is boring without you, without Debbie."

"New York is a pain in the ass right now." I haven't seen Greg Peters in a month. He kisses my cheek as he surveys the entrance to my uncle's home. "Thought we'd check out this family estate you've got. It's better than I expected."

"What did you expect?" I arch an eyebrow, doing my best to appear strong as always.

"Not this. Where's the taxidermy?"

"Fresh out, but you can go pheasant hunting in the halls." I quip.

"Do I smell coffee? I could use a cup if so." Greg drops his Gucci duffle on the marble landing, and I wince at his casual treatment of Norris.

The older man doesn't even seem to notice, lifting Trip's heavy suitcase and Greg's bag. "I'll just take these to the bedrooms."

My eyes cut from the bags to the butler, and I sigh. "They can stay in the east wing, Norris. I'll move Hana's and my things into the west bedrooms."

"Yes, ma'am." He dutifully takes the two bags.

"We're not putting you out, are we, love?" Concern is not in Trip's tone, and I remember why I didn't feel like contacting him.

"Come with me." I lead them past the living room, past Uncle Hugh's study, to the kitchen. "I assume my sister told you we were here?"

Trip gives me an entitled smirk. "We keep up with each other."

It's not a straight answer, but Greg distracts me, scanning the walls and looking in my uncle's study. The combination of his light hair and brown eyes so dark you can't see his pupils gives him a sneaky look. I've never trusted Greg Peters, and his interest in my uncle's estate makes me want to shut the door and lock it.

Unlike monochromatic Trip, who reminds me of a labradoodle with a drinking problem. I've often wondered if he takes anything seriously.

"I'm surprised you've never had the gang out here," Trip complains. "Shame on you for hiding a mansion, stables… What else does this dump have? Hot tub?"

We're in the kitchen, and I take down two additional mugs. "It's my uncle's full-time residence, so I don't think descending on him *en masse* would be very polite."

"Where is your uncle now?" Greg's hands are in the pockets of his brown slacks, and he watches my expression.

I smile and lie through my teeth. "Uncle Hugh is visiting some friends for a few days."

"Too bad, we'll be gone before he returns," Trip takes a flask from his inside jacket pocket and spikes his coffee with what looks like whiskey. "We came to retrieve you for the Belmont Gala. Your mother will stroke out if you and Hana aren't there. Irish?"

He holds the flask of whiskey to me, and I shake my head. "No thanks." I lift my mug, taking a sip of straight coffee. "I'm not going to the gala this year."

"What the fuck? Why not?"

"I haven't heard from Mama in weeks, and I don't feel like

a charity for a racetrack is where I should be with Debbie's situation unresolved."

"Where else would you be? Here?" Trip argues, but Greg remains silent, watching me. "We can't mope around *ad infinitum* while we wait for the cops to tell us what we already know."

"What do we know?" I snap, immediately hating that I've shown my emotions.

Now they know how much I care, which is always dangerous around fucking Greg Peters. Yeah, some friend group. Why do I want to go back to New York again?

Trip puts his arm around my shoulders. "Suicide's a bitch. So much blame. So many unanswered questions. She didn't even leave a note."

"It doesn't make sense." My voice is quiet, and I blink back the sudden heat in my eyes.

Greg's measured voice ends it. "Being together will help everyone get past what happened. Go with us to the gala."

He's completely void of emotion, which pisses me off, and I wouldn't be caught dead at the fucking Belmont Gala with how I feel.

Still, there's no point in arguing. "If you don't want breakfast, Norris can show you to your rooms. Hana's at the stables taking pictures. I'll let her know we have company."

My phone buzzes in my pocket, and I lift it to see a text that closes my throat. *You're running out of time. $500K, six days. -P*

"Everything okay?" Trip's eyes are on me, and I quickly school my expression.

"Of course. So you're staying one night? Two? I need to run to town to be sure we have enough supplies for all of us."

"Shouldn't your uncle have enough supplies if you're staying with him?" Greg watches me, and I shift uncomfortably.

My discomfort skyrockets when the back door leading into the kitchen opens, and two big guys fill the room.

"What's going on here?" Hutch towers over me with scary Scar right behind him.

He's angry, and I silently pray he doesn't say anything about my uncle's house being off-limits to visitors.

Overprotective is a sexy look on Hutch. I want to be glad to see him after our night of passion, but the text on my phone is burning a hole in my hand and Greg Peters has me on edge.

"Greg, Trip, meet Hutch Winston and Oscar Lourde."

"Interesting." Trip's eyes cut from me to Hutch and back again, and he crosses his arms like he knows something. "What exactly are you doing here, B?"

Greg doesn't say a word, and a knot twists in my throat.

Hutch's green eyes laser into mine, and I can barely breathe. "We need to talk. Now."

CHAPTER 10
Hutch

SUNLIGHT SHINES BRIGHT THROUGH MY WINDOWS, WAKING ME.
I slide my hand across the cold sheets to find Blake is gone, and I'm fucking pissed. My hard-on only adds fuel to the fire. Then I see the clock.

"Mother fucker." It's after nine, and I should be in the office.

I can't believe I overslept. Lurlene is my backup for getting Pepper to school, but I feel like a king-sized asshole for not being up to tell her goodbye. Last night was clearly mind-blowing in more ways than one if I forgot to set my alarm.

Moving fast, I'm showered, changed and heading out the door with a coffee in my hand in under twenty minutes.

Scar is at his desk when I enter the small space we use for an office. It's pretty basic, glass double doors with *Winston & Lourde* hand-lettered across the center. Inside we each have a desk and a tower of filing cabinets at the back wall that holds the few paper documents we keep.

Dirk maintains the massive computer server and firewall

that's the brains of the office. Dirk would say he's the brains of the office, and while he is our resident computer genius, he's full of shit. We all bring different strengths to the group.

I'm more old-school. I have four years of military experience, a smartphone, and a gun. I can bench-press 400, and my word is my bond. I'm also the leader, having founded this firm five years ago.

Scar looks up from his laptop, and his wolf eyes narrow. "You seem very relaxed today." He leans back, in his chair, giving me a rare grin. "Hell, I don't think I've ever seen you more relaxed. Does this have something to do with your tardiness?"

"Fuck off." I can't believe that asshole is hassling me for being late for the first time in… *ever*. "Did anything happen overnight?"

Other than my world shifting.

In addition to Dirk's work on that ledger, I've asked the local sheriff's department to update us on cars coming in and out of Hamiltown the night Hugh went missing.

"Actually, I've got something you'll want to see." He rises to his full six-foot-four height, two inches taller than me, and I frown.

"Something off the tip line?"

"Nope." He pulls out a linen envelope. "Slid under the door."

My stomach drops. I'd recognize that stationary anywhere. Snatching it out of his hand, I breathe through the tightness in my chest. I should probably consider what it means that I care more about Hugh van Hamilton than my own damn dad.

Opening it, I see brown ink on cream paper, and in Hugh's unmistakably precise handwriting:

You're on the right track.

Keep going,

Hugh

"What the fuck?" I look up at my partner.

"Turn it over."

I do as he says, and I read in small script at the bottom corner, *Tell Norris I have my pills.*

My eyes narrow, and I don't know if I'm unreasonably furious or completely disbelieving. "Did you check it out?"

"I was waiting for you."

"Let's go."

We hustle out to my truck, and I drive us the short distance to Hugh's house. A white Mercedes I don't recognize is parked in the circular drive; otherwise it looks the same as always.

Exiting the vehicle, I motion to Scar. "No need to disturb Norris. I have a key to the back door."

He lifts his chin, and we walk around to the kitchen entrance. I stop in my tracks, surprised and annoyed at the sight that greets me. Blake is inside serving coffee to two well-dressed assholes I vaguely recognize from her New York crowd.

Her eyes widen when she sees me, and I quickly take in her appearance.

She's fucking hot in shredded jeans that hug her curves and a thin, gray sweater. It has a deep V-neck revealing a lacy black camisole, and my fucking dick responds to the sight. A lock of long, dark hair hangs over her full breast, and I want to slide my hands over it. Hell, I want my hands all over her sexy body.

Opening the glass door, I level my eyes on hers. Her smile is cautious, and the tightness in my chest increases.

"What's going on here?" I almost say *Who the fuck are these assholes*, but I figure that might escalate things too fast.

"Hutch," she quickly introduces all of us, and I file the names away.

I'll deal with these unexpected guests later. At present, my entire focus is on Blake and letting her know about Hugh. "We need to talk. Now."

The brown-haired guy makes a quip, but I'm not listening. Last night changed my feelings for her. She's more than a pampered Upper East Side party girl. Blake is deeper, she has a heart, and I want to save her from that old world—if she'll let me.

"Okay." Her voice is quiet, and she follows me out of the kitchen and down the short hallway to the formal dining room.

"Can we see your uncle's bathroom?"

"That's an odd request." Her nose wrinkles, and she looks around the house. "I have no idea..."

Shit, I feel like a jerk. Of course she doesn't know where it is. It's only the third time in her life I remember her visiting this place.

I catch her hand, stopping her movement. "Where's Norris?"

Her hand moves in mine, turning so our palms slide together, and it feels good—before she quickly pulls it away. "I asked him to set up the guys in the east wing of the house. He's probably still there."

We'll discuss that bit of information in a minute. "Take me to him."

Norris leads us to the master suite, and I rush ahead to the bathroom, taking out Hugh's pill bottles from the cabinet and quickly scanning the dates and the quantities in each one.

Pouring the contents into my hand, I do some quick math and glance up at Scar. "Fourteen days."

He nods, and we turn to Blake, who's frowning as she watches us. Her eyes flit from me to Scar. Norris is beside her just as confused.

"What's going on?" she asks, and I move closer.

"A note was left at the office. It's pretty brief, but it seems your uncle is okay. He's alive, and hell, I don't even think he was kidnapped."

I hand her the paper, and her eyes widen. She scans it quickly before looking up at me again. "You think it's really him?"

"It's his handwriting." I gently turn the page to the back. "And there's this."

She reads the postscript aloud. "Tell Norris I have my pills."

"Oh, thank heavens." We all three look at the old butler, and I realize Norris is the one most in danger of fainting. Luckily Scar is right beside him if he goes down.

The old fellow presses his palm to his chest. "I'm so relieved. He has his pills."

Blake returns to me. "I don't understand—so he *planned* to be gone for fourteen days?"

"Or he took what he figured he needed and left the bottle behind."

"Why would he do that?"

Exhaling slowly, I give the only answer that fits. "So nothing would appear disturbed."

"You mean… He *knew* someone would come looking for him?" Fear is in her eyes, and I want to pull her to me.

I want to take her in my arms and tell her I'll kill anyone who tries to hurt her. But we have an audience, so I keep it professional.

"It's hard to know what he was thinking, but at least we can breathe easier knowing he's alive and well."

And somehow he knows everything we're doing. I glance around the house, wondering where he planted the cameras. My gut says his office.

"Where's Hana?" Scar's voice is sharp, and Blake jumps.

"I think she's at the barn taking photos. She said something about the dawn… I don't know, but it's been a while."

He leaves us without a word, and Norris does a little bow. "I'm so relieved, Mr. Winston. Thank you for this. I'll just finish preparing the gentlemen's quarters. It'll be ready for them in the next few minutes, and Miss Blake, I'll be sure the west wing rooms are stocked."

"Thank you, Norris." She sees him out, and when the door

closes, she rests her forehead on it. "He's right, I guess. This is good news."

Stepping forward, I do what I've been wanting to do all morning. I catch her waist and pull her to me. She turns in my arms and places her cheek to my chest. Tilting my head, I inhale the soft scent of rose in her hair.

My voice is quiet, and I slide my palm gently up and down her back. "I don't know what the hell he's doing, but it seems your uncle has a plan."

She pulls back, looking up at me. "Does knowing he has a plan make it better?"

"It's better than when I opened my eyes this morning. A lot of things are better."

Her lip disappears into her mouth, and she steps away, crossing her arms over her waist. "Are they better? Everything feels more complicated to me."

I don't like the sound of that.

"Hey, look at me." I touch her cheek, and her pretty eyes meet mine. "Are you regretting last night?"

"No. Of course, not." Her shoulders relax and she waves a hand. "I just didn't want to make any assumptions, and with the way things are… that's all."

I feel like that's not all by a longshot, but we can start here. "I'd like to see you again—if you're interested."

"I'm interested."

I like how quickly she says it, and I'm sure my amusement is in my eyes. "Now, who the fuck are those assholes in the kitchen?"

Exhaling a laugh, she rolls her eyes. "Not my first choice of house guests, believe me."

"What do they want?"

"According to Trip, my mother sent them to check on me. Or, if you ask Greg, New York is a nightmare right now. Who knows which is the real story?"

"How long are they planning to stay?"

"A few days? They're headed back for the Belmont Gala."

"Is that still happening?"

"As a matter of fact, my mother is very involved in that annual event. She'll be pleased to know you're so interested." She's teasing, and I let my eyes roam her beautiful face. I like seeing her smile.

"I guess I'm not the gala type."

"To be honest, I'm not feeling much like it myself this year," she sighs. "I was just heading to your house to collect our things. Hana and I'll stay here while the guys are in town."

"I don't like that." I don't know if I'm being possessive or overprotective or both. "We still don't know what's going on around here or why Hugh left the way he did."

"I can't have Trip and Greg here alone, and I'm not telling them what's really going on." She gives me a little smile. "Don't worry, we'll be safe."

"Keeping you safe is my job." I hook my thumbs in her belt loops and pull her against my chest. "I don't want you out of my sight."

Gray-blue eyes meet mine, and she slides her hands up my shoulders. "It's only a few days. I can't exactly throw them out."

"Can't you?"

Rising on her toes, she lifts her lips to my ear. "You're not jealous are you?"

It registers straight to my cock, and I push her back against the door. "I don't get jealous. I get what I want."

Leaning down, I cover her mouth with mine. Her pillow lips part, and she tastes like sugar as her tongue curls with mine. I slide my hands from her waist, circling my thumbs over her pointed nipples, and she emits a soft whimper.

I'm hard as a rock, tracing my lips to her eyebrow and into her hair. "I can't fuck you if you're here."

"What's stopping you?"

I'm ready to jerk those jeans down her hips and nail her to the wall when I hear voices outside the door. Exhaling a swear, I step back, sliding my hand over the boner in my pants.

"Come back to the house for dinner tonight, and bring your guests." My tone is all business, and she's killing me leaning against the door with heat in her eyes, breathing fast. "Lurlene bought a pile of groceries, and she's planning a big dinner for all of us."

Her disappointed smile is very satisfying. I like knowing she wants more, because I plan to give it to her.

"We'll be there." She turns with a sigh, opening the door. "I'll pick up our things then."

I catch her arm, not wanting to leave her with a pout. Leaning down, I press my lips to hers once more, and she melts into me.

My hand rises to her cheek, and I press my thumb to her chin. She blinks her pretty eyes open slowly, and I let her go. "Tonight."

CHAPTER 11
Blake

"**T**WO MEN FROM NEW YORK?" LURLENE FLURRIES AROUND THE kitchen like the house is on fire. "I don't know if this is fancy enough. I need better dishes."

"An additional fifth of vodka will be plenty." I'm only half-teasing, hoping to calm her insecurity. "Trust me, Greg and Trip aren't picky. They'll drink more than they eat."

Lurlene looks back at me as she opens a small cabinet over a partially filled wine rack. "We have a bottle of scotch and this whiskey." She pulls out a small flask. "Hutch doesn't drink much now that Pepper's here."

That nugget of information is unexpectedly satisfying, and I watch as Lurlene lifts the lid from a pan of sizzling pork chops. The kitchen fills with the scent of garlic and herbs, and my stomach growls loudly.

"Damn, Lurlene, what are you making?"

She waves me away. "Just pork chops and gravy. Put those potatoes in the Cuisinart. They need to be mashed."

I carry a bowl of quartered, boiled potatoes from the

counter beside me to the stainless steel mixer and dump them in the bowl. She's preoccupied with the meat, and I lift a yellow box of cake mix, quickly scanning the directions on the side.

"I'm actually not too bad with a box. Want me to whip up the cupcakes?"

"Yes." She doesn't even hesitate, bumping me out of the way with her hip and flipping the switch to activate the massive beater. "Call Pepper in here, and she can help you."

Leaning to the side, I catch sight of Pepper and Hana in the living room playing Uno. Pepper goes out on my sister with a wild draw-four card, and she jumps up to do a little victory dance in her softball uniform. Hana throws her cards on the table, and Scar actually chuckles at her loud complaints.

"I can do it myself." I let the door close, returning to the island in the center of the busy room. It's all so damned warm and homey. Hana's playing Uno and drinking lemonade instead of gambling and smoking pot.

I glance over at Lurlene moving fast as I mix the ingredients. "I never see Pepper playing on her phone."

"Hutch is fighting it." She shakes her head, carrying the mashed potatoes "But he's in a losing battle if you ask me. All these kids are on the TikToks and the Snapchats. She'll be begging for her own phone soon enough."

I think about Hana playing games with this little girl, having experiences we never did. "I can't remember not having a phone."

Hell, I can't even remember playing cards outside a casino.

"I keep telling him the world is changing," Lurlene fusses. "He's stubborn as a mule, but she manages to get around him."

"It's true." My voice is soft, and I glance at her, smiling as I slide the cakes into the oven. "I hope he's able to hold out a little longer."

Warmth filters through my chest as I think about Hutch doing his best to give his little niece a traditional life. The brief time I spent at Bishop I had something of a normal life, since the nuns didn't allow phones. I could use my computer to send emails, but I didn't have social media.

I think about Debbie, and the pain aches in my heart. With the weight of my uncle's disappearance lifted, her loss and that fucking blackmail message have moved to the front burner in my mind.

I want to trust Hutch with these things. Going to the door, I study the group in the living room waiting to eat. Trip and Greg haven't arrived, which doesn't bother me. Our host is quietly sorting his mail at the door.

His hair is damp from a shower, which triggers heat low in my belly, thinking of last night. He's dressed in jeans and a black tee, and my eyes trace from his square jaw down his broad shoulders to his perfect ass.

He's hot as fuck, but he's so disapproving of everything about my life in New York. I can't really blame him, but do I trust him? Uncle Hugh clearly does.

The oven timer dings, and I decide the next time we're together alone, I'll test him out with something simple. I'll share my fears about Debbie, and if he doesn't overreact, I'll take a chance he can help me with the blackmail situation.

Taking out the small pot of frosting, I think about Oscar shadowing Hana like some ominous watchdog. He would definitely put an end to her problems, only, he might burn the whole city down in the process. Would that be so bad? My eyebrow arches as I lick the knife.

We take our usual seats at the table. Greg and Trip finally arrived, and they take seats on the other side of me at Hutch's right. Scar is beside Hana, and Dirk texted he's running late, not to wait, since Pepper has school.

Lurlene let me help arrange the pork chops on a platter, which we place in the center of the table. Crisp green beans are in a white bowl beside whipped mashed potatoes in another serving dish. The pink cupcakes are under glass, and they look pretty damn good if I say so myself.

We're passing the food around, when Trip pops off with his usual arrogance. "I have to say, Blake, your namesake town is a bit of a snooze. I mean, if we were making a documentary, that would be one thing, but what does anyone do around here for fun?"

I glance at Hutch who's loading his plate, jaw tense. "I haven't had a chance to explore Hamiltown since we've been back. I've been… busy. But we have horses to ride, and I baked these cupcakes."

"Quaint." Trip inspects the pink confections and takes another sip of vodka. "So Hutch, you're like the town detective? What's that like?"

Hutch levels his green eyes on my friend, and a block of concrete presses on my throat. Why did I ever think having Trip and Greg here for dinner was a good idea? They're arrogant pricks, and Hutch has zero tolerance for bullshit.

"It's interesting." He consumes a bite of meat, and Trip's eyebrow arches.

"You're kidding. Tell me, what's the worst crime you've handled in Hamiltown?"

Hutch places his fork down and leans back in his chair. "I'm not at liberty to discuss the specifics of any cases, but we have our share of incidents. Mostly my job is about keeping the peace."

"Which you are clearly a master at. I've never been in a place so peaceful. How about you, Grish? Are those crickets deafening or what?"

Hana shifts in her chair, exhaling an uneasy laugh. She's

been on edge since they arrived, and I've been tense, watching her for any sign of relapse. Scar's presence is my only relief.

Greg glances from my sister to Trip, and his eyebrows quirk in response. "Nature's white noise."

"New party game." Trip gestures at Greg and Hutch with his fork, leaning towards me. "Do a shot for every one-word answer they give."

I choke on my bite of pork, convinced I'll never make it through this meal when Dirk waltzes into the room.

"Sorry I'm late, but have I got news for… you…" His voice sputters out as Hutch stands, giving him the eye. The younger Winston smiles as he quickly takes a seat on the other side of Scar, across from Greg. "Hello, I didn't know we had dinner guests."

"They're friends of Blake and Hana's in town for a visit," Hutch answers, returning to his seat.

"I don't think we've met."

A quick round of introductions, and an awkward silence falls over the table. The only noise is the clicking of metal utensils against china, and I don't know why Pepper isn't talking Hana's ear off—or at the very least, Hutch's.

Her little eyes are droopy, and I guess she's been practicing hard.

I'm pretty much done, so I turn to her. "Your first game is tomorrow night, right Pep?"

The little girl climbs onto her knees in her chair and lifts the lid off the cupcakes. "Yep, first game of the season. Uncle Hutch is going to throw the opening pitch."

"I heard about that." I smile at him, and he gives me a brief smile.

Pepper takes a cupcake for herself and one for my sister before sitting back in her chair. Their friendship is cute, but Hana is retreating into herself again.

"What position do you play?" I take a cupcake for myself.

"Shortstop." She nods, getting pink frosting on her nose. "It's like one of the best positions on the team."

"I can't wait to see you play. Maybe we can all go tomorrow." I look from her to Hutch, who's looking at his brother with a neutral expression. "Wouldn't that be fun?"

His eyes flicker to mine, and I can tell he wasn't listening.

Trip, however, heard it all. "Peewee softball? Sounds delightful. Where and when?" His sarcasm is apparent.

"It's not Peewee. It's Little League." Pepper scowls at him fiercely, and Trip holds up both hands.

"Sorry, small-fry. I'm still learning the ropes."

Greg places his napkin beside his plate and stands abruptly. "Thank you for dinner. If you don't mind, it's been a long day."

"Of course," I stand, doing the same. "I'll ride back with you. Hana can bring the golf cart."

Hutch follows us to the door, catching my hand when we reach the landing. "I still think it would be better for you to stay here."

"Looks like you have your own personal watchdog, B." Trip pauses outside the door.

"The thing about watch dogs is they bite." Hutch's dark brow lowers. "Don't give me a reason."

"Is that a threat?" Trip's laugh is loose, and I know he's buzzing.

"I don't make threats."

My friend shrugs, walking away to the car, and I look up at Hutch. "They're harmless. You don't have to worry about me."

"I don't worry." He glances at the car, flexing his jaw, and I think he might. "Still, I'll stop by to check on you later."

"I'll leave the door unlocked."

"Lock all the doors. I have a key."

I confess, his fierce expression is doing it for me. "Even better. I'll wait up for you."

CHAPTER 12

Hutch

"**Y**OU'RE CERTAIN THE LEDGER DIDN'T BELONG TO HUGH?" We're back at the office, and Dirk is filling us in on what he found.

"I didn't discover it until I was in the city." He opens the thin book, pointing to the back cover where VP-K is written in ink at the top corner. "I was able to connect each of these transfers to accounts made by Victor Petrova. The only question I can't answer is how did Hugh get it and why?"

I think about what Blake told me, and I remember that night a month ago and the dead trespasser of eastern European descent. I think I know the answers to both of these questions. "How many days has Hugh been gone?"

"Almost a week, why?"

I retrieve the note and hand it to my brother. "Read both sides."

He quickly reads it and looks up at me. "You checked it out?"

"We counted fourteen days out of the pill bottle. It could

be an exact count or he might have brought extra to cover his bases. Either way, we're in a holding pattern until he decides to reappear and fill in the blanks."

"Not necessarily. The men in this book all have connections in the city. They're pretty good at covering their tracks, but I've been searching the names and addresses. It's mostly gambling and strip clubs."

"Laundering money the old-fashioned way." My tone is grim, and Scar is quietly observing.

I'm about to ask his opinion when the tip line lights up, and a reedy old-lady voice leaves a message. "Hutch? Those teenagers are at it again in the woods behind Willow Run. Sounds like a keg party, but it's too loud on a Wednesday night. They should be at church or in bed. I don't want to call the police, but it's a school night. Would your guys handle it?"

The line goes dead, and Scar looks at me. My mind is on Blake waiting for me at the mansion. Crawling between her luscious thighs is where my mind is, but Dirk just got back in town. It's my turn to take the call.

"Feel like going for a ride?" I look over at Scar, and he takes his boot off his desk, standing.

"Sure."

We're two blocks and a medium stretch of country road before the orange light of a bonfire illuminates the trees behind a new subdivision outside the Hamiltown boundary.

"I bet they don't have a permit for that fire." Scar puts his truck in park and opens the door.

The woods are slowly consuming an abandoned park with a small covered shed off to the side. We've broken up teenage keggers here before, but in this case, the music isn't loud. The fire is burning in a clearing, and a few teens stand around it drinking and laughing.

"She called to complain about this?" I glance over at my partner. "Hardly seems worth the effort."

"Old people forget what it's like to be young."

Together, we slowly cross the dark grass. I don't see signs of a keg, but as we get closer, what I do see stops me in my tracks. At the back of the covered shed, Hana sits on the wall with a half-drunk beer in her hands and that asshole Trip beside her looking more serious than he has all day.

A low noise rumbles from my partner, and I place my hand on his arm. "Come around back with me."

Instead of breaking in on the kids, we follow a path into the trees where we can slip up behind the small pavilion in the darkness.

"You came here because your uncle invited you?" It sounds like an interrogation, and my fist tightens. "Out of the blue? No warning?"

"Blake said we were coming, so we came." Hana sounds high, and I feel the waves of tension rolling off my partner. "Who cares?"

"You know who cares. You left a lot of shit unresolved."

Hana's head falls back, and her eyes closed. "So what."

"So plenty." His voice gets harder. "What does Greg want with you?"

"I don't know him. He only talks to Blake."

"That's probably for the best." He steps away then turns to her quickly. "The last time you saw Debbie, what did she say?"

"I don't remember. I want to go home."

"Cut the crap, Hana." He puts his hands on her arms and gives her a shake. "You'd better start remembering. Greg came here for a reason—"

"What reason is that, pretty boy?" Scar steps into the light.

Trip's head snaps around, and when he sees my partner, his hands drop. "What are you doing here?"

"One of the *quaint* things about Hamiltown is people call me when kids are misbehaving in the woods. If I don't handle it, they call the cops."

His jaw clenches when he looks out at the teens by the fire, but just as fast, his expression melts into his fucking detached grin. "Sounds like it's my lucky day. It was too early to go to bed, so Hana and I decided to go for a drive. Come on, Han. I'll take you home."

He holds out his hand to her, but she wobbles away from him. "No thank you. I don't want to *trip* with you." A woozy laugh huffs from her lips, blowing a lock of hair out of her eye. "Yak yak yak, so many questions. You're no fun anymore."

Scar storms forward and picks her up, holding her upper arms. She staggers a bit before shaking her head like she's trying to clear her vision. He catches her chin, frowning hard as he looks into her eyes.

"It's you." Her voice turns soft, and she smiles, blinking sweetly. "I didn't know you were coming to the party. You're cute."

"You're high as a kite," he growls in response.

Scar's wolf eyes cut to Trip, who immediately holds up both hands. "I didn't do it. Hana's a grown woman. She gets her own drugs."

My partner's expression darkens, and he looks at me. "I'm taking her home."

With that, he holds Hana under her arm and leads her away from the shelter. As he passes through the group of kids, he barks an order for them to break it up and go home.

One look at him, and they immediately scatter, leaving me with Trip. "You're giving me a ride back to the mansion."

He sweeps his arm in an annoying, sweeping fashion. "It would be my pleasure."

As we drive to Hugh's mansion, I study my driver. "You said you came here for a reason? What might that be?"

"To find out what happened to the girls, of course. I've been staying with them the past month while my mother is… between engagements."

I'm convinced I won't get a straight answer out of this guy on anything, but I know one thing. "If you're smart, which I'm not sure you are, you'll stay away from Hana. My partner has taken an interest in her, and he doesn't always color inside the lines."

"Understood." Trip's tone is emphatic, and he adds under his breath. "He's got his hands full with that one."

"What does that mean?" I cut my eyes at him.

"How well do you know her?"

"If you've got something to say, you'd better say it."

His eyes slide up and down me, and he shakes his head. "Listen, I don't like to speak ill of anyone, especially not a friend, but Hana is a user. If your scary partner is smart, he'll keep that in mind or she'll use him the same way she uses all of us."

"How does she do that?"

"In my case, it's money. Hana doesn't come into her trust for another few months, and she owes me a lot of money. She owes a lot of people a lot of money."

"From what I understand, she'll be good for it."

"Maybe." His tone is thoughtful. "Hana likes to gamble and drink—she also likes to forget. Ask her tomorrow what happened tonight, and you'll see what I mean. It's a dangerous combination. Even Blake can't cover for her as much as she tries."

His words tighten my throat. I don't like him talking about Blake or the thought of her covering up shit for her sister.

We're at the house, and he shoves the car in park, tipping an invisible cap before climbing out. "That's all, Dick. Have a nice evening."

"Hold it." I climb out and catch him by his skinny arm before he disappears into the house. "Don't give Hana drugs. Blake wants her sister clean."

"Easy on the threads." Trip shrugs out of my grip. "I told

you, no one controls Hana, not me, not Blake, not even your scary friend. She does what she wants—drugs included."

He takes off for the east side of the house, and I turn my face in the opposite direction. Scar has Hana, and I'm confident in his ability to care for her, even after all Trip told me. Scar's walked through hell more than once and come out on the other side.

She'll be fine for tonight, and I've got my mind on heaven.

Hustling up the stairs, I make my way down the wide hall of the east wing. A light coming from under the door at the end tells me which room is hers.

Tapping on the door, I hesitate. Blake and I've known each other a while, but maybe we're moving too fast. My hesitation dissolves when the door sweeps open, and she blinks up at me, eyes wide and bright.

She's wearing a white lace nightgown, and her hair is loose down her back. She's smiling, and I trace my eyes over her sexy body, her perky breasts and round hips.

"Damn, girl. You look good enough to eat."

She exhales a little laugh, rising on her toes and putting her arms around my neck. Her chin lifts and her lips brush against mine. "Good thing I'm on the menu. What took you so long?"

"Something came up."

"I feel it on my stomach." She slides a hand down, stroking the growing bulge in my pants, and I cup her cheeks with my hands.

"You're going to feel it in your sweet little pussy." My lips brush hers before sealing over them and spreading them apart.

A moan breaks in her throat, and I tilt her face to the side to kiss her deeper. My fingers cut into the skin of her cheeks, and I rotate her body so her back is to me. Sliding my hands down the front of her nightgown, I pause to lift her breasts, kneading them in my fingers and tweaking the tips.

Her mouth breaks from mine, and she drops her head against my shoulder with a low hiss. "Keep doing that."

"You're sensitive." My lips are behind her ear, and she shivers.

"I could come right now."

My right hand lowers, and I lift the hem of her nightgown, tracing my fingers up her inner thigh to her bare ass. Squeezing my eyes shut, my cock is an iron rod in my jeans.

"You're not wearing underwear," I groan, and her fingers thread into the side of my hair.

Her face is at my neck and she kisses and bites my skin. "I've been waiting for you to touch me."

Sliding my fingers around her legs, I feel cream on her inner thighs. I dip two digits inside and she's so fucking wet. "Fuck me," I hiss.

Her back is against my chest, and her lips graze my jawline. "I was dreaming of your cock and playing with my pussy while I waited."

I'm painfully hard as I quickly fish out a condom so I can unzip and step out of my jeans. She starts forward, holding my hand and leading me to the bed.

"Sit." She turns me so I'm sitting on the edge and straddles my lap. "I want to ride you like a stallion."

I'm usually the one taking charge in the bedroom, but fuck me, Blake is blowing my mind right now with her sassy orders and slick cunt. I thought it couldn't get hotter but hovering over my erection, she pulls a narrow ribbon on the front of her gown and her top falls open.

My hands move from her ass to her gorgeous tits on full display in my face, and I lift them, squeezing and massaging before covering a hard nipple with my mouth. I give it a firm suck, and she lowers with a loud moan, taking my dick all the way to the hilt.

"Blake…" My mouth pops off her body as pleasure blankets my mind.

"More," she gasps, lifting her breasts to my face.

I return to nibbling and pulling on her hardened nipples, and her hips buck frantically on my cock. Stars fill my vision, and I'm losing control. I'm about to explode in that fucking condom when I feel her break into orgasm.

"Oh, god… yes…" Her body shudders, and I let go, leaning back so I can drive farther into her as she falls forward on my chest.

Lifting my chin, I exhale a loud groan and come long and hard inside this gorgeous girl. She's better than I fantasized, and we're only getting started.

CHAPTER 13

Blake

"J UST LIKE THAT," I GASP, GRIPPING THE BACK OF THE CHAIR. "Don't stop…"

I'm on my spread knees in an ivory-silk, Edwardian armchair, and Hutch is pounding his massive cock into me from behind.

His hand is between my legs, circling my clit, and he leans closer, scuffing my shoulder with his beard as his lips trace the skin behind my ear. Shockwaves of orgasm flash through my belly at his touch, and I exhale a quivering moan.

Tracing his teeth along my hypersensitive skin, his hot voice is low. "Good girl."

Every ridge tickles my core as he thrusts faster, seeming to grow larger, and my thighs tremble as his fingers pick up speed over the sensitive bud between driving me wild.

"Faster, baby." His lips are hot on my neck.

I'm lost in all the sensations around me. My eyes squeeze shut and I climb higher, as my orgasm grows stronger, tightening my belly. In a quick move his palm moves to cover my breast, squeezing and pulling at my nipple, and I shoot over the edge.

My orgasm electrifies my brain. My elbows bend, but his hand is on my breast, holding me upright against his chest. Another thrust, and he stiffens with a groan. He pulses deeply, and I'm limp in his arms, panting hard and vibrating from the intensity of our union.

I'm secure against his chest as he quickly disposes of the condom and slides his other arm under my knees to carry me to the bed. My head rests limply on his shoulder, and I hold his neck, inhaling deeply of sage and citrus and clean man-sweat.

Salt is on my tongue from kissing and biting his skin, and I feel so deliciously used and sated. I've never been fucked this way. I've never been this hungry for more.

We slip into silky soft sheets, and he pulls my back tight against his firm chest. A round bicep is under my head, and I turn to gaze up at his profile.

"I take it you're spending the night?" I'm teasing, and a smile lifts his cheek.

Knowing this massive man, this broody leader is mine to tease does squishy things to my insides. It's after two in the morning, and I've had four orgasms, starting with the first, mind-altering one when he arrived. I'd been edging, waiting for him to appear. I didn't expect it to be almost midnight.

"It'll be easier to know you're safe if I'm here." His teasing tone sends another shimmer of warmth through my stomach.

A niggling hint of worry pushes at my mind. If I'm not careful, I'll get attached, and that will be problematic. I don't want to worry right now.

Scooting forward, I turn to face him in the bed. "I told you we're perfectly safe with Trip and Greg here."

"I don't like those guys. Why are they here out of the blue?"

"They said it was for my mother, the gala." His eyes narrow, and my lips press tighter. "You're going to make me paranoid if you don't stop being so suspicious."

I should be honest and tell him I was surprised they showed up as well, and while I don't think Trip is up to anything, I don't trust Greg as far as I can throw him.

I should also tell him about the blackmail and what's going on with Hana, but it's all too much for tonight, for what I want to do with him. It can wait.

He gently places his thumb under my chin, lifting my eyes to his again. "That was a long pause. What are you thinking about?"

His voice is so warm, I want to kiss him again. I want to pretend we're starting something easy, a small-town love-affair that might lead to something wonderful. In the light of day, I'll know better, but for tonight…

Wrinkling my nose, I scoot closer. "You're throwing the opening pitch at Pepper's game tomorrow."

"Pepper," he groans rolling onto his back. "She's a hustler. Already knows how to get whatever she wants."

"She's got her work cut out for her being the only girl with all you men."

"All us men?" A tease is in his voice and he leans up, rolling me onto my back so I'm caged beneath his luscious weight. "I'd say she's got us men right where she wants us."

I can't argue with that, and I can't argue with the deep satisfaction rising in my chest at his affection. The way he holds me down is delicious, strong, skin on skin. Lowering his face, he kisses the side of my neck, and it feels so good.

"Do you have to work tomorrow?"

"I'm keeping an eye on things. I was thinking I might show you around Hamiltown, since you've been too busy to get to know the place."

Curling my finger in the soft hair behind his ear, I nod. "Sounds like a perfect day."

Green eyes meet mine, and he hesitates before kissing my nose. "We should rest."

He shifts around so I'm beside him again, and I wonder what changed. Is he struggling with the same tricky realization as me? We both know what we're facing—distance, work, complications, *blackmail*... But he doesn't know about that.

Shaking away the dark thoughts for tonight, I curl into the safety of his embrace. I have a few days left to deal with Papi-O, whoever the fuck he is, and worst case, I have a plan.

CHAPTER 14

Hutch

"**W**HAT GIVES IT THAT FLAVOR?" BLAKE HOLDS THE COFFEE mug close to her nose and sniffs. "It's so warming and addictive."

She's sitting across from me at Steamy Beans, the coffee shop on Main Street down from our office. We each have a cup of their signature blend, and a plate of scones and jam is between us.

"You're going to know the minute I tell you."

"Wait! I almost have it." She holds up a hand, closing her eyes and taking another sip. "I think I know…"

I'm addicted to watching her. She's so adorable, every move she makes. I don't recognize this person I'm becoming, and it's somehow both satisfying and unsettling.

This morning, when I opened my eyes, she was in my arms, breathing softly as she slept. I pulled her to me and kissed her slowly behind the ear, tracing my lips higher as I inhaled her lingering scent of rose.

She woke with a soft moan, arching against me like the

sex kitten she is. I slid my hands up to her full breasts, squeez-ing and holding them as I drove deep into her core, and she reached back, rocking her body as we moved together like the waves on the sea. She's amazing, like her body is made for me, and I need to get a grip before I become attached.

As if I have a choice.

When her uncle sent me her fashion spread two years ago, I memorized every line of her body. I couldn't help myself. Having her in my life seemed impossible to me. We're on the same planet, but in vastly different worlds.

Still, every time we're together, our chemistry is undeni-able. If only chemistry solved problems. In my experience, it only creates new ones.

Her gray eyes meet mine, and she's given up. "Tell me."

"Cinnamon."

"Dammit, cinnamon!" She holds up a hand, and I chuckle. "I even know people who add cinnamon to their coffee when they want a little something extra."

"It's definitely extra." Sliding my hand across the table, I want to touch her. "Keeps the customers coming back for more."

She doesn't pull away, and our fingers thread. A beat of si-lence falls between us as we adjust.

Soft gray eyes meet mine. "What's next on your agenda for introducing me to my family's town?"

"I still can't believe you've only been here three times in your life."

"Mama hated it, and Dad only came to visit Hugh."

Looking down, I slide my thumb over her soft knuckles. "Hugh loved those visits. After the first one, he would always tell me when you were coming to town."

"The one when I was thirteen?" She turns her face towards the window, and pink creeps into her cheeks. "It was the only time I ever saw you here. You must've left town every other time we visited."

I hadn't meant to be so precise, and I shift in my seat. "I started college, then I went straight into the service."

I'm not about to tell her I purposely stayed away when she came here.

"Either way," she shrugs. "We only stayed a day or two, and we were at the estate the entire time. I was with Hana, or I rode around the grounds. We flew, so I didn't have a car."

Standing, I pull her to her feet. "Stop making excuses. It's time you got to know your heritage."

"My heritage." She shakes her head. "Can you even call it that?"

"Can you call it anything else? Your great-great grandparents founded this place, named it after you."

"Weren't your great whatevers founders as well?"

"Mine were present, but the name is all yours." We're out the door, walking down the four blocks of Main Street. "This is the town square."

"Howard's Five and Dime." She reads the hand-painted vintage signs. "Stinky's Hardware? Hang on—is that the same stinky who has the snow cones? Pepper's softball team?"

"Clearly, he's an aspiring mogul."

"I'll say. Hardware, snow cones, *and* sponsoring a sports team? You'd better keep your eye on that guy. He'll be running for mayor next thing you know."

"And giving himself big tax breaks."

She breaks into a hearty laugh, and I catch her around the waist, leaning down to kiss her cheek. "I was wondering what it sounded like when you really laughed."

Blinking fast, she studies my face. "I don't remember feeling this way before—so relaxed and good. I shouldn't feel this way."

"Why not? You deserve to be happy, and I'm glad to be

the one to make it happen." As I say the words, I realize how much I mean them.

"I don't know. After what happened to Debbie and with Uncle Hugh gone, I feel like I should be sadder."

We start walking again, holding hands. "It's okay to take a break from the sorrow, and we're pretty sure your uncle will return by the end of the week."

She nods, but the dark cloud is still over her features.

Lifting her hand, I kiss her knuckles. "Anything else on your mind?"

Frowning up at the storefront, she exhales. "I kind of feel like a failure."

My chest tightens, and I pull her to my side, wrapping my arm around her as we continue walking. "You're twenty three. You've hardly had time to be a failure."

Her chin drops and we take a few more steps before she looks up at me again. A breath, and I think she's going to let me in, tell me what's on her mind.

Instead, she gives me a dazzling, fake smile, tugging my hand towards a small, boutique store. "What's Ruth's Rarities?"

"You'll like this one."

A bell rings above the glass door as we enter the small store crammed with goods, and a young girl pops up behind the counter in the center of the room.

"Hutch? Is that you?" Her hazel eyes go wide when she sees Blake. "You must be one of those New York girls. Mr. Hugh's nieces."

"Carmen Montgomery, this is Blake van Hamilton. Blake, Carmen is Ruth's daughter."

"It's nice to meet you." Blake is friendly, but reserved.

"You're so beautiful." Carmen's voice is filled with wonder. "Are you staying here long? You must be going crazy in this little town after being in New York City."

"It's actually a nice change of pace." Blake smiles, glancing around the store. "I love this place. Are these candles made locally?"

"Yeah, the candles and the jewelry and the art are made locally. We get the quirky stuff like the penis book and the naked president magnets at market."

"Penis book?" Blake snorts and covers her nose.

"Come look. It's hilarious." Carmen grabs her hand and the two jog across the store to where I hear Blake read *Penis Pokey* aloud.

"Oh, no!" She cries. "It's a hot dog."

Glancing up I see them holding what looks like a board book with a big hole in the middle. She cuts her eyes at me, and I shake my head. It's nice to see her getting along with Carmen.

"Is that really hot guy who was in town yesterday with you, too?" Carmen and Blake walk back across the store to the jewelry case. "Lord, he looked like something out of a catalog. Nobody ever wears suits around here."

"Probably." Blake seems indifferent, but I'm curious.

Which of those two dickheads was snooping around Hamiltown and why? I can't say for sure, but I don't think they're here just to check on my girl.

I also make a mental note as Blake admires a necklace featuring a palmetto tree and crescent moon. "This is interesting. It kind of reminds me of something I've seen in Dubai."

Carmen's eyes go so wide, I'm worried they'll fall out. "You are the coolest person I've ever met. I've never even been out of the state."

Blake laughs, and her cheeks flush. "It wasn't that big a deal."

The bell on the door rings, and a cluster of ladies I don't recognize stroll in chatting loudly.

"Tourists." Carmen leans in, speaking low. "Will you be at the softball game tonight? We can sit together if you want."

"Sounds fun." Blake agrees, and Carmen skips back across the room to her spot at the register.

After waving goodbye, we're back out on the sidewalk.

"She's really sweet." Blake smiles up at me. "Is she a Hamiltown native, too?"

"Ruth moved here with Carmen after her divorce. I think they're originally from New Orleans."

"Stinky'd better keep his eye on you. You're more like the mayor." Her eyes shine as she teases me. "You know everyone."

"I've just lived here a long time."

"And you're close to my uncle. He always talked about you like you were his son."

I'm not sure what to say to that, but I know how I feel. "I'll be glad to see him again."

We've reached the end of the sidewalk, and I'm about to suggest we head back to the house when Blake turns to me.

"We've still got time to kill before you show off your expert pitching skills."

"It's little girls' softball. I'll just toss it underhanded."

"That's a letdown." She shrugs. "Either way, we still have time. What's your favorite place in Hamiltown? Show it to me—if you have one? I'm sure you do."

"Actually…" I catch her hand again. "I have more than one, but I'll take you to the closest."

We head down the hill about a half mile from the main drag to a massive wooden structure nestled in the trees.

"A barn?" She squints up at me.

"It's not just a barn." Pushing open the wide, wooden doors, I lead her into the massive open space. "It's the location of all the town activities, the boiled peanut festival, the Frogmore stew competition, the spring dance."

She holds up both hands, shaking her head and blinking fast. "What the hell is Frogmore stew? Does it have frogs in it? And a spring dance? Are there cloggers?"

"This is South Carolina, not Appalachia. They shag here."
Looking down, I pull her to my chest.

"Is that like having sex?" Her arms circle my waist.

"It is how some people do it." I'm liking this little
Hamiltown primer. "There are no frogs in Frogmore stew. It's
named after the town. It's more like a crawfish boil, but with
crab claws and shrimp."

"Sounds delicious."

"I really want to kiss you right now." That persistent
warmth is back, and I can't ignore my feelings for her.

A smile curls her lips, and she rises on her toes, lifting her
chin. "What are you waiting for?"

Our mouths seal together, and something shifts. The lust
burning between us takes on a different form, like a white-
hot blaze settling into a steadily burning fire. I begin to have
thoughts like she belongs here. It's her hometown, and I'll do
what it takes to keep her here.

These are dangerous thoughts. We're in the middle of a
shitstorm, and catching feelings will only make it harder for
both of us. I can't turn my back on my promise to her uncle,
but I can protect myself from third-degree burns.

CHAPTER 15

Blake

"**F**REEZE 'EM OUT, SNOW CONES! FREEZE 'EM OUT!" CARMEN is beside me clapping her hands in an adult-sized, bright-red Stinky's Snow Cones jersey.

I confess, I'm crazy-jealous of her Snow Cones fan gear.

We're sitting in the bleachers in a mix of red Snow Cones supporters and royal-blue Hot Shot fans, and Hutch has just been announced as the special guest pitcher for the first game of the season.

"We want a pitcher, not a belly itcher!" Carmen yells, cupping her hands around her mouth, and Hana snorts a laugh from my other side.

My sister leans into my side and whispers, "I don't know who she is, but she's invited to every party from now on."

Hutch cuts us an annoyed glance that registers as way too sexy for a children's softball game, and I hear a few women around me sighing with delight… or lust. He's delicious in dark jeans that hug his ass and an honorary Snow Cones jersey.

From her spot beside the pitcher's mound, Pepper waves at us so fiercely, I'm afraid her little arm will fly off.

"Go, Pep!" Hana yells, with a volume that surprises me.

I've never heard my sister talk above a Marilyn-Monroe pout, but in Hamiltown, it seems she's a different person. It makes me question ever returning to the city—for so many reasons besides just solving problems.

I notice her dark watchdog at the end of the bleachers glancing over at us every few minutes. Scar has become her self-appointed guardian since we got here, but my sister doesn't seem to find it strange or even notice.

She lifts her camera to her eye and snaps shots of Pepper, Hutch, the outfield players. "I'm going to go down. Coach Perkins said I could stand on the sidelines if I gave them copies of the prints."

"Do it."

I watch her climb down the bleachers and make her way to the chain-link fence. The Hot Shots coach motions for her to enter the field, and sure enough, Scar walks over and leans his forearms on the fence to watch.

"I have never seen that man show interest in anyone in this town." Carmen leans into my ear, causing me to jump. "He is some kind of tortured soul, but no one, not anyone, has ever gotten close to him. Besides Hutch, of course."

Chewing my lip, I study the tall man with the tattoos covering his scars. "Is he dangerous?"

"I imagine he is." Carmen's eyebrows rise. "Just look at all that ink. He's like Bill fucking Skarsgård."

"Who is that?"

"He's the other Skarsgård, younger brother to Alexander from *True Blood* and *Big Little Lies*." I nod, and she continues. "You'd think he'd be drop-dead gorgeous with a hot brother like Vampire Eric, and occasionally he is, but mostly he's creepy as fuck."

"I don't think I know what he looks like."

"Creepy clown in the new version of Stephen King's *It*."

"Oh, god!" I jump back as realization hits me. "I saw that once and I hope I never see it again. That's Alexander Skarsgård's brother?"

"Just goes to show, you never know with siblings. Something went wrong with that one."

I shift in my seat, suddenly uncomfortable. "Yes."

I clear the knot out of my throat when I see Hutch climbing the bleachers, headed our way. As predicted, we'd watched him toss a very slow, underhanded pitch to a little Hot Shot, who nailed it over right field, sending the little players into chaos.

Pride swells in my chest as I watch him shake hands and speak to almost everyone before sitting beside me and threading our fingers. I kind of love how he holds my hand like we're teenagers.

"Really appreciated the show of support, Carmen." He leans forward to glower at her.

"Nice pitch, traitor. They would've got a homer if it weren't for your niece." Carmen claps back, and I pinch my nose to keep from laughing.

Green eyes cut up to me, and my stomach tightens deliciously. "Whose side are you on?"

"Pepper's!" I answer fast, and his frown melts into a grin.

Everything about this is so foreign and so fun. We watch Pepper working her little tail off stopping every short hit and getting three girls out in one catch, ending the inning.

"She's really good." I state the obvious as Hutch buys three hotdogs for Carmen, him, and me. "I haven't seen that much hustle outside Yankee stadium."

Hutch cuts his eyes at me, taking a bite that consumes half his hot dog. "Have you seen any games outside Yankee stadium?"

Taking a more reasonable bite of my dog, I can't argue. "You got me, but she's really good. Does she get that from you?"

"I played some baseball in my day."

"Your day!" I laugh, bumping his shoulder with mine. "You're not even thirty."

He leans in and plants a warm kiss on my lips, shooting fire through my belly, through my groin, all the way to my toes. He holds it a beat, no tongue but pulling my bottom lip with his. It's the best kiss I've ever had.

Leaning back, he meets my eyes. "Sorry, I couldn't resist. You've been too cute all day today."

"Don't apologize." My voice is quiet. "I really liked that. I'd like more."

"I've got plans for more."

I'm about to burst into flames when Carmen lets out a groaning-yell beside me. "Oh my god! You two are so damn cute, I can't eat my hot dog. It tastes like it's got sugar on it."

Straightening in my seat, I fight a laugh as I scoot away from him. "We should watch the game." He gives me a heated eyebrow arch, and I clear my throat, turning to face the field and clapping my hands. "Go, Pepper! Kick their butts!"

It's not the greatest softball cheer, but it earns me an enthusiastic arm-wave from the hardest-working shortstop in the Little League. Hana is right there on the sidelines snapping photos.

The Snow Cones pull a 7-2 win over the Hot Shots, and Hutch treats the team to cupcakes at Shirley's bakery in town. It's a ten-minute walk from the field, and the girls bounce and squeal, reliving their victory the whole way.

"They won't sleep tonight," I note, holding Hutch's arm. "They should have these games on Fridays."

"Can't do it. High school football." He leans closer to my ear. "That was more my game than baseball."

Twisting my lips, I picture him in white football pants. "I'd have liked to see that."

"We'll have to find you a cheerleader uniform."

"We didn't have cheerleaders at Bishop."

"Still, I'd like to see you in one of those little skirts."

The hunger in his tone helps me ignore him being the reason I was sent to that convent school. It sends my mind flying down a rabbit hole of short skirts and football pants and sexy quickies behind the bleachers.

Twelve happy little girls later, Pepper is tucked in her bed at Hutch's house, and he's driving me back to my family estate. "Pony" by Genuine plays softly on the radio of his big, black truck, and I lick my bottom lip, threading my fingers with his on the console.

Without a warning, he takes a turn off the highway onto a narrow road leading into the pine trees.

"Where are we going?" I look over at his profile illuminated by the dashboard light.

"A part of town you'd only know about if you grew up here."

He stops the truck on a hill overlooking a slight valley below. It's semi-secluded, and no other cars are around.

"Are we getting out?" I watch as he puts the truck in park and kills the engine.

"Out of these clothes." A naughty grin curls his cheeks, and he lifts the arm rest, pulling me roughly to him by my waist.

I exhale a laugh that melts into a sigh as he buries his face in the side of my hair. Electricity races down my shoulders, tingling my core at the touch of his lips on my skin, and I glance out the windows to be sure we're alone.

"What is this place?" I gasp as he lifts my sweater, finding my bra and pushing it higher so my breasts spill out, into his waiting hands.

"Makeout Point." His hot tongue circles my hard nipple,

and I exhale a noise of pleasure. "It used to be more popular when I was a kid. I don't know what happened. Kids are driving less. Parents are more permissive."

He punctuates each sentence with a kiss to my sensitive skin, and his hands drop to my waist jerking at the button on my jeans. It's hot and aggressive, and I scoot over so I can shimmy out of the restrictive fabric.

"Tonight would've been a good night for that cheerleader skirt," I mutter, struggling to get the pants off my ankles.

"Tease." He grins, whipping his shirt over his head.

Crawling onto my knees in only my black string bikini panties, I rub my hand over the impressive bulge in his jeans. "Your turn."

A condom is between his teeth, and his jeans are below his hips in record time, allowing his erection to rise, bobbing over his belly. Leaning forward, I can't resist sliding my tongue up the length of his shaft, circling it around the mushroom tip before pulling it between my lips.

"Fuck, yeah," he hisses, threading his fingers in the back of my hair.

Salty precum touches my tongue, and my insides clench, growing slicker with every suck. He's too big to fit all the way in my mouth, so I grip his shaft, pumping as I lick him and take him as far as I can into my throat. His hips rise, thrusting gently as my head bobs up and down in his lap.

"Good girl." It's a hoarse whisper and his grip tightens in my hair. "You suck me so good."

His dirty words make my pussy flutter, and when he sits forward, driving his thick fingers into me, I pop off him with a moan. It's like fuel to his fire. He grasps my face in both hands, pulling my lips to his in a forceful kiss.

His tongue captures mine, demanding and dominating, and I grip his neck in response, barely noticing when he hauls me onto his lap in a straddle. I'm ravenous, kissing him desperately, rubbing my tingling nipples against the coarse hair on his chest.

"I'm going to fuck you now, kitten." His deep voice is in my ear, and a delicious sting cuts into my legs when he rips my panties away.

"Oh, God, yes," I manage to answer just before he drives balls-deep into me with a low, animal groan.

I'm on top, echoes of that song in my head, and I rock my hips, riding his pony as he grips my ass. He drags me roughly, massaging my clit against his pelvis, causing stars to break out behind my closed eyes.

My back arches, and I slide my hands up my body, lifting my breasts as I grind.

"I love your tits." His hungry tone thrills me. "You are so sexy."

I feel sexy. I feel powerful, and as the orgasm blooms hotter in my belly, I ride faster, chasing the pleasure flooding my senses. Sweat trickles along the line of my hair, between my breasts, and I throw my head back as the wave starts to crest.

Large hands squeeze my ass, drawing me closer, and when his mouth clamps forcefully on my nipple, I scream, coming hard on his cock.

"That's my girl." He thrusts up, teasing my spasms, drawing them out again and again before holding, groaning deeply as he comes.

"Blake…" It's the same groan he made in the shower, and a thrill races to my toes.

Falling forward, I clutch his cheeks again, kissing him firmly, dragging my lips across his and curling our tongues together.

He feels so good.

He feels like mine.

And when he groans my name that way, it makes me believe this could work.

Driving back to the estate, our fingers are laced, and I'm buzzing with afterglow. "I like makeout point. It might be my top favorite place in Hamiltown."

He exhales a chuckle, and I look out at the dark trees passing on the road. My mind drifts to my sister so genuinely happy tonight. She skipped around, posing the young players in their softball gear next to super-girly towers of cupcakes and oversized gerbera daisies.

The dirty little players with their pigtails and big smiles—some missing teeth—created a cute juxtaposition, and even though she's only been taking pictures for a short time, my sister has an artistic eye. I can't wait to see what she's captured.

"It's been a long time since I've seen Hana so invested in something." I glance up to catch the muscle in Hutch's jaw moving. His brow is lowered, and he seems angry. "What?"

He cuts his eyes at me briefly. "Nothing."

It's dark, but I can tell it's not nothing. The fizzy glow in my chest cools. "Say it."

Shifting in the seat, he releases my hand, putting his on the steering wheel. "I'm not so comfortable with Pepper and Hana getting close."

Defensive anger tightens my throat, and I lean back, crossing my arms. "What's wrong with Hana and Pepper being friends? I've only seen good things coming from them spending time together."

"For now."

"What does that mean?"

He exhales loudly, looking out the window. "Come on, Blake. Don't make me say things you don't want to hear."

"I think you'd better, since I'm not a mind reader."

"Hana's a loose cannon. Pepper's a little girl." He pinches

his top lip, and even if he looks delectable, the anger tightening my chest kills it.

"You're saying she's a bad influence? I disagree. Hana knows Pepper's only eleven. She wouldn't do anything irresponsible around her."

"It didn't stop her last night."

It's like a splash of ice water in my face. "What happened last night?"

Again, his jaw tightens, and he casts me a withering glance. "We got an anonymous tip at the office, and when we went to check it out, she was there with Trip, high as a kite."

"And you're just now telling me?" Frustration and disappointment war in my chest.

I don't know if I'm more betrayed Hutch didn't tell me or if I'm embarrassed I trusted her, defended her, and she's fallen back into her same old self-destructive habits.

No, pushing back on that, I won't let him try and take the moral high ground. "If Hana has a problem, you're as much to blame for it as anyone else."

His fist tightens on the steering wheel, and he exhales a growl. "How do you figure that?"

"I was the only person protecting her from Victor, and when you sent me to Bishop, that was the end of it. She had no one."

"I thought you said he was already…" His voice drops in volume. "Molesting her before you left."

"I'd heard rumors, but I didn't have any proof. Once you removed me from the picture, he had a free hand."

Hutch's chin drops, and he appears remorseful. "I'm sorry that happened to her. If I could go back and help her, I would." Just as fast, he lifts his chin and green eyes flash at me. "It doesn't change where we are now. She's not a good influence on my niece, and I won't have her misbehaving in my town."

"So it's *your* town now?" I can't decide if I'm shocked or

pissed. "I thought you despised all forms of pretense, town ownership."

"It's not a pretense. It's the truth."

We're at the door of Uncle Hugh's home, and I grab the handle before the truck is fully stopped. "You don't have to worry about my sister interfering with your family or sullying your good name in our town. Goodnight, Mr. Winston."

Pushing out of the truck, I slam the door of the cab, storming to the front door.

I hear the sound of his voice briefly, but I'm not interested. I'm in the house, locking the door and my heart before he exits the driveway.

CHAPTER 16

Hutch

Slamming the door to my bedroom, I wince, remembering it's a Thursday night, and I'm not the only one in the house. I reopen it and listen for sounds of Pepper. After several seconds of silence, I close it again quietly.

My jaw is tight. Hell, my entire body is tight. I don't know how we went from that fucking heaven to the pit of hell so fast.

It's a lie. I know how. I've known from the start this was a bad idea. Blake is stuck in a reality where her sister is the victim with no agency. She sees Hana as a little girl locked in a room of abuse she can't escape.

It's not true, and it enables her to keep doing what she apparently always does, which is whatever the fuck she wants, and Blake cleans up the mess. It's fucking infuriating, but I wouldn't be giving a shit if I hadn't started to care so much for Blake.

She's under my skin, dammit. She's been under my skin since I saw that fucking magazine spread with her breasts wet and barely covered, her pillow lips parted, and her silver-blue eyes saying *fuck me* through the pages.

I answered that call too many times. Now I'm the one getting fucked.

Scrubbing my hands in my hair, my face lowers, and I catch a whiff of roses on my shirt.

"God dammit," I growl, ripping the garment over my head and throwing it across the room.

Hugh did this to me. He's been playing these games with me for years, sending me to check on her, sending me her photographs. Now he's put me in this position, where I have to stay near her to keep her safe. I walked right into his plan.

I'd be raging if it weren't for that damn ledger, if it weren't for what Blake told me about Victor stealing from her father's estate, if it weren't for that dead body. They're the only things keeping this real and not just a fucking matchmaking plot orchestrated by her uncle.

What Hugh doesn't know is I'm through with the games. I'll find out what happened to his niece's inheritance, to his nephew's estate, and then I'm out. Walking away. No more.

Blake van Hamilton can have her life in New York where she's always looking over her shoulder and pretending to be happy. She can enable her codependent little sister as much as she wants. I'm done trying to save her.

I'm tense and angry as I rip back the blankets and climb into bed. For a long time I toss and turn in the sheets—which also smell faintly of roses, dammit—before finally, sometime after two a.m., I slip exhausted into a restless sleep.

Somebody's got something on Hana. Dirk's text is the first thing I see when I open my eyes to the blazing dawn.

"Tell me something that won't surprise me," I mutter, sitting up slowly and rubbing my face. I feel hungover, then I see the clock. "Shit."

Throwing back the covers, I hit the shower. It's after nine again, and I forgot to set my damn alarm again. I missed seeing Pepper off to school—*again*—now I'll have to face Scar's judgmental smirk at the office. *Again.*

I've turned into a model slacker since Blake entered my life.

The anger I brought to bed with me returns full force, and I'm out the door in less than ten minutes this time.

"Not so relaxed today." Scar squints at me. "Still look like you didn't sleep, though."

"If you know what's good for you, you'll drop it."

"Is that a threat?" His expression is somewhere between amused and ready to kick my ass.

"I'm saying I don't want to talk about it." Scar and I are an equal match, but with the level of pissed-offedness I'm feeling right now, I'm pretty sure I could take him.

Still, fighting with my best partner is the worst form of unprofessionalism—right up there with fucking the woman I've been hired to protect.

"What do you know about this text from Dirk?" If anyone will get to the bottom of this shit, it's Scar.

"I didn't get a text from Dirk."

"He sent it at around four a.m. Probably wanted to let you sleep." Passing him my phone, I glance over at my brother's empty desk.

I need to know what he's discovered, but if I know Dirk, he's just closing his eyes.

"Let's go." Scar is on his feet, and I figured this would happen.

Without looking back, he grabs his keys, and we head for the door.

My brother's place is on the outskirts of town, set back in the woods. He bought an old garment factory, and while the first floor is abandoned ruins, he fixed up the second floor into a three-thousand square-foot loft apartment. He says he'll do the rest at some point.

We enter through the wooden double-doors, sliding them open and leaving them open as we pass a wall of cloudy windows to a wooden staircase at the back wall.

"You got a key?" Scar glances back at me as he jogs up the wooden stairs to the second level.

"Pretty sure he doesn't lock it." My boots scuff on the old steps as I follow him.

I'm right. The heavy wooden door opens easily when he turns the handle.

"Dirk?" I call, but the lights are all off.

We walk into the front part of the studio, which is designed to be a living room. A kitchen and dining area are in the center, and all the way in the curtained-off back corner, my brother is facedown on a king-sized bed.

He's not snoring, but he's breathing loud when Scar jerks back the heavy curtains covering the massive windows. Sunlight bathes the entire space, and Dirk lets out a low groan before rolling over. "I'm going to kick your ass."

"Vampire," Scar growls. "Somebody's going to come in here and stake you one of these days."

"Not in wholesome Hamiltown." He rubs his eyes, yawning.

The hair on the back of his head is scrubbed into a little nest, and for a second, I remember when we were kids, how protective I always felt towards him. My chest tightens, and I push back on that damn nostalgia. I'm not letting it change how I feel about Blake. She's wrong.

Hana needs to grow up and get help, and she's not going to do it with her sister bailing her ass out all the time.

"What's this shit about Hana?" Scar's voice is fierce, and I glance at him, wondering how he's planning to handle the problem.

Dirk clears his throat, standing and scratching his butt through his boxer briefs as he walks towards the kitchen. "Last time I text your ass in the middle of the night."

"I didn't know it was private." I follow him to the sink.

"It's not private, but it's not on fire either. You could've let me get a few hours sleep."

He turns on the water, filling a kettle before putting it on the stove. We're waiting, arms crossed as he grabs his iPad pro. "I've been tracking this guy Ivanov."

"One of the guys from the ledger?"

"A relative, I think. He's into horses and strippers. And porn."

Scar's arms lower, and his fists clench. "Go on."

"He's pretty sloppy at securing his data. I found chatter between him and this other guy Sidorov about throwing a loop over a honey pot. Instead of names, they're Honey and Black. I'm pretty sure Honey is Hana." He swipes across the screen, showing us the texts. "They think they can get Black to pay them to kill an mp4 labeled with the initials *3L*."

Protective rage surges in my chest. "You think Black is Blake?"

"It fits, right?" Dirk blinks up at me. "Two rich socialites, one a bit of a loose cannon with a lot of gambling debts."

"You think it's a porn film?"

"*Licking Lady Liberty?*" He arches an eyebrow. "I don't know what else it could be. I've been trying to access this file, but whoever encrypted it knows what they're doing."

"Is that everything?" Anger tightens my throat, and I'm ready to hunt down this Ivanov asshole.

"It looks like he's made contact with Black, but she's not playing ball. I don't know what their threats are, but I'd be willing to bet they're bearing down hard. They're hoping for half a mil from her."

"Must be a pretty sick porno."

"Or something they don't want all over the media."

"Mother fuckers," Scar exhales a hot breath. "I want to know who these assholes are, where they live."

Dirk turns serious eyes on me. "Has Blake said anything to you about it?"

"No." I'm pissed someone's threatening her, and I'm more pissed she didn't tell me.

On top of that, I'm pissed my first thought is *Nobody fucks with my girl*, especially after my decision last night.

"That's all I got." Dirk pours boiling water over coffee grounds. "I plan to spend today tracking down more info on who this Ivanov might be."

"Let's get started." Scar pulls out a chair. "I'll help you search."

"I'm going to start at Hugh's place." Taking his keys, I head for the door. "It's possible the answer might have come to us."

Even if it hasn't, Blake is going to tell me what the hell she's hiding.

CHAPTER 17

Blake

"**W**HERE DID YOU GET IT, HANA?" MY SISTER'S BLUE EYES OPEN slowly, and she frowns up at me.

"What time is it?" Pushing off her pillow, she digs out her phone.

"Time to get up and start telling me the truth. I can't believe I thought you'd changed."

After storming into the house last night, I went straight to my sister's empty room and began searching. I pulled out every drawer in her lingerie chest, searching the spaces between the drawers as well as the contents. Nothing.

I opened and inspected every container in her cosmetics bag and her toiletries case. I opened every book, shaking them so the bookmarks and pressed flowers fell out onto the desk. I didn't find any drugs or paraphernalia, so I sat on her bed fuming, waiting for her to appear.

Finally, when she still wasn't home after midnight, I gave up and went to my room where I punched on my pillow several times, pretending it was him. Then I pulled it to my chest and hugged it as angry tears coated my cheeks.

How dare he be right? How dare she make him right? I look like a fucking fool. After a long time, sleep took me away from the pain and frustration.

Now I feel torn and shaky. I'm tired of carrying this burden alone. I'm pissed that Hutch would judge my sister, and I'm annoyed that he might be right.

Either way, I'm not letting her do this again. I'm still trying to put out her last fire.

"I don't know what you're talking about." She flops back against the headboard. "Go away and let me sleep."

"Hutch said you were out with Trip two nights ago. He said you were high. Is that true?"

Her dark brow furrows, and she lifts her thumb to her mouth, chewing on her cuticle. "Did I see Hutch two nights ago?"

Reaching out, I grab her hand and pull it down to her lap. "We've had dinner at his house every night since we've been here."

Her pink lips pout, and she rolls her eyes towards the window. "I don't know what you're talking about."

"Who gave you drugs? Was it Trip?"

"I don't remember." She shifts her body away from me, pulling the blankets over her shoulder.

I'm so not in the mood for this act. Reaching for her shoulder, I pull her over to face me. "You can't keep doing this, Hana. You've got to take responsibility for your life and start acting like an adult."

"What does that mean? Acting like an adult." Her voice rises. "Who gives a shit what we do?"

"I give a shit. I want your life to have meaning. You have talents. Find a way to use them to contribute or at least to find happiness."

"That's what I'm trying to do. What are you doing?"

My head hurts. My heart hurts, and I'm so tired. "You have no idea what all I do."

"You have no idea what I do." She turns away again, and I don't pull her back or try to engage anymore.

There's no joy in protecting her.

Leaving the room, I walk down the hall to the main house. I'm so tired, and I have no one to lean on. I've lost the one person I could maybe go to for help. Now I'm facing a blackmail deadline and the very real possibility my sister might never get better.

I'm not ready to give up, but this ache in my chest is so strong.

Rubbing my hand over my forehead, I'm considering going back to bed when I see the light on in Uncle Hugh's office. My brow furrows, and the low tone of male voices drifts to me. Hope squeezes my chest, and I break into a short trot.

Is it possible—is he back? Oh, God, it's exactly the help I need. I round the corner then skid to a stop, ice replacing the hope in my veins.

"It's all law books and leather-bound classics." Trip leans against the desk holding a copy of *Great Expectations*. "You're wasting your time. Hello, B."

"Trip." I'm breathless from my jog. "What are you doing here? Where's Norris?"

"We let ourselves in." Greg levels his gaze on me in a way that makes my heart beat faster.

"Why?" My eyes go from him to Trip, who breaks into that casual grin.

"Just looking for a book. What's your favorite Dickens?" His eyebrow arches. "I like the one with Pip. He finds out the person helping him is also a convict."

"I don't have a favorite." The pity party consuming my

mind is gone, and I'm back to the bad bitch who protects her family. "You're not to be in here. It's my uncle's private office."

Greg steps between us, and his tone is sharp. "Tell me, Blake, where is your uncle again?"

"I told you, he's visiting friends."

"Yet he invited you and Hana here for a visit. Why would he do that if he planned to be gone?"

"Maybe we got our dates crossed."

"I don't think you did." Greg steps closer, and his black eyes sear into mine.

I don't know what he's looking for, but the scar tingling above my eyebrow reminds me I'm not intimidated by bullies. "I don't care what you think."

Trip stands, but Greg doesn't move. His eyes go from my face to my uncle's disheveled desk and back to me again before he blinks. "Your uncle has something that belongs to me."

Pulling my chin back, I try to think. "Does my uncle even know you?"

"That's a good question." He watches me, waiting, and the skin on my neck tightens.

"You think I know what you're talking about?"

"Do you?"

Huffing a laugh, I shake my head. "This is bullshit. Tell me what you're looking for, and perhaps Norris can help us find it."

"I'm not talking to Norris."

Trip interrupts with his usual nonchalance. "Here's the mystery I want solved. What's up with you and the big guy? How long has that been going on?"

I blink away from Greg's persistent stare. "Nothing is going on with Hutch. He's a friend of my uncle's. We've known each other since we were kids."

"Don't lie to me, old chap." Pushing off the desk, he wraps an arm around my shoulders, guiding me to the door. "Has the town detective taken you behind the barn yet?"

My cheeks heat, and I shrug out of his embrace. "I'm on my way to the kitchen for coffee. Would you join me?"

"No thanks." Greg's shoulders relax, but his eyes are still cold. Walking to the door, he hesitates beside Trip. "We're heading back to New York. Now."

"Ah, yes. The gala." Trip shoves his hands in his pockets and turns to follow his friend. "I guess this is *au revoir*, B. You and Hana will be missed."

Greg Peters is not getting off that easily. He's up to something, and I intend to find out what it is and what it has to do with my uncle.

Squaring my shoulders, I follow them out into the hall. "I've decided to go to the gala. I just need to pack a bag."

"Make it quick." Greg doesn't turn. "We're leaving in twenty minutes."

"I'll be ready in ten."

CHAPTER 18

Hutch

Hana's in the kitchen when I use my key to enter. Our eyes meet, and she gives me a careful smile. "It's like you live here or something."

Her voice is soft, and she sips a mug of what I presume is coffee. It could be anything.

"Your uncle gave me a key." My focus is on finding Blake, and I quickly scan the room to find us alone.

"It's kind of crazy how he disappeared like that. Any idea where he went?"

"None." I don't have time to hang out and chat.

I start for the door when she puts her mug down, standing straighter. "I got some cute shots of you and Pepper last night. I'll run them by your house when she gets home from school."

My conversation with her sister is on my mind. She must read it on my face, because she quickly adds. "Or at dinner. If we're still doing that, I mean."

"Of course. Lurlene is expecting you."

She nods, looking down before quietly adding, "She's a really great kid. "

"I think she is. Thanks."

"My life went to shit after my dad died." Her voice drops, and she says it again. "She's lucky to have you."

I don't know Hana very well. I haven't made up my mind how I feel about this girl who's normal one minute then high as a kite or mixed up in a gambling-porn-blackmail racket the next. I know she's important to Blake, and while I disagree with her reasons, it makes me want to try.

"I'm sorry." Clearing my throat, I take a step back to where she's standing. "I'm sure that was hard for you."

"Our past makes us who we are today, right?"

"And the choices we make." She doesn't respond, so I put it out there. "I don't want Pepper around things that could hurt her."

She doesn't meet my eyes, but she nods. "Blake is like that."

"You could be a little more like that yourself."

"I don't want to hurt anyone." Her brow furrows, and she looks up at me. "I want to have experiences. I'm an artist."

"Art isn't about gambling debts and porn films."

The color drains from her face. "What do you know about that?"

It's enough to draw me closer. For the first time, she might choose to remember. "What do you know about someone named Ivanov?"

Her body is tense, and her eyes flutter away. She seems to be closing in on herself. "Nothing. I don't know him."

"But you know it's a him?" Her chin lowers, and she starts chewing her thumb. I've seen her shut down this way before. It's annoying as fuck, and I don't have time for it. "Where's Blake?"

"She's not here."

"Did she go into town? I need to speak to her."

"She left with Trip and his friend. They went back to New York."

"New York?" Cold filters through my veins. "Did she say why?"

"Trip said they were going to the gala, but Blake said I had to stay here." Hana turns her back and walks to the window. "We always go to the gala together."

Knowing what I know now, I'm pretty confident the gala is not why Blake went to the city.

"Listen to me," I catch Hana by the arm and turn her to face me. "I need you to think. Who would Blake go to see in New York?"

Her brow furrows, and she shakes her head. "I don't know."

For once it's possible she's telling the truth. "When is the gala?"

"Tonight at nine. Are you going?" She studies my face. "Can I go with you?"

"I think your sister's right. You'd better stay here. I'll have Scar and Dirk keep an eye on you. Spend the night at my place if you don't want to stay here alone."

She pulls her arm out of my grip and walks away, but I don't have time to waste.

CHAPTER 19

Blake

CAMERA FLASHES STROBE IN OUR FACES AS I STEP OUT OF THE SMALL limo on the royal blue carpet leading into the convention center. For a split second, I'm plunged into the last time I stepped out of a limo into a rainbow of flashing lights.

Debbie.

My heart seizes, but Trip catches my hand, helping me out of the vehicle. I exhale slowly, holding the side of my sheer, red Versace gown. I chose it in memory of her. The annual Belmont gala was one of Debbie's favorite events of the year, and according to Hana, she'd already chosen the Versace dress she wanted to wear.

I never saw it.

Grief swells in my chest, but I hold it back. I'm here to get to the bottom of all the bullshit. On my way into the city with Greg and Trip, I got the final text from Papi-O, **Welcome home. Time's up.**

I haven't responded to any of the threats, but my suspicions are confirmed. They're tracking my movements. Only three people knew I was coming here, and after my encounter with Greg, I'm convinced he's involved somehow.

He doesn't know that I know about my uncle's ledger. I also know Dirk came to the city to investigate the names in that book. More importantly, my uncle wanted us out of here, which all adds up to one thing: Returning to the city is the only way to get the rats to come out and play.

I'm the cheese.

I have the money, but I know paying a blackmailer never stops the blackmail. It only encourages him or her. I have to find out who it is.

Trip pulls my hand into the crook of his arm as I scan the room of familiar and unfamiliar faces. "You're very J-Lo in that dress, B. You make me look good."

Glancing up, I give him a tight smile. "You're welcome. I'm sure you could've found any number of attractive debs to hold your arm. Natasha or Rainey, for example."

"Natasha is so boring, and Rainey's a child."

"She's eighteen last I checked."

He lifts two flutes of champagne off a passing tray, handing one to me and finishing his in a single gulp before grabbing another. "And yet I chose you."

"You're supposed to sip it, not shoot it."

The gala hall is breathtaking as it is every year. The black and beige marble floors are polished to a high shine, and massive jeweled chandeliers are lit in a row down the center of the high ceiling. Windows soar to the roof, covered in long sheer curtains, and a dance floor is in the center of the enormous space with a full jazz band playing standards accompanied by a Kenny G type on the tenor sax.

It's a black-tie affair, and the pedigreed class loves to take this opportunity to show off their Fashion Week finds. The ache in my chest fuels my desire for answers.

"I'm not surprised you changed your mind about being

here. One can only stand so much of that corny, Hamiltown snoozefest. Poor Hana. I'm sure she's climbing the walls."

My eyes narrow, and I study his face. "She was doing very well until you showed up. I heard you took her out and got her high your first night in town."

"You were misinformed. I did no such thing."

"You're saying Hutch didn't find my sister high with you two nights ago?"

"Oh, he found her high." He's already on his third glass of champagne, and I've only taken two sips. "I had nothing to do with it."

"Why did you take her out?" I watch him as I sip from my glass.

"As I said, Hamiltown is as boring as being alive. Even that attempt at frivolity was a bust."

"Are you blackmailing me?"

I catch him mid-guzzle, and he almost does a spit take. "Are *you* high? Why the fuck would I want to blackmail you?"

"Is Greg?"

Shaking his head, he finishes his drink. "Greg has more money than God—and in cash."

"Why was he digging around in my uncle's study?"

Trip's lips pucker, and he glances around the room. "He has his reasons."

"Which you know?"

"Maybe."

We walk farther into the crowd, closer to the dance floor, when I stop and pull his arm, forcing him to face me. "I've been generous with you. Now it's your turn. What do you know?"

His jaw sets, and his eyes level on mine. "I know you're a target because you won't lose. Hana is at rock bottom and still digging, but the honey all comes from the same pot."

"You know who's behind this?"

"I don't know for certain, but I can guess. Ask yourself who needs the money, and you'll find him."

"So it's a him?"

He shrugs, answering me with that annoying smirk.

"What does Greg Peters need?"

All signs of mirth fade, and he glances over his shoulder before leaning closer. "Answers, and he's determined to find them. You'd better keep your sister on ice if you care about her safety."

My throat tightens, and I take a sip of champagne, doing my best to act indifferent. "What does he care about Hana? They barely know each other."

"His uncle is missing, presumed dead, and he believes either Hana did it or she knows who did."

"Hana isn't capable of murder."

"Have you seen her high?"

Chewing my lip, I don't like to think about it. "Even if it's possible, you have to have a motive. I've never even seen her angry at anyone."

"Just because you haven't seen it doesn't mean it doesn't exist. You can't see the wind, can you? But it's blowing some bad shit your way."

Shaking my head, I try to make this make sense. "Who the hell is Greg's uncle?"

"Your mother's old accountant." *Victor.* Now I am sick, but I hold my expression steady as he continues. "According to Debbie, Hana had a motive. According to Greg, Debbie said Hana got her revenge. He was going to confront her, but that tattooed freak was always hanging around blocking. He even blocked my attempts."

Debbie told Greg? Could it be true? Inside I'm spiraling, but I force a laugh, rolling my eyes like he's lost his mind. The truth is, I'm scared as shit.

"Whatever Greg *thinks* Debbie said, it won't matter. Hana never remembers anything."

"What did she forget about Victor Petrova?"

A large hand slides around my lower back, and I jump forward with a little yelp. Trip catches my drink, and when I turn, my eyes fly wide.

"Hutch… What are you doing here?"

"And why am I not surprised?" Trip exhales heavily.

"I was going to ask you the same thing." Hutch's brow is lowered over his intense green eyes. His dark hair is perfectly messy, and he's gorgeous in the requisite black tie and tux. "If you'll excuse us, Trip."

"Take her. I've got my own business to manage." Trip waves me away with a flick of his wrist, and I know he's hooking up with his gambling connections. "Goodnight, Blake."

Hutch takes my hand and pulls me tight against his side. The band is playing George Gershwin's "Someone to Watch Over Me," and I don't even go there with the coincidence.

We're at the dance floor, and he turns to face me, still not smiling. Merging with the other dancers, his palm is flat against my lower back, and our hands are clasped. I hold his shoulder, lowering my face to his broad chest as sage and citrus and sexy man-scent flood my senses.

I'm frustrated and still angry at him, but I'm relieved to see him—and I'm pissed that I'm so relieved.

"You left town without telling me." His stern voice is at my ear, and I lift my chin, meeting his arrogance head-on.

"I didn't know I had to check with you before I did anything."

"I promised your uncle I'd keep you safe. How am I supposed to do that if you leave without telling me?"

"Perhaps it's time I paid your bill. I don't like being a prisoner."

"You're not a prisoner, and you're not my client." His warm

breath tingles against my bare shoulder. "Your uncle hired me to protect you, and I never charge him for my services."

My lips press together. He's so fucking infuriating. Our eyes meet, and mild amusement is in his. Exhaling, I decide to make the most of his presence. After what I've learned from Trip, I need all the help I can get.

"How much did my uncle tell you about why he wanted us out of New York?"

"Not much. He said it was for your safety, and he made me promise to come and get you if his letter didn't do the trick."

That makes me laugh. "He thought I would go with you?"

"I told him you wouldn't, but he insisted I convince you."

"Why would he do that?" I scan the room.

"He trusted me, Blake. Don't you think it's time you did the same?"

My fingers tighten on the expensive fabric of his Armani suit. It's the first time I've been in the city since Debbie died, and I feel like I'm clinging to the only lifeboat in a sea of sharks.

His arms are around me and the power of him seeps into me with the lyrics of the song. Lifting my face to meet his, I slowly nod my head.

Soft as butterfly wings, his lips brush the silver scar above my eyebrow, and he murmurs, "Good girl."

Those words falling from his lips heat my blood, but it's killed by a shrill voice calling my name.

"Blake!" My mother sways up beside us on the arm of a man I don't recognize. "I didn't think you were coming. Where have you been?"

"I was visiting Uncle Hugh in Hamiltown." I hold steady as she kisses my cheek.

"Why on Earth would you go to that odd little hamlet? I've never understood Hugh's fascination with it."

"It's our family place. It's part of who we are."

"Darling, I have family in the hills of West Virginia, but you don't see me running off there."

I swallow my annoyance, and Hutch cuts in. "I don't know about West Virginia, but most people find Hamiltown relaxing. It's definitely more real than New York."

Mama's eyes narrow at Hutch. "Hoyt's son." She holds out her hand. "I see you're as arrogant as ever. Are you here to tell us all what to do again?"

"I'm simply stating my opinion." He shakes her hand briefly.

Her eyes move from him to me and back again. "You've always been so interested in my daughter. Are you two together?"

"We just bumped into each other," I answer quickly.

Her gaze turns to me. "Where is your sister? Is she also in Hamiltown? Her birthday is right around the corner, and I—"

"I think we'll spend her birthday at Uncle Hugh's. She's doing well there, taking pictures, staying clean. It's a better environment for her."

"Well, I just don't know what to make of this." Mama places a hand on her chest as if she's astonished. "You girls always hated the country. You said the sound of crickets gave you the itch."

Blinking down, I exhale a laugh. "I guess I've grown up since then."

Hutch clears his throat, and my mother's eyebrow arches. "Well, I understand grown-up feelings. Whatever makes you happy, darling. I'm leaving for Cannes in a few days. Let me know if you need anything."

"It was nice to see you, Mrs. van Hamilton."

"Good heavens, call me India. You're over twenty-one."

A flurry of air kisses, and she swirls away, leaving me as alone as I've ever been. For years my mother's indifference bothered me. I longed for her approval, yet I only received criticism and dismissal for my efforts. She's never been any help to me or any kind of role model for Hana. It's exhausting.

Hutch takes my hand firmly in his, and I look up at my designated protector. "We have things to discuss."

I nod slowly, allowing him to lead me away from the crowd. Maybe I'm still angry with him, and maybe we don't see eye to eye, but it looks like trusting him is my only choice if I'm going to save us.

CHAPTER 20

Hutch

"**W**HERE DID YOU LEAVE IT WITH THEM?" WE'RE ON THE balcony just off the grand ballroom, and I'm listening as Blake fills in the missing details of the blackmail story.

She's gorgeous in a sheer red floral dress with her dark hair hanging loose down her back. Two narrow strips of fabric barely cover her full breasts, and her back is completely bare to the waist. The long skirt has a high slit that shows off her shapely legs, and her beauty is intoxicating.

Her arms are crossed, and she faces the water, while I lean beside her against the railing. I want to be angry with her for skipping town, but the story she's unfolding and what I know of my brother's work shoves all my feelings aside.

"I haven't replied to his texts. The number is blocked, but he's following me. He knew I was here tonight."

"You know it's a male?"

"Trip seems to think it's a man. He says it's about Hana's

gambling debts. He said they're after me because all our money comes from the same 'honey pot.'"

She makes a face like she's quoting him, and my ears perk up. It's the same language Dirk found in the intercepted texts.

Anger tightens my jaw, and I'm ready to kick Trip's punk ass into next week. "He knows who it is?"

"Not exactly." Her arms drop as she exhales. "He said he can guess based on who needs money. Knowing my sister, it could be any number of people."

"You'll have to make a payment. How much do you have?"

"I can send twenty-five thousand."

Nodding, I check my phone. "Dirk can trace it once you make the transfer, and he thinks this guy's sloppy enough it'll lead us right to him."

"I don't want to give them any money. I don't believe Hana would make a porn film. My sister does a lot of things, but she wouldn't do that."

Her eyes flash defensively, and I look down. I won't say what I'm thinking, since it only leads to more fighting. I don't know what her sister might or might not do, and I'm not willing to put anything past her, especially not after all I've seen.

"It's the best chance we have of finding the guy. We can get your money back."

"I need you to give me some space for a few days."

That pulls me up short. "Give you space? We're just about to bust this guy."

"There's something worse than blackmail going on, but I'm not going to be able to find out what it is if you're always hanging around me."

"Out of control gambling debts and porn films aren't bad enough?"

Silver-blue eyes meet mine, and she's determined. "I'll send the payment tonight. That'll get you what you need. I need you to give me what I need. Will you do that for me?"

My jaw grinds, and I'm ready to fight. "Space?"

"Please."

Standing straighter, I rise to my full height. "I don't like this. You're not strong enough to handle these guys."

"And you're not always right."

My body is tense. "I'm not leaving the city."

"As long as you keep your distance." Blinking towards the ballroom, she nods. "If I'm right and they're watching me, I need to send a strong signal that we've parted ways. For good."

Everything in me says this is a bad idea. I'm tense, ready to argue, but she looks up at me again, pleading.

My shoulders drop, and I take a beat. "How are you going to make it look like we're not working together?"

"I'm sick of you following me around!" She begins to shout. "I don't care what my uncle said. If you won't leave me alone, I'll report you to the police!"

I guess I have my answer.

It's a damn convincing display of anger, and as much as I hate it, I follow her lead. "You'll do as I say, or—"

Smack! She cuts off my reply with a stinging slap across my face.

I'm stunned by the force of her blow, and rage explodes in my chest. Grabbing her upper arms, I give her a shake. "Don't ever hit me again."

Our eyes meet, and while her mouth is set in defiance, her eyes glitter with confidence. I release her with a little shove, then I step in close, speaking under my breath.

"Don't do anything stupid."

Her response is equally low. "Don't believe everything you see."

Flipping her hair over her shoulder, she spins on her heel and storms away, leaving me on the balcony. She doesn't make it to the oversized French doors before two girls scurry out, huddling at her side.

"Blake! What happened? Are you okay?" The darker one holds her chest, worried eyes flitting from her to me. "Isn't he that private investigator?"

"Natasha, it's nothing." Blake takes her arm, raising her voice again. "Some people don't know when their services are no longer necessary."

The little one beside them, holds her dress, looking panicked. "I can call security if you want?"

It's my cue, and I take it. Striding towards them forcefully, I pause before passing. "That's the last time I stick my neck out for you."

"Fine!" she shoots back, and it takes all my willpower to keep walking.

This feels like a mistake, but I'll give her what she needs—for forty-eight hours.

"There's one intelligent person for every five or six in these groups." My brother talks absently as the noise of his fingers tapping the keys fills the background. "It's why criminals always get caught. This guy is not the leader—he's one of the weak links."

"We need to find the leader."

My chest is tight, as I wait on the line for my brother to work his magic. He verified she made the payment late last night. Now he's waiting for it to move.

I feel like I've betrayed my promise to Hugh. Blake is out there doing who knows what, and I'm allowing it. "Keep an eye on her, Dirk. Don't let her out of your sight."

"From what you've told me, it sounds like Trip might be the skeleton key to all this. Why don't you try and find out what he knows while you're waiting?"

"It'll at least give me something to do. I'll catch up with

him tonight. For now, I want to see what Dad knows." Glancing at my watch, it's after noon. "He's always easier to talk to after his two-martini lunch."

"Keep me posted."

My father's office has a view of the Statue of Liberty. When I was younger, I thought he must have the best job ever to have such a view. As I got older, I learned more about what he did as a day trader, the lies, the women, the alcohol, and the drugs, and my opinion changed.

"All these NFTs." I watch Hoyt Winston slide his finger across the screen of his computer. "I can't decide if investors are dumber now or if they simply have so much money, they don't care what they do with it."

"Isn't that the majority of your client base?" My arms are crossed, and I'm looking out his window at the ferry miles below headed out to Staten Island.

"Competition is at an all-time high." He grumbles like he doesn't love his work. "It's the eighties all over again. Greed is good."

Blake is on my mind, and I'm anxious to wrap this up and check in with my brother, be sure she's okay. "What do you know about Victor Petrova?"

Turning to face him, I see his brow is furrowed as if he's trying to remember. "Hell, I haven't heard that name in a while. He was a regular Bernie Madoff. Last I heard, he got what was coming to him."

"You think he's dead?"

"He's been gone so long without a word, I think we've all come to the same conclusion. He cheated the wrong person and got nailed for it." Leaning back in his chair, he surveys me. "Why do you ask?"

"Doing some work for a client. He embezzled money from their estate."

Dad nods, studying me. He doesn't remark, rather he looks down at his computer, exhaling a laugh. "I never dreamed I'd have a son like you."

He's slim and fair, more like Dirk than me, and I'm not sure how to take his judgment. "I guess we don't always get what we want."

"Are you getting what you want?" His eyes are on me, and I meet his hazel gaze.

"I'm on the right track. How about you?"

"I don't know." He rises out of his chair, rounding his desk and leaning on the edge. "Still searching for that magic pill, I guess. Lord knows I've made enough money to buy it."

"Good luck with that." I don't shake his hand. I'm not even sure why I came here. I could verify Victor's status without his help. "See you later, Dad."

Descending in the elevator, something Hugh told me crosses my mind, Money doesn't buy happiness. It only reveals your true character.

I'd add the way a person makes his or her money is another indicator—if anyone's paying attention.

I'm paying attention, and I quickly text my brother. *Headed out to find Trip. Got a 20?*

Gray dots float, and his reply appears. *Found him. Dropping a pin.*

I open the maps app before tapping my next question. *Everything good with Blake?*

More dots, only this time, I don't like what I see. *She's on the move.*

Concrete is in my gut, and I decide Trip can wait. I need to keep my promise. *Send me hers as well.*

In less than a second, I've got both pins, and I know where I'm going next.

CHAPTER 21

Blake

MY APARTMENT DOESN'T FEEL SAFE ANYMORE.

The city doesn't feel safe.

After what Trip told me and the clear signs I'm being watched, I want to finish this as quickly as possible and get back to Hamiltown, back to Hana. Walking around my empty apartment, I shake my hands, doing my best to remind myself Scar is there. Dirk is there. They'll keep an eye on her, and they have more muscle than I do.

Last night, after our little drama on the balcony, Natasha and Rainey accompanied me home. They're more Hana's friends, having come on the scene while I was in Connecticut with the nuns, and I've never been fully comfortable with them.

Still, I have to play the part for now. I endured Natasha stroking my hair and commiserating how men can be so insensitive. She asked me how I'm feeling since Debbie. It all sounded caring, but I felt an undercurrent of fishing.

Rainey is simply young and clueless. She's eighteen, old enough to be in the group, get in the bars owned or influenced by the guys, but she's not very sophisticated. She follows Natasha around like a puppy trying to make Fetch happen.

I pretended to be sad. I pretended to be frustrated with Hana's antics. When the clock struck two, I pretended to be tired, and they finally went home.

Once I was alone, I transferred the money to the fucking account of that idiot Papi-O. It burned in my chest to send that money. My conversation with Trip made me realize I'm a mark, and these morons are convinced they can threaten me with anything if it will keep my sister out of the tabloids.

My one consolation is Hutch's promise Dirk can get it back. I'm counting on that.

Today, I've been counting down the minutes until I can confront Greg. Natasha and Rainey are my link, as it seems the asshole is already dating Natasha. Debbie's not even cold in the ground—or ashes in her family's mausoleum—and he's already moved on.

I'm pacing my room when my phone lights up with a text from Natasha. ***Hanging at Gibson's tonight. See you around seven?***

My heart beats faster, and I quickly reply. ***Who's in the group?***

Don't know. I'm meeting Greg. You in?

It's all I needed to know, and I quickly tap out a ***yes***.

I'm taking a big chance confronting him, but I've never been one to cower in fear. He's fucking with the wrong van Hamilton.

Gibson's is an old-school cigar bar, which is saying something these days. Smoking is banned in all bars and restaurants in New York City, but in Gibson's, with it's wine-colored leather furniture, carpeted walls, and heavy velvet curtains, the air is thick with cigar smoke. The counters are lined with whiskey and bourbon and assorted spirits, and the atmosphere is something out of a bygone era.

Frank Sinatra's "Summer Wind" plays softly over the speakers, and a low roar of voices comes from clusters of men of all ages dressed in suits and gathered along the brass-studded, wooden bar or sitting in round, leather booths.

Women in high-fashion, skimpy cocktail dresses drift through the room carrying glasses of champagne. Their hair is perfect, their makeup on point, and they're clearly escorts for hire.

"It's like stepping back in time," Natasha giggles, holding my arm as we descend the stairs to the basement bar.

A velvet rope lines the entrance on street level, but the crowd is sparse. Patrons are permitted by invitation only at Gibson's. You can wait all night in the cold winter air, but you're not getting in unless you know someone.

I know Greg, and my intention is to find him. I plan to tell him to back off Hana and then go home. I'm not looking for conflict. I only want him to leave us alone.

I'll go back to my apartment, shower the cigar smoke out of my hair, pack my things, and leave this city. With all that's happened, New York doesn't feel like home to me anymore.

The doorman doesn't even question us as we enter the smoggy, open bar area. He knows we're Greg's friends.

Laughter erupts from a table in the far right corner. I can't see who's there, but I see a bald guy in a suit smoking a cigar with a pretty brunette draped over his shoulder. It's impossible to know if they're together or if she's looking for a daddy.

"Want a martini? I'll order us martinis." Natasha clasps my hand and drags me with her to the bar.

She's dressed up in an emerald green bustier over a wide-striped black and white, long-sleeved dress. I'm in a simple, black silk sheath with spaghetti straps. We checked our faux furs at the door, and we blend in well with this vintage venue and its patrons.

Leaning against the bar, I scan the crowd of mostly white men for his face. They all blend together, entitled men of privilege showing off their ability to flout the rules in an environment where anything could happen.

Natasha puts a slim cocktail glass in my hand and hisses, "There he is!" like she just spotted Elvis. Or Old Blue Eyes himself.

Greg descends the stairs in a solid maroon suit and black shirt and tie that set off his pale features and black eyes. I shoot my martini, ready to get this done, when Natasha laces our fingers and drags me to where he takes a seat in one of the booths.

"Hello, handsome." She slides into his side, and he lifts an arm to allow her proximity.

I sit, straight-backed like a soldier at the outer edge, tracing my fingers along the stem of my now empty martini glass. I'm starting to feel the effects of shooting straight gin.

"Did you have a nice time at the gala, Blake?" His lazy voice reaches me from the bowels of the wine-colored leather.

Blinking up, I meet his dark gaze. "I saw my mother."

His brow quirks, and he smirks over at Natasha. "Always a plus, I presume."

Natasha snorts into her glass, and I clear my throat. "Can I speak to you for a moment? In private?"

Without missing a beat, he slides to the edge of the circular booth. "I was waiting for you to ask."

I'm sure you were. The thought drifts through my mind, but I follow silently as we walk to the back of the bar, through a set of wooden double doors, into a small, solid-black room with bench seats against each wall. It appears to be a peepshow room, if there are peep shows at Gibson's, which I've never heard of before.

"What's on your mind?" He sits on the black velvet bench, spreading his arms wide like I'm about to give him a lap dance.

"I heard you're looking for my sister."

Tilting his chin, he exhales a laugh. "I already found your sister."

"I heard you're after her for a crime you think she committed."

"My uncle is missing. I've searched all his records, and they all lead back to your family, specifically your sister." I've never noticed the touch of an accent in Greg's voice, but I hear it now, crisp eastern European.

"Your uncle stole from us. He hurt her. That doesn't mean Hana had anything to do with whatever happened to him."

He leans forward, resting his forearms on his legs. "I think it does. And you've come to me, knowing full well what I'm seeking."

"Because Trip told me."

Leaning back again, he exhales a laugh, revealing too many teeth. "You Americans have loose tongues and no loyalty. I follow the old ways. My people don't allow our brothers to go down unavenged. No one gets in our way, no man… or woman."

His black eyes glitter, and ice shoots through my veins. Old ways? His people? What the fuck? All at once, I realize I need to get out of here. Now.

"You're one of them." My voice is barely a whisper. "What is this? Russian mafia?"

"There's no such thing as a Russian mafia." He stares at me with the coldest eyes, and my stomach dips.

He's saying it, but I'm not stupid enough to believe it.

A shudder moves through me, and I step backwards to the door. Rising to his feet, he holds me in a death glare as he closes the space between us. His hands rise, and I think he'll grab me when the double doors part, and a deep voice breaks the moment.

"I'm here to collect my client." Hutch catches my upper arm, pulling me to his chest. "Sorry for the disruption."

He holds me firmly as he leads me out, wrapping his thick wool topcoat over my bare shoulders to hide my shuddering. The temperature inside Gibson's is eighty degrees. I'm not shaking from the cold.

My coat is forgotten as Hutch moves with purpose, sweeping me from the back room through the main bar and up the stairs to a silent, waiting black SUV.

"I'm sorry I didn't give you more time." His deep voice is quiet, but I'm not worried about his interference.

My mind is swirling, and as much as I search for a way out, I can't find one.

This is bigger than gambling debts. It's bigger than blackmail, and I can only think of one way it will end.

CHAPTER 22

BLAKE'S GAZE IS FIXED ON THE GLITTERING NIGHT SCENERY FLYING past her window in my black SUV. She doesn't speak, and I think she's finally coming to terms with the danger of her situation.

My driver stops at the entrance to her apartment building, and I wait, unsure if I should follow her out or leave her at the door.

"You should come up," she says softly.

I step out of the vehicle, pausing only to tell my driver I'll call him if I need him.

We walk into the lobby in silence. It's a beige circular room with a desk and a doorman who tips his hat.

Elevators line one wall, and a small room to the right contains the mailboxes for the building. Blake goes straight to the elevators, and a short, gray-haired man in a green uniform opens the doors.

"Miss Blake," he greets her, and we step inside.

We're silent in the small box, and her eyes are downcast.

Even though her confidence has taken a hit, I can see she's doing her best to regroup, and I can't help admiring her fortitude, even if I believe it's misguided.

I know from experience there's only one way to handle men like Greg Peters, and it's with brute force. His kind only responds to the biggest dick on the block, which he's going to learn is mine.

The bell dings at her floor, and she steps forward to touch the elevator operator's arm. "Take us to the roof, Rusty."

The older gentleman nods, and the doors close again. He turns a key and we rise higher, stopping inside a hooded metal cage. The doors open, and he steps out, parting the shaky metal gate.

"Just buzz when you're ready to come down," Rusty says, and she nods, giving him the faintest smile.

The doors close, and we're alone. She reaches out and takes my hand, leading me across the slab of concrete as wide as the building below.

"You showed me your favorite part of Hamiltown." Her voice is quiet. "I'll show you my favorite part of New York."

My shoulders relax, and I let her lead me. "I'd love to see it."

I want her to tell me what Peters said tonight, but more than that, I want things to be the way they were between us, before the fighting.

The roof is lined with a shoulder-high ledge of beige clay tiles. She walks to where a planter stands holding a pot with viney leaves spilling out of the top and leans her forearms against the barrier looking out.

Glancing back at me, she motions for me to join her, and I walk to where she stands in her sexy black dress that shows off all her gorgeous curves. Her arms are crossed, and I can't tell if she's cold. The wind sweeps her long, dark waves away from her shoulders, and when I look out, the view of the skyline is breathtaking.

The city streets are far below, and straight ahead, the lights of New York ripple out like a magic carpet of glittering white and neon. Skyscraper upon skyscraper is illuminated in a mosaic of gilded yellow squares. One way looks out to the Hudson, the other, to the East River. It's a panoramic view of the city that never sleeps.

"I used to think I was a part of it." Her voice is resigned. "I used to think this was my town. I was Carrie Bradshaw or *Gossip Girl*. I was a fool. This town belongs to the men with the money and the hate to run it. I've only ever been one wrong step from being a victim here."

My brow furrows, and as much as I dislike the corruption, I'm not sure her words are entirely true. She's feeling overwhelmed, and I'm here for that.

"What can I do?"

She lifts her pretty eyes to mine. "What if I told you I killed a man?"

Pulling my chin back, I arch an eyebrow. "I'd find that hard to believe. You're controlled, and you're very strong. You'll do whatever it takes to keep your family safe, but you're not a killer."

"What makes a killer?"

"Determination, resolve… Uncontrollable rage. Passion, belief in some greater good. A million different things."

"Have you killed anyone?"

"Yes, in the military. I didn't know their names or their faces. Still, it took a piece of me."

She's quiet, not looking up, still holding the doors partially closed.

"I can only carry you so far, Blake. At some point, you're going to have to tell me everything."

Her eyes lift slowly to mine, and she blinks several times.

"They're after Hana for more than porn. They think she murdered a man… Or somehow participated in his murder."

Stepping back, I slide my hand over my mouth. This is news, and it makes partial sense, knowing what I know of Hana. But I'd as soon believe Hana is a murderer as I'd believe Blake is one. "Do they have any proof?"

"I don't know. I don't think so." Her eyes fall to the ground. "But they know what happened to her, what Victor did."

"How could they know that? Did she tell them?"

"Trip implied Debbie told them, but I don't believe that." Anger sets in her jaw. "He probably bragged about it. She's a beautiful young girl. I'm sure having her was an ego boost, a testament of his virility… or his cruelty."

"I feel like you're angry with me."

"I'm angry with what he did, and what they're trying to do now, justifying it as some code of honor. It's a code that victimizes a young girl then makes it her fault if she does anything to protect herself."

Holding out my hand, I approach slowly. "Are you saying you think she's guilty?"

Shaking her dark head, she wraps her arms around her waist and shivers. "I don't want to believe it. I don't believe she'd have the strength to do something like that, but I've never been abused that way. I don't know what it makes you capable of doing."

"We can get her help. I know places she can go, places for people like her—"

"People like her?" She flashes at me. "I'm not shipping her off somewhere to be treated like a criminal. I know you don't approve of her, but not everyone has had a privileged upbringing like you."

Exhaling slowly, I gentle my tone. "You were as privileged as I was growing up."

"It's not the same. You had the power to control your world. We had none."

"Maybe," I nod. "Still, you can't excuse her for what she did—if she did this. Being a victim only gets you so far. You can't protect her from the consequences of her actions."

"Yes I can!" Her voice rises, but it breaks as she continues. "I will protect her. I'm the only one who will."

Her shoulders fall, and I'm there to catch her. "I'll help you."

"No." She twists in my arms, and I loosen my hold. "You don't care about her. You're just like them trying to control us, trying to make us do what you think we should do, behave how you want us to behave."

"I'm not like anyone." Catching her face in my hands, I slide her silky hair off her cheeks. "I do care, and we're going to make something better. Together."

She hesitates, blinking up at me. Her full lips part, and she's breathing fast, her beautiful breasts rising and falling rapidly against my chest.

A spotlight passes across the sky, illuminating the mist glistening in her eyes, and I lean forward, covering her lips with mine, sealing my promise in the language we speak best.

"Hutch..." A soft whimper escapes her throat as she turns her face, and I slide my hands up the back of her thighs, lifting her skirt as I lift her off her feet.

Her legs wrap around me, and I back her against the wall, dropping my face to consume her mouth. Her arms surround my neck, and our kisses rise and dip, tilt and dive, tongues chasing and curling together.

It's sloppy and sensual. I suck the tip of her chin before dragging my teeth along the line of her jaw. Her hips rock against my growing erection, and she moans, pushing the jacket off my shoulders.

"Are you wet for me?" She nods quickly, and I lower her to her feet. "I want to taste you."

Dropping to my knees, I lift her leg over my shoulder before burying my face in her bare pussy, dragging my tongue slowly up the line to her clit.

"Oh, God!" She hisses, and her knee buckles.

I brace her against the wall with my palms, spreading her open as I kiss the crease of her thigh. Moving higher, I trace kisses along her lower belly, scenting the faint rose on her skin.

Slim fingers stab into my hair as I move lower again, sliding her lace thong down to her ankles. My tongue covers her clit again and again. She whimpers as I consume her delicate ocean taste, touching her lightly with my teeth before releasing her leg and testing her core with my fingers.

She rises on her toes, bucking her hips against my face, coating my hand in her juices. "I'm coming…" She gasps, and I pull away, rising to my feet as I unfasten my jeans.

"I want your come on my cock." Gripping her ass, I lift her again, holding her against the wall before sliding fully into her slippery depths.

She gasps a loud *Oh*, and I groan, holding a moment to find my balance as her hot body grips me.

I rock into her slowly gaining speed. "You're so wet… So tight."

Her sweet pussy massages me, and her legs flex around my waist. Dropping her head back, her entire body tenses and she breaks into loud moans and orgasmic spasms.

"That's my girl." I slide my palm over her forehead, pressing her head against the wall as I kiss her deeply.

She's my favorite drug, and I can never get enough of her. We're *not* like anyone else. She's mine, and I claim her this night with my heart, with my soul, and with my cock.

Two more thrusts, and I'm gone, pulsing deep, filling her so that it spills down onto my legs. Her soft lips touch my cheek, my temple, my eyebrow. Her fingers lace in my hair, and I lift my chin to taste her mouth one more time.

Our breathing calms. She's in my arms, and the stars light her pretty eyes.

She's so beautiful. I can't get enough of looking at her. Her body is made for me, and I'm aroused whenever she's in my presence. Hell, at the very thought of her.

Resting an elbow on my shoulder, she teases the side of my hair with her finger, a little smile curling her lips. "Why don't you have a girlfriend? Or a wife? You're definitely old enough."

It's unexpected, and it makes me chuckle. I lean forward to kiss her lips. "Are you insulting me?"

"It's just, you seem like the type to be so traditional…"

"Maybe I haven't had time for tradition."

"Maybe?"

"Maybe I had other things on my mind."

"I don't believe you." Her eyes lift to mine, dark and tempting. "You fuck me like you can't get enough."

Heat sizzles in my belly, and I'm very aware of her body against mine. "You're something I waited for a long time."

"I like to think of you waiting for me. Jerking off for me." She leans closer, her voice drops as her lips brush my skin. "You were the first man to make my pussy wet."

My dick rises to life. "We should head down to your apartment now. I want to fuck you properly in a bed."

Soft palms cup my cheeks, and she looks into my eyes. "Take me home, Hutch."

My brow furrows, and I'm not sure I understand. "Where is home?"

Looking over my shoulder, she exhales. "I don't know anymore." Her eyes return to mine. "Would you take me back to Hamiltown?"

Satisfaction fills my stomach, and I kiss her soft cheek. "Yes, I will."

CHAPTER 23
Blake

SUNLIGHT WARMS MY FACE, AND I OPEN MY EYES TO THE DAWN streaming in through Hutch's window. Glancing to the side, I see I'm alone in his enormous bed, but it's okay. I stretch my arms over my head, sliding lower in the blankets as recent memories fill my mind.

Last night, we left New York, boarded a private jet and landed in Charleston less than four hours later. A short drive, watching the headlights trace his square jaw and perfectly straight nose, my fingers laced with his on the console of his truck, and we were here.

It was after two, and he carried me straight to his bed, where I curled up in his arms. He kissed me softly on my head, removed all my clothes, and we made love sweetly, gently, confidently.

He's right we're not like anyone else. What's happening between us changes everything. Our families have been adjacent for so long. They've built a town, feuded, made slow progress towards reconciliation, and in us, they unite.

Perhaps I've always been his. Perhaps the circumstances of our lives have been leading us to this point all along, even when we were far apart, even when I was furious at him for interfering with my life. Now I can't imagine being without him.

One thing is left—I need my uncle back. I need him to tell me how he got that book and what he knows about the disappearance of Victor Petrova. I need him to help me clear Hana's name, or protect her.

My brow furrows, and I sit up in the bed trying to figure out a way to make it happen when the large wooden door opens. My frown melts into a smile when I see Hutch standing there in jeans and a gray Henley holding a mug of coffee.

"Not disturbing you, I hope." His low voice soothes my insides, and I rearrange the pillows so I can lean back against them.

"Are you bringing me coffee in bed? I feel like a princess."

A sexy grin reveals straight white teeth, and he sits beside me, passing over the mug. "I watched how you prepared it at Steamy Beans."

"Mmm…" I sniff the warm brew. "Is there cinnamon in it?"

"No cinnamon." His voice is gentle, and his large hand covers my bare foot as I take a sip. "Do you like to ski?"

I tilt my head to the side. "I've only ever snow skied."

"It's a beautiful spring day. We're going to the lake. Get dressed, and I'll run you by your uncle's to grab a bathing suit and Hana. Let's go."

A smile splits my cheeks and in spite of everything, it feels kind of perfect. "Okay!"

Setting my mug aside, I throw back the covers and hop out of bed.

"The sun feels so good on my skin." Hana leans back on her elbows on a towel, closing her eyes behind dark, oversized shades.

We're on a long, wooden pier watching Pepper being pulled behind Hutch's glistening, polished-wood speedboat. It's a gorgeous craft, slicing through the dark waters with hardly a bounce. Dirk is at the wheel beside his brother who's watching their little charge. Scar is behind us, keeping watch from the picnic area farther up on the bank.

"It always feels so good after a long winter." I'm considering the metaphor to our lives as I finish applying sunscreen to my chest. My hands are covered, so I lean over to rub the excess on her pale skin. "You'll burn if you don't reapply."

She sits up fast, blocking me with her hand and laughing. "Okay, Mother Hen, I got it."

I pass her the bottle before leaning back in the lounge chair I've placed beside her. She's wearing a tiny, white-lace bikini that's only a few shades darker than her pale skin.

By contrast, my olive skin is already bronzed. Still, I have a wide-brimmed hat, and I'm covered in sunscreen from head to toe in my high-waisted black two-piece.

"Look at me, Hana!" Pepper yells, waving her hand so hard she almost loses her balance. My sister erupts with laughter when the little girl lifts one of the giant waterskis, crying, "One hand and one foot!"

Hana drops the sunscreen and grabs her camera off the towel, snapping photos. "Do it again!" she yells, and I grin as I watch them.

Hutch agreed to back off his judgment that my sister is a "bad influence," as long as I promised to keep an eye on Hana's extracurricular activities. So far, so good.

"She's amazing. Pure joy." Hana looks down at her camera, sliding through the shots. "I've never known a kid to be so athletically inclined. It's like she can do anything."

"I love how close you are." I'm quiet, watching her as she lifts the device and takes more shots of the men in the boat, and the little girl sinking into the water as they slow. "She really looks up to you."

"I don't know if that's true." Dark blue eyes meet mine before returning to the camera. "We have a lot in common. We both lost parents when we were young. We both come from these super-rich families..."

"That's about as far as it goes. Pepper goes to public school, she gets dirty, she's never even been to New York."

"She's also really thoughtful, and sensitive. Just because she's playful, people don't realize she can be hurt, too."

Her voice is quiet, and an ache is in my chest. I know Hana is sensitive. I see it in her art, and I know it's what provokes her self-destructive behavior.

"You were hurt pretty bad at her age." I say it quietly, like I'm approaching a wounded animal, waiting to see if she'll engage or shut down as usual.

To my surprise, she answers. "I was a little older than her."

"Not much." I hesitate, hoping I don't go too fast. "I'm sorry I wasn't there to make it stop."

"No one could stop him. He was stronger than everyone." She leans back, lowering the camera.

Her words conjure the image of a small child, a little girl, told by a dark monster she'll never escape him, no one can save her.

"Somebody was stronger than him. He's gone now." I study her eyes, closed behind her dark shades, and she doesn't flinch.

She's calm as the lake before we launched the boat and disturbed the waters.

"Hana?"

Her dark eyes open slowly and turn to me, too wide, too round.

Still, she gives nothing away. "One less predator."

The boat cruises up, and I'm still watching her for any show of emotion—fear, hesitation, satisfaction. I get nothing.

"Who's ready for a burger?" Dirk calls, steering them closer to the pier while Hutch reaches for a post to toss the rope around.

"Me, me, meeee!" Pepper's voice is loud, and Hana turns away.

"You're always hungry!" A huge smile breaks across my sister's face, and she jumps up to grab Pepper's hand as she skips across to the wooden planks.

I exhale slowly, disappointed that we were so close. Then my eyes flicker to the flex of Hutch's muscles as he ties up the boat. He's in swim trunks and a tee, and I picture us swimming in the lake, our bodies sliding together in the cool water, trunks sliding lower, bathing suit bottoms gone…

His eyes lift to mine, and a wicked grin curls his lips. He hops up on the pier and walks straight to where I'm sitting, placing both hands on the arms of my chair and leaning close.

"You'd better stop looking at me that way or I'll have to take you somewhere private."

"I'm ready when you are."

He leans closer, sealing his lips to mine and giving me a quick taste of his tongue. He's salty and smells like coconut from the sunscreen, and I reach up to cup his scruffy cheeks.

"Okay, keep it PG, people." Dirk teases us as he thuds past us on the pier.

Exhaling a laugh, Hutch reaches for my hands as he straightens. I let him pull me up, grabbing the white cotton cover-up off my chair as I follow him to where Scar already has burgers going on one of the outdoor grills near the picnic area.

"Silent but deadly," I tease, holding Hutch's arm as we approach the group.

"It's all true, but I'd trust him with my life."

"I'm trying to decide if I trust him with my sister."

Hana stands away, holding Pepper's hand, and Scar hands them two paper plates with thick hamburger patties on buns. She eyes the food, and my throat tightens, remembering her disordered eating.

"I made it for you." Scar's low voice draws her attention, and her lips tense before relaxing into a cautious smile.

"Thank you." She looks up at the towering beast of a man.

He touches her forearm lightly. "I'll join you in a minute."

"This looks GREAT!" Pepper shouts, marching to where Dirk has unpacked condiments on a wooden table.

He hands her a soft drink before twisting the cap off a bottle of Abita Amber and taking a long drink. "This might be a perfect day."

Scar glances at us, and his wolf eyes stutter my heart. He really is intimidating. He's a few inches taller than Hutch but slimmer. His body is long, lean, inked muscle.

"Burger or hot dog?"

Hutch glances at the picnic tables and calls to Dirk. "Cole slaw?"

"You know it!" His brother holds up a plastic container.

"Give us a couple of dogs." He gives me a wink. "I'll make you a southern style hot dog."

"It's not southern style if there's no chili!" I give his arm a little shove, and his eyebrows rise.

"Listen to you knowing so much."

"You act like I've never been here before. I know how to make a South Carolina hot dog."

Holding up both hands, he flashes me a white smile. "What will the lady have?"

This time I give him a wink. "We'll have a couple hot dogs, please. Just don't call them southern style."

"Yes, ma'am." Hutch chuckles low, and it makes my stomach squeeze.

I haven't had a chance to see the playful side of him. It's

sexy, and a welcome reprieve from the pressure of the last few weeks.

Scar places two red hotdogs on buns and hands them over. Hutch hesitates, and the big guy exhales a laugh before adding another one to his plate.

"For a minute, I thought you were trying to put me on a diet."

"Your pants still fit," Scar quips.

"If they didn't, what would happen?" Hutch stands to his full height.

"You'd be too big for your britches." Scar's voice is low and husky with a touch of an accent.

Hutch chuckles. "Asshole."

Watching them interact like brothers, I have so many questions, especially when I turn to see my sister's eyes on us as she takes a bite of her oversized hamburger.

Our dogs are prepared with coleslaw and onions, and Pepper's on her knees at the table. "Gross!" Mustard is on her nose as she voices her loud objection. "I hate coleslaw!"

"You'll have better taste when you're bigger." Dirk pulls her wet pigtail, and she bats his hand away.

"Old people like nasty stuff."

"I can't decide if I'm offended because I've been food-shamed or because she thinks we're old." I lift the hot dog and carefully take a big bite, doing my best not to get coleslaw in my lap.

"Everybody over thirteen is old to Pepper." Hutch finishes his dog in two bites and is already picking up the second one.

"Slow down." I lean into his shoulder. "You'll give yourself indigestion."

He taps a dab of mustard on my nose. "I've got a stomach of iron."

"You did not do that!" Laughing, I take a napkin to wipe the yellow smear off my nose.

Hana sits across from me, and it's the first time in a long time I remember seeing her laugh. I'd almost say she's happy, and I want so much for it to last.

"I got another letter asking me to teach at the college." Dirk straddles the bench facing Pepper as he downs two hot-dogs and starts on a burger. "I'm thinking about saying yes this time."

Hutch nods as he polishes off the last of his dog. "Computer science? Data analysis?"

"Criminal psychology."

My ears perk up at his answer. My undergrad degree is in psychology, and I didn't know Dirk had experience in the field.

"Do it." Hutch nods, lifting a leg over the bench to strad-dle it, pulling me closer to his chest.

His chin is at my shoulder, and fizz tingles in my veins. I look up at him, and when our eyes meet, I see something differ-ent in his—calm resolve, ownership. It warms me to my toes.

Without hesitation, he leans forward to plant a brief kiss on my lips. "I'm going to help clean up. Take your time."

He stands gathering our plates, and I can't take my eyes off him. He's gorgeous and fierce and kind and so damn sexy. His broad shoulders stretch the gray tee, and his ass flexes in his nylon swim trunks fanning the heat rising into my chest.

"Pepper, bring me your trash," he orders, and when I turn back, I catch Hana watching me.

Clearing my throat, I try to be cool. "Want to walk down to the water?"

"Sure."

We stand, and I wrap my cover up around my body, feel-ing exposed and transparent as glass. We reach the end of the pier, and our feet scuff softly over the smooth boards.

"I've never seen you this way with a guy." Hana slants her eyes up at me.

Exhaling a little laugh, my conditioned response is to be

defensive, tell her she's imagining things. I don't get silly over men. I'm serious, focused, independent.

"I might be falling in love with him." A thrill of fear hits my stomach, and I turn to face her. "It's terrifying."

I'm blinking fast, and her eyes shine. "I don't think you need to be afraid—not from what I've seen."

"I can't help it. I never thought I'd meet anyone I could feel this way about. Not ever."

"I'm not sure you could in our old life. But here, things are different."

"It's all following the plan." A loud, craggly old voice calls to us from the bank.

My heart jumps to my throat, and a little yelp escapes my lips when I see him.

Standing on the end of the pier, dressed in a khaki, seersucker suit, leaning on his cane with his short-brimmed Stetson hat cocked to the side, is the man I came here to see.

I take off running, my feet thudding on the wooden planks beneath me. His low chuckle greets me before I've made it to the grass, and he holds out his arm for a hug.

I race straight into him, wrapping my arms around his narrow waist as my cheek presses to his bony chest. "Uncle Hugh."

CHAPTER 24

"Victor Petrova died of a heart attack." Hugh's hands are clasped behind his back, and he paces the small space between his desk and the bookshelf in his office. "He was found in his bed in his Manhattan apartment, cold as a stone. No evidence of foul play."

Blake's brow furrows, and her expression mirrors my response. "I mean, at his age, he could've had a heart attack. It just seems so…"

"Wrong?" her uncle asks.

"I was going to say anticlimactic, but we can go with that."

"I don't believe it. Foul play was definitely involved. My guy in Kazan has been digging deeper, following the money. Seems our crooked accountant racked up a lot of debt—mostly to the wrong people."

"Which would explain the embezzlement," I muse.

"It doesn't explain how you got his book." Blake cuts straight to the chase.

Hugh exhales his confession, "I arranged to have it stolen

and brought to me. I wanted to see if I could figure out what he did with your inheritance."

"Stolen by…" she urges.

"No one you know." His expression is grim. "No one anyone would know… or will know."

"It was the body." My voice is quiet, and he nods briefly.

Pressing my lips together, another piece of the puzzle snaps into place.

"Stop!" Blake is on her feet. "Too much has happened, I've juggled way too much garbage for anyone to keep secrets. What body?"

The old man rounds the desk, placing both hands on her shoulders. "Calm down. It's none of your friends or acquaintances—"

"Don't tell me ignorance is safety. I've learned over and over these last few weeks knowledge is safety, and I need to know everything."

Lowering his hands, the old man returns to his chair. "He was a minor player. His name was Andre something. Anyway, he got me the book, but when he delivered it, he got greedy. Figured he could make some money off it. He basically said I'd have to pay a certain amount above what we agreed to before he'd give it to me. I told him no, and he became violent."

"He threatened you?" Anger tightens my chest. "This is why you should only run shit like this through me. We're ready to handle it."

"Well, my bodyguard handled it—a bit too forcefully, but it's done now."

Blake turns wide eyes on me. "You knew about this?"

"I knew a piece of this. Not everything."

She stands, crossing her arms, but her uncle extends his hand. "Blake, please." He starts to chuckle. "I've worked so hard getting you two together. You can't fly off the handle over things you didn't know."

"Worked so hard." She shakes her head, and I knew it.

"You did all this for us to be… in the same place?" I can't say *together*. It's so specific and way too soon.

The old man tilts his head thoughtfully. "I did all this because I've gone as far as I can with these guys. I'm too old and sick to fight gangsters, so I'm passing it to you two. I think you make a great team—in more ways than one."

"So you invited Hana and me here, then you disappeared without a word so I'd be forced to stay with Hutch?" Blake's voice rises.

"How else could I get you to see what I've seen for years? I wasn't sure what it was going to take, but I'm glad to see a little forced proximity worked nicely."

She exhales a frustrated growl. "You scared us to death."

"Terror is a potent aphrodisiac, yes?" Her uncle winks, and I can't even with him.

With a low exhale, I start, "You old—"

"Don't say it!" He laughs, cutting me off.

"Where did you go?" she insists.

"I have a friend with a place near the Biltmore. He'd been offering it to me for years, and I figured it was a good time to follow up with him."

"Biltmore." Blake drops into her chair again. "You ditched us to go to the Biltmore?"

"I left you in very capable hands." The old man lifts his chin, giving me a fond smile. "I'd trust Hutch with my life, even more with my two beautiful nieces."

One beautiful niece in particular, who he's been taunting me with for years. "I'm glad you're back safely." Calm is in my voice. "Still, it wasn't right to scare us that way. You almost gave Norris a heart attack."

"I'm sorry, my boy. I tried to send you the message that I was fine as soon as possible, without attracting unwanted attention."

"But I don't understand." Blake's brow furrows. "How did you know we were coming?"

"That was the easiest part. Once you checked in using the ticket I bought, I knew you were on the way, and I had to get out of the way so you could get together."

"Sneaky old man," Blake grumbles, going around to hug him. "You're lucky I love you."

"I love you. Your happiness is my highest priority." He gives her a warm smile before turning to me. "Where do we stand on everything?"

Shifting into professional mode, I run down the latest. We fill Hugh in on the secondary, blackmail scheme.

"Dirk is monitoring the payment Blake transferred to the blackmailer. It's possible they know we're watching, because the money hasn't moved. The account is a dummy—registered to a Jane Doe address in the Bahamas. We've set up an alert for any withdrawals, and I have a solid hunch on their point man in the states."

"Good work." Hugh nods, but Blake turns wide eyes to me.

"You didn't tell me that. Who do you think it is?"

"Scar figured it out after our last dinner together. *Grisha* is the Russian diminutive for Greg."

Her jaw drops, and she's on her feet. "Greg is the blackmailer? But Trip said—"

"I don't think Greg is the actual blackmailer, but I think he supervises the money laundering for this phony Russian investment group. The blackmailer could be any one of his lower-level flunkies."

Fire is in Blake's eyes, and I know what it means. Crossing the room, I take her hand, holding it firmly. "I know you're angry, but you have to let me handle this." She doesn't answer, her jaw doesn't relax, and I feel her vibrating with adrenaline. "Will you trust me, Blake?"

Her chest rises and falls with two deep breaths, and I know

it's a big ask. I know she's spent a lifetime protecting her sister. It's not an easy habit to break.

Blinking several times, she drops her chin. Her jaw relaxes, and she nods slowly.

"Yes." It's only a whisper, but it seals her place in my heart.

A low chuckle from behind the desk draws our attention.

I look up to see Hugh sitting back in his chair with a smug grin. "It's all following the plan."

Eccentric old coot. He'll be the death of us.

Several hours later, Blake's standing on my porch looking out at the oak trees. "I can't possibly go out after all that's happened."

It's a warm spring night, and she's wearing a high-necked blue dress that leaves her arms bare. Her dark hair hangs in a wavy ponytail over her shoulder, and an ivory shawl is wrapped around her upper arms.

"We can't sit around just waiting." Stepping closer, I place my hand on her waist. She's so beautiful in the periwinkle twilight. "I'd like to show you off."

Her full lips press together, and pink brightens her cheeks. "I guess I should get to know the nightlife in Hamiltown a little better. Can Hana come? I'd like to see her having fun in a healthy way."

"Of course. I'll message Scar to get his ass out of the house."

Slim Harold's is a knock-off of a shag club in Myrtle Beach. It's a restaurant with a dance floor in the center. A thin layer of sawdust covers the floor to make it slippery for the dancers. They're mostly old couples who can still do the dance to the sixty year-old "beach music," as they call it. "Rave On" by

Buddy Holly comes from the old jukebox in the corner play-ing original, vinyl records.

"This is amazing." Blake leans on my arm as we enter the semi-crowded place. "It's like they're doing the twist but with little twists mixed in."

"I thought you might like it." Leaning over, I kiss the side of her head. "I'll get us a few drinks. What would you like?"

Her nose wrinkles, and she's too cute. "A margarita?"

"Be right back."

I'm on my way to the bar, when I see Hana rushing up to her sister. "Why didn't I bring my camera?"

She's in a white lace dress that reminds me of the bikini she had on earlier today. Holding her sister's arm at the edge of the dance floor, she seems so young and innocent. I have to remind myself appearances can be deceiving.

Scar joins me on the way to the bar, and I lift my chin. "I guess you know what you're doing."

He orders a Yuengling and a coke then turns to me with a neutral expression. "I'm doing what you said, making sure she's safe."

"Nothing more?"

"She's not twenty-one."

"For a few more months." My eyebrow arches, and I'm not sure I'm buying it. "She's over eighteen."

He nods slowly. "In many ways, she's older than that."

A hunger is in his gaze as he watches the girls while I wait for Blake's margarita. They're at the edge of the dance floor watching the gray-haired couples spin and kick to the classic rock-n-roll music.

Scar and I don't talk much about our private lives, but in the past, I heard rumors he was into darker activities behind closed doors.

"Hana's been through a lot." I stop short of warning him to be careful with her.

He might be into darker kink, but I've never heard any complaints. In fact, he's had a few past liaisons who didn't want to let him go.

"For now, I'd like to see her healthy."

The bartender slides the margarita to me, and I take my beer. Tapping my bottle against his, I make a short toast. "To happier times."

A brief nod is my only response, and I follow him to where the ladies are waiting.

CHAPTER 25
Blake

"Hey, girl, haay!" Carmen's familiar voice slides up beside me. "I haven't seen you since the ball game."

"Hey!" I give her a brief, side-hug while I watch the older people dancing on the floor at Slim Harold's. "How did I not know about this place? It's amazing."

"You think so?" Her nose wrinkles. "I guess I'm used to it. Still, it's the best place for thick-cut bologna sandwiches and fried corn on the cob."

My eyes widen, and I almost laugh. "I've never even heard of those things."

"And you call yourself a town founder."

"I'm not really. We only visited a few times when I was young, and we never came into town. My parents were too snobby."

Hutch joins us, handing me my margarita then sliding his warm hand along my waist. It's possessive and perfect, and I feel all warm and fuzzy inside.

Carmen arches her eyebrow at me. "I need a strawberry margarita with some sugar on the rim."

Rolling my eyes, I take a sip of my tangy drink. "See you in a minute."

Scar hands my sister what looks like a Coke, and I glance up at Hutch. "It seems like she's trying."

His eyes are on his partner. "Pepper talks about her nonstop. Hana's teaching her to develop photos the old-school way, in a dark room."

"She's such a fun little girl. What happened to her dad?"

Pausing, he takes a sip of his beer, and I study the sexy line of his square jaw. "Judy came home pregnant, and never left. She didn't tell us his name, and no one ever came looking for her."

"I'm sorry. I assumed he died. I didn't know."

"No need to apologize." He gives me a tight smile. "We're doing our best to make up for it."

Tucking my hand in his arm, I rise on my tiptoes to kiss his cheek. "You're doing an amazing job. I mean, for starters, this is the first time I've seen you have a drink since we've been here."

"It's Friday night." The music changes, and he takes my hand, leading me to the dance floor. "We need to blow off a little steam."

The jukebox fires up a Backstreet Boys hit, and my eyebrows rise. "Open-minded group."

The older dancers don't miss a beat, twisting and shuffling their feet to the rhythm of "I Want It That Way." I hold his shoulder, watching them move.

"It's a good song." He pulls me closer, humming in my ear. "Tell me why…"

Heat tickles my lower stomach, and I think he is definitely my one desire.

My eyes drift around the rustic establishment. It's a mix of young and old patrons, couples of all varieties. Sawdust covers the floor, and the menu consists of burgers and bologna. It's about as far from a posh New York City gala as you can get, and I kind of love it.

"I wish I could do that fancy dance." An older couple beside us take turns twirling under each other's arms.

"Maybe I'll teach it to you one of these days."

"I'd like that." Our eyes meet, and another charge warms my stomach.

"It's pretty simple. Like most things around here." He's watching me, and I can't take my eyes off him. "Is that something you think you might like?"

Blinking back to the setting, I think about his honest question. Hana stands beside a hightop table with Carmen, who's belting out the lyrics to the song, and Scar sits on a stool watching her take photos of the crowd with her phone.

Uncle Hugh's sprawling estate has horses and the grounds I grew up visiting, but even here in this little village, people are friendly and welcoming.

"I don't know." The idea of moving my life feels daunting but more possible every day. "Would you be here?"

"Of course."

My bottom lip slips between my teeth, and I nod. "In that case, I think I could."

He slides his thumb along my chin, tugging my lip free. His green eyes darken with hunger I feel all the way to my core. "You asked me once if I loved your uncle."

"You said yes." I remember it well.

"I'm starting to love another member of your family as well."

Rising on my toes, I lean into his ear. "Would you take me somewhere private and kiss me?"

"God, yes." The night air is warmer with spring drawing closer, but it's nowhere near as hot as the fire in my belly as Hutch drives his massive cock into me from behind.

With every thrust, I rise onto my toes. I'm standing outside his truck in the woods around Makeout Point.

We didn't make it all the way to the clearing. I was too horny and climbed over the console to nibble his ear while I slid my hand up and down the growing rod in his pants.

With a loud swear, he pulled off into the trees, jammed the truck into park, and hauled me out the driver's side door. I couldn't help a laugh, until he turned me around and bent me over the seat, ripping my skirt up and my panties off.

At that point, I was all fire and lust and need, until he filled me to the hilt. Now he's behind me pumping fast, sending me to heaven.

"Good girl." His lips are at my ear, and his hands lift and knead my breasts, pulling and teasing my nipples, sending fiery sparks of pleasure racing through my core.

My eyes are squeezed shut, and I lean my head back against his shoulder, rotating my hips around his dick. His mouth closes on my neck, biting and sucking, and a flutter of spasms breaks out in my pussy. I'm so close to coming, I whimper and tremble with every slide of his cock through my wetness.

Sliding my hand down my belly, I massage my clit, and my orgasm erupts. My mind goes blank, and I see stars behind my closed eyes. His hot breath turns to low groans as Hutch draws closer, punctuating every thrust with a sound of pleasure until he breaks as well.

Large hands grip my hips, and he holds me still as his cock pulses, filling my trembling core.

We're both panting as he leans over me, sliding my long hair away so he can kiss the back of my neck. His beard scuffing against my skin provokes another round of flutters inside me, and he groans, pulsing once more.

We are fire and energy and completion, and I know I'll never be with anyone else ever again. It's impossible.

Lifting my limp body off the seat, he wraps strong arms around my waist, holding me in a hug against his chest. "Little vixen. You almost made me wreck."

"I just needed you." Turning my face, I kiss his cheek, sliding my nose into the side of his hair, searching for his familiar man-scent I adore. "I couldn't wait any more."

Warm lips press to the side of my neck. "I'll never make you wait. Let's head back to the house."

Several hours and several orgasms later, I'm snuggled in Hutch's big bed with his big, warm body beside mine. My eyes open, but the room is quiet. I have no reason to be awake. It's 4 a.m., the witching hour, and I do what I know you should never do when you can't sleep at night. I pick up my phone.

Checking my social media for the first time in days, Natasha tagged me in pictures from the gala. Studying the faces in the background, I notice Trip beside Greg.

I use my fingers to zoom in on their faces. They're having some conversation, and Greg's expression is stony. Trip's ever-present grin is missing, and I'd give anything to know what they're discussing.

If Hutch is right, and Greg is behind the blackmail scheme, everything Trip has said to me is a lie. Anger burns in my throat when I think about how generous I've been with him, giving him a place to stay when his mom acted out. I want to slap his face.

Hana might put herself in bad situations, but Trip is like our brother. He should be protecting her, not taking advantage of her.

My heart beats too fast, and I know I'm not going back to sleep. Hutch is so peaceful, I don't want to wake him. Sliding out of the bed, I quietly slip on my dress, take my shoes off the floor and tiptoe out of the room.

CHAPTER 26

"IT MOVED." DIRK'S FINGERS FLY OVER HIS KEYBOARD, AND I'M pacing the office.

My brother's call snapped me awake before dawn, and looking around, I saw I was alone in bed, which agitated me more. Now we're at the office in town, and I'm waiting as he fills me in on what happened overnight.

"The transfer was made at approximately 10 a.m. GMT, five our time, to a new account number not on any of the lists."

"Must be why it sat for so long." My jaw is tight. "They knew we were watching it."

"How could they have known? Did Blake let it slip?"

My mind skips back to the last time we were in New York, getting Blake out of that dive bar with Greg. "It could've been my fault. How long will it take to identify the account owner?"

"I'm working on it now, but if they went to this much trouble, chances are, it won't lead anywhere helpful."

"Let me know what you find out. I've got my phone."

Starting for the door, I'm frustrated by this turn of events, and I'm confused by Blake's absence when I opened my eyes this morning. Why would she slip out without a word? Did something happen?

I'm in my truck studying, trying to decide if I should go to Hugh's place and check on her, or if I should give her space to come to me. Things got pretty intense last night. I all but said I was falling in love with her. Perhaps it was too much.

Scrubbing my fingers over my eyes, I think about all of it in the light of day. Blake van Hamilton, the queen of New York City society, here with me, in Hamiltown. Is that even possible? Would she seriously want to give up her life in the city to move here or was it the margaritas talking?

Serious discussions should not be had over alcohol. Still, she was smiling when we fell asleep. At no point in the evening had she seemed upset or uncomfortable or pressured.

I sound like a teenage sitcom. Tossing my phone on the passenger's seat, I decide to let it sit for now. I've got more important concerns at present. The only problem is my concerns take me to Hugh's place, where she lives now.

Fuck it. It is what it is.

"You have to go to New York if you're going to put an end to it." Hugh's voice is solemn, and he sits at his desk, listening as I fill him in on what happened today.

"I don't even know what we're dealing with." The truth is, after my last trip to the city, meeting with my dad, I decided I'd had my fill of New York and all the players in it.

"Gangsters." Hugh's voice is level. "They're high-tech, with all the gadgets, but underneath all of it, they're old-fashioned gangsters."

"They are high-tech. All their shit is online, which means

we can bring them down just as easily from here as we can there."

"I disagree. The only thing men like this respond to is a strong hand. You're going to have to look these guys in the face and deal with them."

His watery gray eyes level on mine, and I remember he's from a different era, a time when violence was the only response to violence.

Shaking my head, I look down at my lap. "I'm not a vigilante, Hugh. If they break the law, I can have them arrested. If not—"

"If not, the monsters like Petrova continue, roaming the city, picking off one victim after the next. These boys are their protégés. They have to be stopped. Tell me you have the stomach to do what needs to be done."

"I'm not afraid to pull the trigger if it comes to that. I'm a Marine, for God's sake." Frustration twists my stomach. "What you're asking is for me to be judge, jury, and executioner. That's not how I operate."

"Maybe it should be. I can't think of a more just, fair person than you. You're not a hothead. I'd let you clean up the streets of my town any day."

"If I get down on their level, I'm a thug just like them."

"You didn't feel that way about defending your country."

"It's totally different."

"Is it?"

I'm prepared to argue it out with him, when my attention is cut off by the beautiful woman standing in the doorway.

Blake's dressed in jeans and a light sweater, and her silky brown hair is tied back in a loose bun. Her eyes are focused on me, and despite my frustration, I can't stay angry. She's the most beautiful thing I've ever seen.

"Hutch." She walks straight into the office like she owns

the place. "Did I hear you say you're going to New York? I need to go with you."

"Good." Hugh leans back in his chair. "It's all settled, then. You can take my private jet."

"No…" I shake my head, looking from her to her uncle. "It's not settled. Why do you need to go to New York?"

More importantly, I want to ask where she went this morning, but not in front of Hugh.

"Well, for starters, all my clothes are in New York… and Hana's." She turns to the side, looking down at her clasped hands. "We came here thinking it was for a week-long visit, and it's turning into something longer. I think?"

Her chin lifts, and when she looks at me, a question is in her eyes. Does she need me to confirm what I said last night?

It's funny, I spent the morning thinking she'd run out because I'd come on too strong. It didn't occur to me she might be worried I spoke in the heat of the moment, and I didn't mean what I said. The idea that I could have it backwards relaxes the fist in my stomach.

"It's definitely turning into something a lot longer." My voice is low, and I take her hand. "I'm glad to take you, and I'll help move your things."

She blinks away with a little smile on her lips, pink touching her cheeks. I want to cup her face in my hands and kiss her. Instead, I think about logistics and not wanting to make return trips.

"Does Hana want to join us? I can get Scar or Dirk to come as well."

"I hadn't thought about it, but yes. Hana needs to come so she can decide what she wants to have here."

"How soon do you want to leave?"

"The sooner the better." Her silvery eyes meet mine, and it's decided.

Hugh chuckles quietly as if to remind us of his presence.

"I'll arrange the flight now. My pilot will be ready when you are."

Blake leaves the room, and the old man gives me a smug grin. "I knew you'd make a great team."

"You've been pushing for it long enough."

All the humor leaves his face, and he grows serious. "And what will you do when they go after her?"

Unreasonable anger hits in my stomach like a punch, and I know he's right. These assholes are circling closer, from theft to blackmail, and now we're headed right back to the city.

I might not be a thug, and I'm not a vigilante, but the thought of someone hurting Blake changes me into a man I don't recognize. She once called me the Dark Knight, but from my internal response, it's possible I'm more like the Hulk.

Hugh reads the change in my expression, and nods as if he's satisfied. "That's all I needed to know."

"But you'll miss my game." Pepper's arm is around my neck, and she's giving me her best pout. "You've already missed seeing me off to school twice this week. It's like I don't even know you anymore."

"That's laying it on a little thick, even for you." My brow arches, and I give her waist a little tug. "Your game isn't until Thursday. I'll be home by Wednesday at the latest."

"Hana's going with you? What am I gonna do while you're all gone?"

I want to point out that Hana has only been in Hamiltown a few weeks, but I don't. "Uncle Dirk has promised to have dinner with you every night. He'll take you to get cupcakes, and we'll be back before you have a chance to miss us."

She slides off my knee, standing between my legs to face me and putting both hands on the tops of my shoulders. "I know! I'll go with you to New York." Her eyes flash. "It'll be educational—like a field trip. I can visit the MoMa and the Statue of Liberty. And Alexander Hamilton's grave!"

My hands are on her little waist, and I guess this is what parental guilt feels like. "It's not that kind of trip, Pep. I'm working on a case. I won't have time to take you to those places."

Her lips flap as she blows air forcefully through them. "It's never been like this before. I think you like Blake better than me."

It hits me all at once—I am not prepared for her to get older. "It's different with Blake. Mr. Hugh hired me to keep her safe, and part of the reason I have to go is some bad men are trying to… do some bad things."

Pepper's eyes go wide. "They want to kill her?" Just as fast her bottom lip trembles, and her voice gets thick. "Do they want to kill you? If that happened, would I live with Uncle Dirk?"

"No!" *Jesus!* Exhaling slowly, I pull her to my chest in a hug. "Nobody's trying to kill anybody. It's more like special adult-style theft. It's called embezzlement. Nobody is getting killed, okay? I don't even want you to think that. I'll be back Wednesday, and I'll go to your game, and that's all you need to worry about, okay?"

"Hana, too?" Her little voice is muffled against my neck, and I slide my hand up and down her back.

"Hana, too, and Blake. The whole reason they're going with me is to pack their things so they can move back here and live with Mr. Hugh." She sniffs a few more times, and I nudge her back to meet her eyes. "Everybody's going to be okay, you hear me? Now no crying. Give me a smile?"

Her lips press into a little pucker, but she blinks hard and nods, forcing a smile.

"That's my girl. Hardest working shortstop in softball." I pull her in for another squeeze, holding her close until I feel her relax. "I'm going to need a big, goodnight hug to last the next few days, okay?"

Her arms tighten around my neck, and I'm relieved and sad when she does a little grunt. I do the same, hugging her and pretending to strain.

Lifting her head, she whispers in my ear. "I love you, Uncle Hutch."

It hits me straight in the heart, but I have to go. "I love you, too, peanut." I pull her back, giving her little fanny a swat. "Now get to the kitchen. Lurlene has your dinner, and Uncle Dirk is on his way."

She nods and takes off running through the house. Rubbing my hand over my forehead, I think about my promise, about Hugh's line of questioning.

No one is getting killed.

We'll be back in three days, this shit is going to be settled, and we're all going to a softball game. Together.

On my way out the door, I slip my Beretta into my duffel.

CHAPTER 27

Blake

HANA STANDS BESIDE HER BED, LOOKING DOWN INTO THE SUITCASE. "It's odd to think about going back there. The last time we were in New York together, Debbie died."

My stomach cramps, and I hate that we still don't know what really happened to our friend. I will never buy the official line that she jumped off her balcony after a night of partying and pills. Debbie wouldn't do that.

But in the absence of more evidence, there's nothing I can do to clear her name. It's frustrating as fuck. We always looked out for each other—Debbie and me, and Hana as much as she could.

"You don't have to pack anything but toiletries. Maybe not even that. We're packing up whatever we want from the apartment and bringing it back here for the time being."

Her blue eyes meet mine, and she nods, solemnly. "New York doesn't feel like home anymore, does it?"

"No." It hasn't for a long time, I think to myself. "Hana?"

She glances over at me as she carefully puts items into an

overnight duffel. When she sees my serious expression, she stops. "What's wrong?"

"I'm just wondering, when you would go out with Trip, the nights I wasn't there, who all was with you? Natasha, Debbie, any other guys?"

"I don't remember."

Anger burns in my throat at her go-to, cop-out response, but my sarcastic *whatever* dies on my lips when I see her face.

Her brow is furrowed, and she's focused on the sequined top she's holding like she's genuinely trying to remember something.

"It's okay." I speak gently, going to her and taking her hand. "Try to relax. See if it comes to you."

She blinks several times before closing her eyes. "Greg would be with us sometimes, and another guy, Ivan…" Her lips tighten, and she shakes her head, opening her eyes again. "Ivan is all I can remember."

"That's okay! That's good, actually." I sit on the bed smiling up at her. "We'll call him Ivan X."

A little smile relaxes her face. "He'd probably like that. He was always trying to be a big shot like Greg. But he wasn't."

She adds the last part softly, and my chest is so tight. I've never gotten this far with her before, but I try to control my excitement. I don't want to pressure her and make her shut down again.

"Do you remember what Ivan did? For work, I mean."

Her small nose wrinkles, and she looks at the window. "He said he was studying film? Or he was making a film. I don't know." She shakes her head fast. "It was something about a film. Debbie and I split a button of mescaline, so it's all kind of hazy."

Inhaling slowly, I hold onto my shit. "That's okay. Can you remember anything he said?"

"Not really." She looks down. "I was never smart enough

to follow their conversations. They always talked about things I didn't understand."

Frowning, I try to imagine what that could be, if there were any business deals she heard about that I could piece together. "You don't remember any of the words they said? Maybe I can figure it out."

She starts to say no, but then she inhales quickly. "I remember one thing! He was a germaphobe… I think."

My chin pulls back, and I don't know how that's useful—or if it's even real since she was tripping on mushrooms. "Why did you think that?"

"He was always talking about stuff being clean or cleaning stuff." Her brow furrows, and she taps her forehead. "Maybe he said it needed cleaning."

It takes all my power to hold my expression neutral. "That's good, Hana." I squeeze her hands. "One last question. It's a hard one. Okay?" She watches me, waiting, and I proceed with caution. "Did they ever mention Victor? Or did you and Debbie ever see Victor or hear about him being with them?"

Her face pales, and her round eyes blink away. Lifting her hand out of mine, her thumb is on the way to her mouth when it stops.

Lowering it slightly, she looks from her digit to me and does a little smile. "I remembered."

My breath picks up. "What did you remember?"

"Not to chew my thumb."

"Hana!" My breath rushes out in a hiss. "About Victor—what do you remember about him?"

"Nothing." She grits her front teeth, and anger lines her face. "I never want to remember him as long as I live."

"Okay." I exhale slowly as I stand, pulling her into a hug. "You don't have to. You've done really well. I'll take it from here."

Our New York apartment is the same as when I left it after the gala—clean, shining wood, somewhat familiar, and completely uncomfortable.

I'm glad Hutch and Scar are with us, even if the guys are preoccupied with tracking down Trip and our new mystery man, Ivan X.

I filled Hutch in on everything my sister told me on the short flight from Charleston, and he relayed the information to Dirk, who's running searches on this new name from his place in Hamiltown.

"Are you going to see Trip or meet him somewhere?" I watch as Hutch uses a tracking app on his phone to locate our friend. "He lives a few floors down, so he's probably there now."

"Yep, just checking to see if this thing works." Even in simple jeans and a black tee with a black jacket on top, he looks like a model.

He's so tall and broad, and the muscle in his square jaw moves as he thinks. Despite the shitty timing, I can't help wanting to trace my tongue along it. He's so lickable.

"For now, while he's unaware of our presence, I'm going to watch where he goes and hope it leads somewhere incriminating."

"Did you have anything in particular in mind?"

He hesitates a moment before answering my question. "There's an ATM in Brooklyn that handles cryptocurrency. Dirk traced several transactions in the accounts we're monitoring to that machine. My hope is he's the person making them, or one of the persons."

"It's all so confusing. What are you going to do once you find the men behind it all?"

"Not what your uncle wants me to do," he grumbles.

"We're going to obtain warrants for their arrest and hope we can build a case that will stick."

A sick, uncomfortable tightness is in my stomach, and I almost hate to ask. "Is there any chance of recovering our money? Or the money I sent that blackmailer?"

Intense green eyes hold mine. "Absolutely. If we're able to prove they took it, we'll recover it from whatever holdings they have. I said I'd get your money back, and I will."

Smiling, I walk to where he stands, placing my hand on his arm and kissing his cheek. "I'm not worried as long as you're here."

He slides his thumb along my jaw, looking deep into my eyes. "Have you thought about what I said the other night?"

My chest squeezes, and I nod. Standing here completely sober, in the light of day, I remember him saying he was falling in love with another member of my uncle's family.

"I've been thinking about it pretty much nonstop."

"No matter what happens, I want you to remember it. Okay?" A trickle of dread filters through my chest, but I nod as he continues. "You're mine to protect. Hana is part of that deal. I won't let anyone hurt either of you."

Sliding my arms around his neck, his words replace the fear in my veins with calm satisfaction. When he turns my face and covers my mouth with his, my satisfaction turns to lust.

He might be falling in love with me, but I know I'm falling in love with him.

CHAPTER 28

Hutch

THE TONE SHIFTS THE MOMENT WE TOUCH DOWN IN NEW YORK. It's in the tension in my muscles; it's in the hardening of Blake's expression, like she's preparing for battle. It's even in the way Hana is more fidgety and nervous. Scar is the only one quietly resolved, but his expression never changes.

I'm glad he's with us. Heaviness and danger are all around, and I'm preparing to move the minute Dirk gives me the word.

I've filled Scar in on what Blake learned from Hana before we left. Ivan X could be anyone. Hell, once Blake told me her sister was on mushrooms, I realized his name might not even be Ivan. Either way, we're starting with what we know.

"You've met this guy." I'm sitting across from Scar, giving him the breakdown of Trip my brother sent us on the flight over.

He graduated from Iona Prep, dropped out of Columbia after two years. He's into horses, gambling, and philandering, but no established criminal behavior. He doesn't need to be a criminal. He's a bored, entitled, trust-fund asshole who associates with shady as fuck characters.

With a low exhale, I realize the same could be said for Blake and Hana, the only difference is they're trying to get out. Trip seems happy to stay right in the middle of it.

"Is he smart enough to be the leader?" Scar's low voice is thoughtful.

My brother's theory on mobster hierarchy drifts through my mind. "He's smart, but I don't think Trip's the head vampire."

Scar's wolf eyes meet mine. "The problem with lesser vampires is they're still fucking lethal."

The problem is, I don't think Trip's necessarily lethal either. He's something in between. "He's the skeleton key."

Blake orders Asian takeout and has it delivered. Beef and broccoli for her, miso soup for Hana, sushi for Scar, and sweet and sour pork for me.

"It's ecumenical," she laughs, pulling the white paper boxes out of the brown bag. "All Asians are welcome here."

I love that she's making the best of a tense situation, considering the pressure we're under. I know she's worried about her sister, she's worried about her friend, and she's worried about the money.

I want to sweep her up in my arms and carry her away from this mess, but we have to settle these matters before I can do that. I've promised to get her money back. I promised her uncle to get these guys behind bars. I intend to keep both.

"How did the packing go?" My voice cuts through the shuffling of boxes and plastic cutlery.

"I'm all done." Hana looks up from where she's sipping chicken broth with a few chunks of tofu and seaweed.

"I'm pretty much done." Blake bites the head off a steamed broccoli stem covered in deep brown gravy. "I have a few things left to pack, mostly books and items I don't want left here unattended."

"We'll give it a day, and if nothing happens, I'll go to Trip and get the ball rolling."

"Natasha texted me wanting to get together." Blake looks to Hana, who makes a face like she's gagging. "I don't know if we'll follow up, but I don't like not answering. It's possibly the last time we'll see her for a long time."

"I didn't think you liked Natasha." Hana's voice is soft, like she doesn't want to speak in front of Scar and me. "You said she was an opportunistic mean girl."

"She's definitely fake." Blake polishes off a thin slice of beef. "But she's been really nice since Debbie. I think she's trying to be a friend—as much as she knows how."

Dinner is finished, and cleanup consists of carrying our trash to the bin in the kitchen. I'm all prepared to suggest Blake and I visit the roof while I wait to hear from my brother, but just like a good cock blocker, Scar catches my arm.

"Looks like our man is headed out. You ready?"

"We'll give him a minute and follow." I leave the Beretta in my duffel, strapping the Glock to my ankle.

I don't expect to need it, but it's always good to be prepared. Hesitating before we head out into the night, I go to where Blake's standing in the kitchen holding a glass of wine.

"I don't know how long we'll be out. I want to track this guy everywhere he goes."

She nods, setting her glass on the island. "Sundays aren't typically party nights. Hopefully you'll find what you're after."

"If not I'll confront him. I won't keep us here longer than necessary."

"I'll be glad when this is over."

"If you decide to go out, just let me know where you are."

A little smile curls her lips, and she nods. I hook a finger under her chin, lifting her face so I can plant a light kiss on them. "Be safe."

The Vogue is a typical, live music venue. A stage is in the back corner, and wooden tables and chairs line the walls. A VIP section is in the back, separated from the rest of the club by velvet ropes.

Naturally, that's where Trip is headed. I come to attention when I see he's meeting a guy I don't recognize from any of our previous encounters.

New guy is dressed in jeans and a denim jacket off his shoulders. His flat-brimmed hat is tilted, and he looks like a low-rent gangster wannabe. It reminds me of what Blake told me about Hana's memory. Ivan X always tried to be a tough guy like Greg.

This guy is nothing like Greg, but he's definitely trying to look tough. Trip seems unaffected. He's dressed in his usual slacks and blazer, this time in a rust-brown silk over a white shirt. He sits at the small table and signals the waiter.

"We can't hear what they're saying," I grumble, turning to face the bar. "Not sure how useful this is going to be."

Scar is hidden from Trip's view by a thick column, and the low light and semi-crowded venue makes me hope he doesn't recognize me. Not that I'm particularly worried about being spotted. It'll simply up the timeline.

My phone buzzes, and I look down. It's a text from Blake. ***Decided to hook up with Natasha and Rainey. Won't be late.***

I quickly reply with ***thanks***, and my attention returns to Trip nursing a tumbler of clear liquid I assume is vodka. The new guy pulls out his phone and appears to be bored as he taps the screen several times.

Trip sits up and takes his phone out of his breast pocket, examining the screen and nodding. The guy shoots the beverage he was holding and stands, abruptly leaving. Trip remains seated, finishing his drink at a leisurely pace, a satisfied grin on his face.

My eyes go to Scar's, and he lifts his chin. I'm not sure what this means or what to do until my phone buzzes with another text. It's Dirk. ***$25K just moved from the new account to Trip's.***

It's all I needed to know. I turn my phone to Scar, and his brow lowers. His expression goes dark, and I look back to where Trip has just polished off the last of his drink and stands, straightening his blazer.

We're on our feet, following him out into the damp night. My friend is breathing like a bull on red, and when Trip takes a sharp turn down a narrow alley, Scar moves so fast, it's a blur.

With a sharp *slam*, Trip is pinned against the wall by the neck.

Scar's fist closes over his windpipe, and Trip's expensive loafers dangle, kicking against the wall as he struggles for his life. "You're the asshole blackmailing Hana?"

My partner's head tilts to the side like he's about to take a bite.

Trip claws at Scar's fist around his neck, his face red and grimacing. "Stop," he snorts.

Slowly, I approach where my partner is strangling the life out of this piece of shit. As I told Hugh, I don't condone violence. I don't think of myself as a vigilante, and I certainly would not take someone out unprovoked.

I've been provoked.

"Let go..." Trip grunts, trying to push Scar off with his foot.

My partner won't be moved. "You were her friend. You exploited her, assaulted her—"

"NO…" Trip's nose is running, and his wild eyes meet mine. "Trying to help."

As much as I want to let Scar continue, I exhale slowly, and put my hand on his shoulder. "Let him speak."

It's a hard order to follow, but my partner releases him, stepping back with a growl. Trip falls to his ass on the wet pavement, dropping back against the brick wall of the alley. His knee is bent, and he's holding his neck as he gasps for breath.

"Choose your words wisely," Scar warns.

I'm not going to hold him back if this piece of shit doesn't say what we need to hear. I've had enough of his lies, pretending to be Blake's friend.

"I'm trying to help them," he finally croaks out.

Scar makes a move like he'll grab him by the neck agan, but I shoot out my hand, holding him by the chest, even though I could never stop him in a rage.

"How are you helping?" Disbelief drips in my tone.

"Blake told me she was being blackmailed." He lifts his chin, regaining his strength. "When she said it was a porn racket, I knew who it was."

"Who was it?"

"Ivan is the only one who does film."

My eyes meet Scar's, and we hesitate. "Continue."

"I was getting her money back." Trip scowls at me like it should be so obvious.

I'm not buying it. "You expect me to believe you?"

"I don't give a shit what you believe. It's the truth." He rubs his hand over his eyes. "Blake's been good to me. I owe her."

"You're damn right you do." I grip the front of his shirt, pulling him closer. "I don't like your friends, and I don't like your looks. If I find out you're lying to me, I'll take it out of your hide."

His eyes close, and he shakes his unfeeling head. Releasing

his shirt, I shove him back against the wall, rising to my full height.

Scar is still glaring hard like he doesn't care if this guy is telling the truth. He'll do anything to protect Hana. I get that.

Trip shakes his head, still managing to put on the act. "You let that guy do these things?" His voice is raspy from the near-strangulation he received.

"He's working his angle. I let him."

"What angle is that?"

"You messed with his girl."

Trip's brow furrows. "But I thought you and Blake were—"

"Hana. He's going to protect Hana."

A bitter laugh rasps from Trip's damaged windpipe. "Good luck."

It's not the first time I've gotten that response to helping Blake's sister, but I know how important she is to Blake. So she's important to me.

"You've got twenty-four hours, then I'm coming for you." I signal to Scar, and he hesitates before taking a step to follow me.

Trip slowly pushes himself to his feet, leaning against the wall and narrowing his eyes. "Hey, what would you say to a little three-way split? I could skim it right off the top, and you could still be a hero."

Anger roars to life in my chest, and I catch him by the front of his silk shirt. "Didn't you get enough or are you asking for more?"

He does a little snap-point with his finger. "That was a test. Just making sure you're not secretly a bad guy."

"Are you familiar with the phrase 'morally gray'?"

"Yes, and it's not you. That guy," he nods towards Scar. "One hundred percent. But you? Brutally moral."

Pulling him closer, I get right in his face. "Blake belongs to me now. You mess with her, you're messing with me." I release him with a shove. "Return her money, all of it, or you'll see how brutal I can be."

We start to go, but his voice stops us.

"One thing I don't understand." Pausing, I turn to see what he'll say. "You big shot detectives never asked why."

I'll take his bait. "Why what?"

"Victor Petrova stole millions from Charles van Hamilton. Grisha manages a whole operation to launder the money. Some two-bit minion goes after Hugh's niece, and you're called in like it's a mob war. Why?"

Scar's fists are balled, and he's ready to snatch him up again, but I hold him back. "Are you trying to say you know something?"

"No." Shaking his head, he looks down, exhaling a chuckle. "But I'd be asking why all of this is happening. What's the bad blood? It's something I'd want to know."

"I'm not you."

We leave him sitting on the damp street, but his words itch in my brain. As soon as we're back, I'll ask Hugh about what Trip is saying, whether there's more to this than I thought. In the meantime, it's after two, and I have one more visit to make.

CHAPTER 29

"**L**OOK AT THIS ONE—IT'S YOUR FIRST VIRGIN CRUISE!" HANA cries with a laugh. "You were a virgin on the Virgin!"

"Shut up. I was only thirteen."

"Who allowed me to wear those glasses?" She turns the phone so I can see her cat-eye purple frames on her tow-headed, ten year-old self. "I look like an elf."

"You look adorable."

We're sitting on the edge of my bed swiping through old photographs when Natasha's text appears on my phone. *You're back, beesh! Let's celebrate. Meet me at Gibson's in twenty.*

Glancing down at my sister, she rolls her eyes before falling back on the bed. "Nooo!"

"Come on. I don't want to leave you here alone."

"Natasha is fucking annoying. She's such a suck-up, I feel like she's sucking my soul whenever I'm around her."

"So, ignore her. Have a few drinks, and I'll tell them goodbye."

"I don't understand why I can't just stay here. I could pack some more."

"You said you were finished packing. Now put on a dress, and come with me."

Thirty minutes later, we're stepping out of a car in front of the underground cigar bar. Hana is dressed in an ivory shift dress with iridescent panels mimicking fringe all over it. I'm in a conservative, long-sleeved beige bodysuit with wide-legged black slacks.

"Blake!" Natasha's shrill voice cuts through the roar of old men's voices and Rat Pack singing. "You look amazing. Very nineties DKNY."

A few heads turn to look at us, and I make my way to where she's on her knees in the booth.

"Already so fucking obnoxious." Hana exhales heavily at my shoulder. "How long do we have to do this?"

"Thirty minutes," I say emphatically. "If it continues to suck, we can leave after thirty minutes."

"I'm setting my timer."

Natasha pulls me into a firm hug. "It's so good to see you! You know you left your coat last time we were here. I know you want it back. It's Givenchy!"

"I didn't even miss it." My mind returns to that night, my encounter with Greg, and Hutch saving me.

"Still," Natasha loops her arm through mine. "It's a nice coat. I have it for you."

"Can we get some drinks over here?" Hana waves at the waitress in the old-school, thigh-high dress with a low-cut top. She makes her way through the smoky room to where we stand. "Martinis all around."

Sliding cautiously into the round, leather booth, I glance around the room, wondering if Greg is here, wondering what might happen if he does appear.

"I heard the most ridiculous rumor after you left last time."

Nat puts her hand on my forearm, eyes wide. "You're back with that big guy from the gala, the one you were yelling at? Is that true?"

The waitress reappears to place three martinis on the table.

Hana scoops hers up and quickly shoots it, motioning to the young woman. "Three more, please!"

Arching my eyebrow, I take my glass, sipping it slowly. "My uncle hired him to protect us."

"Mmm, lucky you!" Natasha scoops up her martini, stirring her olive around in the glass. "He is yummy! Is his *thing* as big as he is?"

Hana takes my glass, drinking it faster than me as she scans the room. Her brow is furrowed, and it reminds me of being in her bedroom at Uncle Hugh's, the way she held her shirt like she was on the verge of remembering something.

"I don't like this place." Her voice is urgent. "We need to get out of here."

My heart beats faster. "Why? What happened?"

The waitress is back with three more martinis. I still haven't finished my first, but Hana has already drunk half. She switches to the fresh one as she falls silent.

Natasha is preoccupied with the table to our right, and I'm focused on finding out what my sister knows. She's drinking too fast, and I take the martini from her, polishing it off so she can't.

"This place isn't what it seems." Her dark blue eyes widen and meet mine, and her tone is ice filtering through my veins.

"Tell me what you remember."

She frowns into her empty glass. "It was a night, a strange night, almost a year ago? I was here, but not here." She gestures to the room where we're sitting. "There's another room. It's smaller and all-black with a little slit like a window."

My stomach roils. The last time I was here, I was in that room with Greg. "What happened?"

Placing her fingers on her eyes, she rubs them gently. "It could've been a dream. It was like I was watching an art film with old men sitting on benches. Or maybe I was in the film?"

She blinks hard, looking in the direction of where I know the back room is located. "I was holding a torch like a statue, and one of the old men was on his knees between my legs…"

Her eyes squeeze shut, and she wobbles to her feet. "I've got to get out of here."

I jump up to catch her arm. "I've got you. Let's go."

We're making our way to the door when Greg appears. He's coming down the stairs in front of us, and when our eyes meet, terror grips my throat. Evil glitters in his grin like he's caught us. He starts to move in our direction, but a cluster of girls pushes between us, starting up the stairs for the door.

I hold Hana's arm firmly and guide her into the mob, hurrying us up the stairs with them. I have to get her away from this place. When we reach the top, I look down. He's still looking up, but his smile is gone. When I scan the room, I see Natasha is watching us as well. Her expression has changed. Her eyes are cold, and she's staring like she knows something.

Dread is ice in my stomach, and I guide us out into the misty rain. I don't know what's happening, but I'm not sticking around to find out. I only know one person who can protect my sister—maybe two, and they're not here, which means it's up to me.

Back at the apartment, Hana goes straight to her bathroom and turns on the sink. I'm a little wobbly from shooting half my martini then finishing hers, but I need to know the rest of the story.

"Hana?" I tap lightly on the door. "Are you okay?"

She's leaning over the lavatory, lifting handfuls of water and holding them to her face. I go to where she's standing and switch off the tap before passing her a towel.

Without makeup, she looks younger, but her eyes are still haunted by whatever memory we triggered. She follows me silently to the room we're sharing, and I wait as she lets her dress fall to the floor. She's not wearing a bra, so she pulls on a T-shirt and crawls between the sheets.

Sitting beside her, I gently move a spiral curl out of her eye. I've already figured out this was the night of the porn film, and clearly she had no idea what was happening. I'm ready to kill all of them, but I need to know.

"Hana?" My voice is quiet, gentle. "I need to ask you one more thing about that night."

Her shoulder rises, and she presses her cheek against the pillow. "I don't remember any more."

"I know, honey, but just one more question." My stomach is burning and tight.

She shakes her head, scrubbing her eyes. "Nothing happened. It was a dream."

"Was Victor there?"

"Victor is dead."

My throat closes up. I know for a fact Hana wasn't in the room when my uncle told us Victor died of a heart attack, yet somehow she knows he's dead?

"What makes you say that?"

"I saw him on the floor." She turns away, quietly adding, "The man said he was dead."

"What man?"

"I don't remember."

I let it go, but her story makes my stomach churn. I don't

know what to do without Hutch here. Two things are clear—she was present when Victor died, and the sex tape Ivan X was using to blackmail us was filmed in that back room at Gibson's.

It's just after midnight, and I study my phone. I haven't heard anything from Hutch since he left, so I shoot him a quick note. ***Back at the apartment. Hope you're making progress.***

Hanna is asleep, and I'm sitting in the bed in my black tank top trying to figure out what to do. The alcohol is slowly leaving my system, and I need Hutch to hold me. I'm so afraid, and I know having his arms around me would at least help me sleep.

Taking out my phone one last time, I send a text. ***Wish I could kiss you goodnight. Maybe good morning?***

The apartment is so quiet, and I glance at the clock. It's one-thirty. Hana is breathing heavily from the other side of the bed, and a little buzz indicates I have a text. My stomach relaxes, and I'm sure it's Hutch.

Tapping in my code, I'm all ready to see his reply when my heart stops. Cramps filter up the sides of my stomach, and I sit up fast not believing what I'm seeing.

It's a text from Debbie, and I swipe so fast, I almost drop my phone. I can't breathe as I read the words. ***Very bad traffic in Milan. Vv bad. Grisha is here, not getting out.***

It was sent the night she died, but I'm only seeing it now. Shaking my head, I try to understand. *Why am I just now getting this? Was it delayed somehow?*

The scar above my left eyebrow burns, and the fear in my chest twists into anger. I've never backed down from a bully, and after what I've learned about Hana, now this? He's a fucking liar. He's a devil and a killer, and if he thinks he's getting away with it, he's wrong.

Tears heat my eyes, and I'm out of bed so fast, I don't

even consider the consequences. I scoop a pair of jeans off my pile of clothes, pulling them over my hips without stopping. I'm running through the house when I see the duffel bag Hutch brought sitting on the table.

It's unzipped, and my eyes land on the steel-gray handle of his gun tucked in a side pocket. Grabbing my coat off the back of a chair, I take the heavy gun from his bag and shove it in the inside pocket. Then, I step into my shoes and head out into the night.

I've only been to Greg's loft in SoHo one other time, with Debbie. It's a third-floor walk-up on Prince Street, and the rain has stopped when I step out of the cab in front of the twelve-story building.

Hesitating on the wet concrete, I slip my hand inside my coat pocket to touch the handle of the Beretta. Doubt tried to creep in on the short ride down, but justice strengthened my resolve. This ends tonight.

Tucking my chin, I go to the front door and press the buzzer. He doesn't even ask. He simply presses the release button allowing me access to the building.

Jogging up the stairs, I walk down the narrow hall to where his door isn't even locked. When I enter, he's standing in the kitchen with his back to the entrance, pouring a tumbler of vodka.

"I wondered how long I'd have to wait before you came here." Turning slowly, he gestures to me with the bottle. "Can I fix you a drink?"

"No, thank you." My voice is level, and he arches an eyebrow.

"Funny, last time I checked you were a fan of Mamont."

"I'm not here to socialize." The noise of my footsteps

is muffled by the thin Persian rug covering the dark brown wooden floors.

His loft is a single, long room divided into thirds by exposed brick half-walls. The front is the kitchen-dining area, and I watch as he strolls into the middle, living room. I don't want to get too close, so I stand just inside the brick wall.

"Why are you here? Did you come to confess what I already know, or is this something else?"

"You killed her."

"I'm afraid you'll have to be more specific." His thin blond hair is smoothed back from his pale face, and his black eyes show no emotion.

Swallowing the lump in my throat, I do my best to steady my voice. "Debbie sent me a text the night she died. You were there."

He takes another, slow sip of alcohol. "I've already established I was out of town the night she died."

"You *were* there. You threw her off that balcony, and I want to know why."

My heart beats faster as his eyes turn deadly, and he takes a step closer. "Be careful hurling accusations, Blake. You might go too far."

"She was my best friend, and you were supposed to love her."

"Was I?" His gaze is so flat, so devoid of emotion, so terrifying.

He takes another step closer, and I take a step to the side, putting a chair between the two of us.

Setting aside his now-empty glass, he watches me. "There's an essential cruelty in the universe. No one expects the killer whale tossing a bloody, baby seal in the waves to be concerned with its pain. Or the cat playing with the mouse."

"So you're saying you never cared about her? You were only playing with her?"

"Debbie knew too much. She asked too many questions. I don't like people who ask too many questions." We're slowly circling his narrow apartment, getting closer with each rotation.

"You're a psychopath." Tremors move through my chest, but I won't show any signs of fear. I won't feed his hunger.

"I'm neither of those things. Debbie got in my way." His lips spread in a sinister, toothy grin. "Don't get in my way, Blake."

Slipping my hand inside my coat pocket, I know what I have to do. My fingers close around the gun, and my voice grows stronger. "Is that a threat?"

"It's a warning."

"I have a warning for you." Pulling the pistol out, I hold it steady. He's close enough that I have it leveled on his heart. "Stay away from my family."

He takes a step back, dark eyes go from the gun to me. "Or what? You'll shoot me? I'm not afraid of you, little girl."

"You'd better be afraid." At the sound of Hutch's deep voice, I almost collapse, but I don't.

My eyes stay focused on my target, as Trip enters the room followed closely by my smoldering knight.

"Why the fuck did you bring him here?" Greg hisses.

"I didn't. He followed me." Trip casually goes to the kitchen. "Why, yes, I will have a drink. Thanks for offering. What's this I hear about you murdering Debbie?"

"Idiot. I told you I was at Gibson's with Ivanov." Greg's black eyes flash from Hutch to Trip and back to me, and for the first time, I see him flinch.

It renews my strength. "You're losing track of your story. You said you were out of town that night."

"Perhaps he went out of town after going to Gibson's." Hutch's smooth voice takes on an edge, and my confidence strengthens.

"Blake's guard dog. Always a few steps behind." Greg is slowly backing towards the wall, and I notice a hollow in the bookcase—a perfect hiding place for a weapon. "Please know I say this with the deepest respect. I'm not afraid of you."

I haven't taken my gaze off his dead, shark-eyes, and I'm closing the space between us, ready to cut him off if he pulls out a gun.

Hutch remains calm, even cracking a grin. "You know, Grish, the thing about being licensed to kill is I don't need a reason to take you out. All I need is probable cause."

"So many threats and so few brains." Greg slides his hand into the books. "I'll take you out."

"Not so fast." My finger curls on the trigger, but Greg lunges at me fast.

"Get back, bitch."

He slaps me so hard, I'm off my feet. My hand holding the gun flies to the side and goes off with a loud *BLAST!* Light flashes behind my eyes as my head hits the center column, and I'm on the floor.

"Stay down," Hutch orders.

I'm vaguely aware of yelling and the shuffling of bodies. Lying on the floor, I see Greg's feet kicking as Hutch holds him off the ground, punching him repeatedly in the face. Trip is collapsed against the wall, and his chin is on his chest. Blood covers the front of his white shirt.

Oh, God... Did I shoot Trip?

A dull thud sounds above my head, and I try to get my bearings. I try to lift my head to see what's happening, to help, but I'm so dizzy.

I try to understand what's going on as Hutch tucks the gun I fired into my coat pocket again before lifting me easily in his arms. "You still with me?"

Worried green eyes meet mine, and I'm doing my best to

fight through the pain in my temple. "I'm okay. I'll be okay now."

Now that you're here, I think.

"Yes, you will." He pauses, and I look around the room to see Greg out cold against the wall beside Trip, who also appears to be mumbling something.

"We're all finished here." Hutch's voice is level, and he carries me out of the apartment, down the stairs, and into the rain.

Tucking my face into his neck, I grip his shoulder as he holds me in his arms, carrying me across the street to a waiting SUV.

CHAPTER 30

Hutch

'M COMPLETELY SOAKED, RIDING IN THE BACK SEAT OF THE BLACK SUV with Blake's head tucked into my shoulder. She got a pretty bad hit, but her pupils aren't dilated, and she hasn't vomited. I don't think it's a concussion.

Pulling out my phone, I dial the number of the Brooklyn police department. "Hey, Louie? Hutch."

"Hey, man. Long time no see." Louie Jackson is a police detective who taught the six-week course I needed after retiring from the military to get my PI's license. We've kept in touch ever since. "If you're calling me at this hour, it can't be good."

"I've been working a case in Manhattan. What's the status of that socialite who wound up on the pavement outside the Andover earlier this month?"

I hear the low drone of the office behind him and the tapping of computer keys. "Case closed. Suicide."

"Better reopen it and head over to Prince Street in SoHo. I've got a couple of warm bodies laid out for you. One of them is the killer."

"I'm sending a unit over now. What's the number?"

As I fill him in on the details, we pull up to Blake's building. She lifts her head and opens the door slowly. "The one with the bullet hole will verify his verbal confession. Let me know how it goes. I'm available tomorrow to make a statement."

"I'll be in touch."

We disconnect, and I pay the driver before stepping out and sliding my arm around Blake's waist. "How's the head?"

"How does it look?" She pauses inside the door, and I tilt her chin gently, holding her face to the light.

Her hair is wet from the rain, and her pretty eyes are tired with little flecks of black in the corners. The start of a lump is on her temple, but she's still the prettiest thing I've seen. "He barely laid a glove on you."

A smile relaxes her forehead, and she steps into my chest. "You should see the other guy."

Exhaling a chuckle, I wrap her in my arms. "Trust me, I did. You messed that guy up good."

"More like you did. I'm exhausted."

"Let's get some ice on that thing and get you to bed."

Lifting her chin, she shakes her head slowly. "Take me to bed or lose me forever."

"Music to this fighter's ears."

Blake is curled at my side sleeping when I open my eyes the next morning and check the clock. It's almost noon, but we didn't get to bed until three. She showed me the text she got from her friend, and I bit my tongue on scolding her for going over to that asshole's apartment alone.

She could've been killed, but she wasn't. I guess it means I'm evolving that I let it slide.

Gently tilting her chin, it appears our makeshift ice bag

did the trick on the lump at her temple. It's a lot smaller today, and more importantly, her face is relaxed. She seems at peace.

I'll be glad to take her home as soon as she's ready. We've essentially wrapped up all our loose ends.

Dirk hasn't alerted me that Trip made the transaction, but I'm willing to give him a few extra hours, considering he took a bullet last night.

The only item outstanding is finding Victor's killer, not that I give a shit about getting justice for that piece of human garbage. I just don't want his nephew causing any more problems for my girl.

Sliding out of the bed, I pull on my jeans and a tee before going into the kitchen to start a pot of coffee. Scar's lying on the sofa in the living room holding up a paperback with Hana curled up in a ball beside him asleep.

He's so big and long, she looks like a little white kitten at his side, and he idly twists one of her spiral curls in his fingers as he reads.

"Any luck last night?" I ask, filling the carafe with filtered water.

He lowers the book, shaking his head. "He gave me the slip at a club, and Dirk wasn't tracking him."

Scar and I parted ways shortly after midnight last night when I noticed Trip was on the move again and not headed back to his apartment building. Scar wanted to continue searching for Ivan X, and I let him go for it.

He has to handle that situation or it will never give him peace. I can't say I blame him. Sex-tape blackmailers are the lowest criminal life form in my book, only slightly above pedophiles at the bottom of the scumbag rankings.

I don't like the dark path this might lead him down, but I have to let him go there. He appears to be the only savior Hana might allow to help her.

"Where did the asshole go?" Scar's deep voice rumbles Hana awake, and she starts to stretch.

"No surprise, he went straight to Peters's place." Although, I was surprised to find Blake there.

"Any idea why?"

Entering the living room, I give Hana a nod as she goes into the bathroom and shuts the door. "Greg killed his girlfriend."

"The one who jumped off the balcony?"

Lifting my chin, I correct him. "She was thrown."

I'm all ready to tell him the rest when my phone buzzes on the kitchen counter. Returning to get it, I'm not sure who this will be, my brother about the money or Louis about the arrests.

It's the latter, and my brow furrows as I read the words.

"What is it?" Scar sits up on the sofa studying my face. "What's wrong?"

"Greg Peters is dead." I scrub my fingers over my forehead. "Louis said he had a heart attack."

Scar's all the way up, and I'm tapping the call button on my phone.

Louis answers on the first ring. "Hey, man, you got my text?"

"Yeah, it's why I'm calling. Greg Peters was what? Thirty?"

"Not even. When the officers got to the apartment, he was already dead, and whoever bled all over the place was gone. What happened there last night?"

"When I left it was an argument that got out of hand. The dead guy confessed to killing his girlfriend, and I got my client out of there. Then I called you."

"Well, I guess the case is closed again. The killer's dead."

"But who killed the killer?" *And where is Trip?*

"Looks like natural causes, but I can request a toxicology report if you want it."

"Thanks, Lou. I'm headed back to Hamiltown today or

tomorrow. Let me know if you need anything before I go, or you can contact me there."

We sit in silence a moment after I disconnect, and I don't know what to think.

"Could be congenital if Victor was his uncle." Scar's voice is as doubtful as I feel about that possibility.

I'm about to text my brother when the devil beats me to it. My screen lights up before I can unlock it. *$25K just transferred back to Blake's account. Case closed?*

Shaking my head, I exhale through my teeth. I don't know how to answer him. It looks like all the loose ends are tied up, but it's only left me with more questions.

"So everything's taken care of, and my nieces are home." Hugh leans back in his chair, looking satisfied. "You are truly the best in the business, Hutch."

"I don't know about that. We still have several unresolved issues."

"Do we?" He goes down the list, counting on his fingers. "We settled the blackmail situation. Victor's death is closed, and as an equal bonus, we discovered who murdered the girls' friend. And he's now dead as well."

"Under very questionable circumstances," I counter.

Hugh leans forward in his chair, lifting a paperweight off his desk. "Does it matter? These men were criminals operating in highly volatile situations. They reaped the consequences of their actions."

"Sow the wind, reap the whirlwind." Scar's deep voice adds gravity to his words.

"Exactly." Hugh points to my partner. "Not all questions are going to have answers."

I don't like it. In my experience, unanswered questions usually lead to new problems down the line.

Hugh rises slowly and closes the space between us. "Most importantly, Blake and Hana are here." He grasps my shoulder with a smile. "If necessary, we can look out for each other the same way anyone else in the world does. Life is full of hazards."

My arms are still crossed, and I think about what Trip said. "Why did it happen?"

Hugh's brow furrows. "I'm not sure I understand what you mean."

"Why was Victor after Charles's money? What made him target the van Hamilton estate?"

"Are you asking me what makes criminals choose their victims?" The old man exhales a chuckle. "In this case, it seems pretty obvious. Three wealthy women are left alone, a widowed mother and two beautiful daughters. Along comes an opportunistic monster, and next thing you know…"

"Maybe." I'm not satisfied it's as simple as that.

Also, I've got a lot of experience with this old man and him keeping secrets. Trip was sending a message.

"Hutch, my boy, you are a true detective." Hugh starts for the door. "Take my advice and enjoy the successful resolution of this case. Your next problem will arise soon enough." He pauses before leaving us. "If you're looking for something to do, I know a young lady who would enjoy a night on the town with you."

He leaves, and I shake my head, glancing over to my partner. "What do you think about all this?"

Scar's heavy black boot is propped on the edge of Hugh's ornate desk. His dark hair is tied back in a small samurai bun, and he's sliding a silver pocket knife back and forth behind his thumbnail.

"I think your lady's out of danger." He flips the knife closed and rises with an exhale to his full height. "You should be grateful for that. I've still got an asshole to track down."

"Right." I follow him to the door and into the hallway. "Do what you need to do, and let me know how I can help."

"I will—if I need your help." He slides the knife into his pocket. "You should do as the old man said and live your life. It's time."

"That's not exactly what he said."

"Close enough. See you at the game."

CHAPTER 31

Blake

"He's so beautiful." I slide my hand along the rich brown hide of Training Day, my uncle's prized thoroughbred. "Hold that pose." The sound of my sister's camera lens clicks in the quiet barn.

It's the first time I've visited the stables since we came back to Hamiltown, and the familiar smells of leather and hay and the faintly pungent manure reminds me of being a girl here.

"Remember when we would spend every visit riding horses from sunup to sundown?"

"Yeah." Her voice is quiet.

Resting my face against the soft neck of the powerful, gentle horse eases the pain that resurfaced with Debbie's text.

Dirk said he couldn't figure out why it appeared on my phone weeks after her death. He said it was possible Debbie's phone had been switched off before her message was sent, and then it was switched on again for whatever reason, and the text went through. It made me wonder if Greg outed himself by keeping her things or if he summoned me.

"Why did she say she was in Milan?" Dirk had asked, and I told him about the night we'd been out partying, when she'd told me if she ever texted anything about traffic in Milan or traffic anywhere, she was in danger.

I'm still ashamed I thought she was being silly or drunk. I should've asked why she would be in trouble. I was so naive, and now she's gone.

Last night when I said I was showering, I lay on my bathroom floor and cried for a long time. She loved him, and he killed her. He was a monster, and I'm not sorry he's dead.

"We were never allowed to touch this guy." Hana slides her hand over Trainey's velvet nose. "Your colors blend perfectly. Put your cheek beside his again."

I do as she says, looking down as I slide my hand under his neck. She takes several different angles before she's satisfied. "These are going to be really good. I can do different effects in the darkroom and blow them up. I'm sure Hutch will want one."

Her voice is soft, and she glances up at me.

"Maybe," is all I'll say to that. "How are you feeling now that we're back?"

She shrugs. "Scar told me not to be afraid. He's handling things."

It's the first I've heard of him being involved. The blackmail money was returned to my account as Hutch promised, but as far as I know, the video is still out there. Ivan X has disappeared into the underground, and I thought it was a lost cause.

But Scar is scary-intimidating. If he says he's on a case, I feel confident he'll get his man, especially if Dirk is helping him. I've watched that guy with Hana, and he's motivated to help her.

"You like him?" We step out of the horse's stall and stroll up the passage to the tack room.

"I like knowing he's looking out for me." She blinks up with a little smile. "He's very strong, inside and out."

"What happened to him? With all the scars, I mean."

"I don't know." She leans against the doorjamb while I take down a bridle and loop it over my shoulder.

"It's never come up in conversation?"

"He'll tell me when he's ready."

I lift a padded blanket and saddle off a nearby sawhorse. "Just be careful. He doesn't seem entirely safe to me."

"I don't think he is, but he would never hurt me." We're back in the alley, and she continues on in the direction of the main house looking through her camera lens.

Watching her go, I can't help wondering if she's met her match, someone as wounded as she is but still willing to find a way to survive, to fight the demons.

When Hutch appears in the doorway, a flutter of happiness replaces the tension in my chest. A cap is pulled low on his head, accentuating his square jaw, and when he smiles, the flutter turns to heat filtering low into my stomach.

"I've been looking for you." He closes the space between us.

"It felt like a good day to take Dancer for a ride." I continue towards the stall where a palomino horse is peeking her golden head over the door.

"Let me help you with that." He lifts the saddle right out of my hands, ignoring my protests. "You shouldn't be lifting heavy objects. You just had a head injury."

"It was barely a scratch!" I can't help a laugh.

"You had a nice-sized lump on your head." He places the saddle over the door, turning his cap around, which somehow makes him look even hotter.

I open the narrow stall, going inside and running my hands over Dancer's golden coat. "Why don't you come with me? I'm sure Uncle Hugh wouldn't mind you riding Training Day."

"Your uncle would have my neck if I touched his prized stallion. You know he gets a fifty-grand stud fee for that guy?"

"Wow," I make an *oops* face. "That's almost as much as Shadow used to get."

Shadow of the Moon was my father's race horse, and after winning the Belmont Stakes, he could fetch as much as a hundred thousand dollars per breeding dose, sometimes even more—until he failed a drug test and was stripped of his titles.

"Regency's Honor shouldn't get you in trouble. Saddle him up and let me finish here with Dancer."

He lifts my chin and squints at my eyes like he's checking for signs of concussion. "If you think you can handle it."

"I'm fine." Rolling my eyes, I'm startled when his lips cover mine in a warm kiss.

"I want you to take it easy." His nose touches mine, and my knees melt just before he turns and leaves me swooning in the stall.

Ten minutes later, we're loping side by side, headed towards the backwoods of my uncle's property. Dancer is a drop of honey on the green grass, and a warm spring breeze pushes my hair behind my shoulders.

Regency is part Friesian. He's black as night with a gorgeous long mane and tail, shiny coat, and big hooves like a draught horse.

We pull them to a stop when we reach a narrow creek dividing the pasture land from the start of the denser trees. I slide off Dancer, allowing her to take a drink of water and glance up at my companion.

Hutch sits straight on the horse's back, surveying our path. Holding the reins in his large hands, his biceps stretch his short-sleeve shirt and the muscle in his square jaw flexes. His dark hair moves in the breeze, and on that horse, I can't help thinking he's like a prince—or a knight.

A silly swoon tightens my stomach, and I tuck my chin so my hair will cover the heat in my cheeks. "Is it warmer today?"

Green eyes land on mine, and his dark brow furrows attractively. "Does your head hurt?"

"No, I'm good. I was just wondering." I lead Dancer away from the water and climb onto her back again.

We take a slower pace, leading the horses across the water and into the trees. "What did my uncle say when you told him about the case?"

"He says it's all settled, and we should put it to rest."

"You don't sound happy with that decision."

He's not smiling, but he's still so handsome guiding the gorgeous horse. "It's possible he's right. We've managed to extract your family from this criminal enterprise, and some of the more dangerous players are now dead."

"But?" I wrinkle my nose up at him.

"Others are still out there. I don't like loose ends."

I think about everything that happened to us in New York. "It did take an unexpected turn. What will you do now?"

We ride a bit farther in silence, and the only sound is the dull thud of the horses' hooves. "Your uncle says I should take a break and enjoy my success."

"You've certainly earned a break." I give him a little wink. "Did you have anything in mind?"

"Well, for starters, I need to be at Pepper's game tonight. Would you like to go with me?"

That makes me smile. "Like on a date?"

"Sure, if you want to call it that." Seeing my smile fading, he quickly adds. "I'd rather save the term *date* for when I take you out to dinner tomorrow night, which I'd also like to do. If you're interested."

My smile is back and bigger. "I'd love to. Oh!" I shriek when Regency breaks into an unexpected trot, and a splat of mud flies up and lands on my arm.

Dancer startles at my yell, and within a few steps, my legs

are covered in sticky brown mud as are the legs of Hutch's jeans.

"Ho, boy." Hutch catches the reins, easing his horse to a stop. "Way to scare the horses."

"It wasn't my fault!" I can't help laughing now that I'm covered in mud.

Turning his giant horse so he can get closer, Hutch reaches out and wipes a clod of mud off my cheek with a grin. "It's nice to see you getting dirty for once."

Reaching down, I scoop a plop of mud off the side of my thigh and wipe it across his cheek. "Right back atcha."

Green eyes flash, and he makes a lunge like he'll grab me, but I'm too fast. I turn Dancer quickly, giving her a squeeze with my thighs, and we shoot off in a gallop, headed in the direction of the barn.

"You'd better run!" Hutch yells from not too far behind me, and an excited laugh bursts from my chest.

"Come on, Dancer!" I give her a little kick.

Regency might have characteristics of a draught horse, but he's nimble and fast. We're only slightly ahead of them when we blaze into the wide alley of the barn laughing and breathing hard.

Dancer slows to a trot then goes straight to the door of her stall like she is so done. My legs are wobbly from the exertion as I slide off, opening the door so she can walk inside. I'll have to track down Uncle Hugh's groom and ask him to wash the mud off the horses.

Hutch is right behind me, grabbing me around the waist and lifting me off my feet. "You're lucky she's fast. I was ready to wrestle."

The idea of mud wrestling with him sends a charge straight through my core, and I wiggle out of his embrace, turning so I can put my arms around his neck.

"If I'd known what you had in mind, I might not have run

so fast." He backs me against the post and leans down to cover my mouth with his.

Lips part, and our tongues slide together in a kiss that lights my entire body on fire. It's slow and gentle, pulling my lips with his and surrounding me with his sexy man scent. Lifting his chin, he looks down at me, and I want to climb him like a tree.

"As much as I want to keep going with this, I've got to take care of the horses, and I need to shower if I'm going with you to the game."

"We could share a shower." His hot voice has my insides dripping.

"No," I shake my head. "I have a surprise for you." That makes him frown, and I slide up to kiss his lips again. "Maybe after the game you can take me to Makeout Point?"

He lowers his head, running his nose along the side of my hair and sending chills skating down my arms. "Let's make that a *definitely* after the game."

CHAPTER 32

Hutch

"**H**IT IT, PEPPER, YOU GOT THIS!" I SHOUT FROM THE STANDS as our favorite shortstop enters the batter's box.

Blake gives my hand a squeeze before releasing it to clap. She's outfitted in a red, adult-sized Snow Cones jersey with a white, pleated miniskirt, and her hair is styled in two side ponytails at her shoulders with red and white ribbons.

"Freeze 'em out, Snow Cones!" she yells, and I lean closer.

"Where did you get this outfit?"

"Carmen helped me. I'm a cheerleader." She dips her chin, and makes a little sexy, pouty mouth. "You like my skirt?"

Shit. My dick twitches in my jeans. "I like all of it. You're hot enough to melt a snow cone."

That makes her laugh, and I have to focus on the game and not what I plan to do to this naughty cheerleader at Makeout Point later.

Carmen chants from her other side. "We want a catcher, not a belly scratcher!"

"We want a pitcher, not a belly itcher!" Blake joins, and I shake my head.

"I can't decide if Carmen's a good or bad influence on you."

"We're supporting our team!" she argues adorably.

Pepper is all over the field as usual, pausing periodically to wave or do a little dance when she makes a triple play. Hana is inside the gate taking photos, and after the ones she showed me from last week, she might become the official team photographer. She's really damn good.

It's a fast game, and the Snow Cones pull out a squeaker win at 6-5 over the Sea Turtles. The players line up to shake hands, and we head to our favorite bakery for celebratory donuts and chocolate milk.

Hana dances through the group as usual, taking pictures of the pigtailed players holding oversized, sprinkled donuts in front of their eyes and striking silly poses.

Scar took off after the win, telling me he'd be away for a few days. Dirk is helping him try to locate Ivan X, working off the theory he could be the *Ivanov* in Hugh's ledger.

Last I checked, they hadn't established a definite link, but it's a logical place to start. They both insist I stay out of it and take a break, which I'm all too happy to do—for a little while.

I want to spend time with Blake and see if there might be the potential for something more between us besides "hired protector," or even "hated teenage nemesis who ruined her life." That last one makes me cringe, but I'd do it again in a heartbeat. She was not safe in that house, and it was the only way I could have any peace of mind.

But when I watch her sitting with Pepper, sharing sprinkled donuts, it hits me our situation might be more complicated than I'd considered.

Up until now, I'd always thought of my situation with my sister's child as a team effort between Lurlene, Dirk, and me.

We all share responsibilities and pinch-hit as needed. The truth is, Pepper is legally mine.

Blake's only twenty-four years old. She's a society girl and probably plans to pursue a career. What reason do I have to think she'd want to be part of an instant family, especially one that includes an eleven-year-old going on thirty?

She looks up at me and smiles. Sitting there in a Snow Cones jersey with her pretty lips painted red and her dark hair tied with red and white ribbons, I wonder what she might say to this dramatic change in her lifestyle.

"What's got you so worried, big guy?" Carmen sidles up to me, and I straighten quickly.

"No worries. Looks like the girls might be headed to the state championships this year."

"Pepper's a pistol. She's going to carry this team all the way." Carmen takes a sip from her mug. "But that's not what's on your mind, I can tell."

"I just came off a pretty complex case, Carmen." My tone is dismissive, intended to shut down this line of questioning.

"Nope." She looks at the table where Pepper and Blake have traded donut halves. "You're worried about that right there."

Shifting my stance, I'm ready to tell the town gossip to keep her nose out of my business, instead I opt for diplomacy. "It's a school night. I'm only worried about getting Pepper home in time to get a good night's sleep before the first bell."

I start to move away when she catches my arm. "Listen to me." She levels her hazel eyes on mine. "No woman spends that much time with a child unless she likes it. You've got nothing to worry about with Blake. She's yours. Now put a ring on it before it's too late."

With that she walks past me to where Hana is taking pictures of the outfielders pretending to catch fly-ball donuts with the help of their teammates.

"Hold it right there!" Hana directs. "A little higher. I can still see your fingers. Move them to the back a little more."

My thoughts are a jumble with all that's happened in the last twenty-four hours, but Carmen's words feel right. When I look again, Pepper leans forward to throw her arms around Blake's neck, and Blake wraps her arms around the little girl, pressing her lips together in a happy smile.

Hell, leave it to the town gossip to see what's right in my face.

The girls chatter all the way back to the house. Hana has her camera, and she's in the backseat with Pepper, showing her the pictures she took. Pepper squeals and bounces in her seat, and I'm sure she's had way too much sugar—even if she did burn a million calories on the field. She's headed for a crash. Blake is turned in the front seat as if she doesn't want to miss a thing.

"And when you went down in that squat pose like that to stop the line-drive." Hana holds her camera over to my niece. "Holy crap. What do you call that pose?"

Pepper's eyes are wide. "I don't know. I just knew I had to stop that ball, or the game was over."

"It was an amazing play," Blake says, and my eyes fall to her silky thighs exposed in the pale light of the dash.

Talk about amazing, Blake in that cheerleader skirt is pretty fucking amazing. I've been on edge all night.

"What did you think, Uncle Hutch?" Pepper's eyes meet mine in the rearview mirror, and I remember a time when it was only Pep and me driving home after games. She was just getting started then, not nearly the superstar she is now.

"I think you're a rockstar, Pep. I couldn't be prouder."

Pepper falls back with a quiet smile on her lips. Hana nods, looking out the window, and Blake shifts around in the passenger's seat, giving me a look like I just found the cure for cancer.

We're at my house, and I put the SUV in park. "Come on, Pep, I'll walk you in."

Pepper unbuckles her seatbelt and flies across to give Hana a big hug. Then she rushes to the front to catch Blake around the neck, eliciting a startled laugh. Blake hugs her back with a fake grunt like Pepper and I always do at bedtime, and my worries melt a little more.

I take my niece inside doing all the hugs and carrying on we do at bedtime, before passing her to Lurlene. The last stop before Makeout Point is dropping Hana at Hugh's place.

Few things are less exciting than getting rid of all the kids so you can have sex, but every time I glance over at Blake in the passenger's side, her hourglass figure swiveling in the seat, tits stretching that red jersey, tiny white skirt scooting higher on her thighs, my dick reminds me it's worth the wait.

"See you in the morning," Hana teases as she gets out of the backseat. "Or not."

The door closes, and Blake's across the console, with her arms around my neck and her lips at my ear.

"Finally," she exhales hotly, and I've got a steel rod in my pants. "I didn't think we'd ever be alone."

Makeout Point is barely two tenths of a mile from Hugh's driveway, and I pull in, braking at the edge of the clearing and throwing my truck into park. I've just gotten the seat all the way back when Blake hops across the console, straddling my lap and covering my mouth with hers.

Cupping her thighs with my hands, I slide them higher, under her short skirt, to discover. "Oh, shit." She's not wearing underwear.

Her bare ass is soft and juicy, and I'm ready to get my pants off.

"I've been waiting all night for you to touch my naked ass," she teases, leaning back to meet my eyes. "I love our families, but shew, talk about cock blockers."

Reaching up, I hold her cheeks, pulling her lips to mine and kissing her slowly.

"Blake," My voice is heavy even though my cock is aching. "It's all settled now. You can go back to your life in New York."

She slows, cupping my cheeks in her hands, mirroring my movements. "Is that what you want me to do?"

Fuck no screams in my mind, but I'm a grown-assed man. Even with this gorgeous woman on my lap with tits I can't get enough of and an ass for days, I can't set myself up for that level of pain. I know how the world works.

"I want you to do what's going to make you happy."

Her thumbs slide lightly across the tops of my cheeks, and she leans in closer, every bit the sex kitten she's always been as long as I've known her.

"I'm about to do just that." She pulls my bottom lip with her teeth before sealing our mouths together.

Our lips part, and we're sloppy, licking, kissing. Her hands tug on my shirt, and I sit forward to quickly whip it over my head.

Silvery eyes darken, and she slides her hands over my chest, curling her fingers so her nails scratch my skin. She traces the outline of my ink, while I slide my hands over her ass, loving the feel of her in my arms, on my skin.

"Your turn." I take the bottom of the jersey, sliding it up her waist.

She lifts her arms, and I exhale a groan. The bra she's wearing only covers the bottom half of her breasts, and she slides her fingers down along the cups, pulling them lower so her pointed nipples peek over the tops. It's all I need.

My mouth is on her tits, kissing and pulling them into my mouth, teasing them with my teeth. Her back arches, and she slides her bare bottom back and forth over the bulge in my jeans, moaning.

"Take off your pants," she hisses. "I want to ride your cock."

"I have something better in mind." Reaching for the handle, I open the door, turning to the side and lowering her down to her feet.

She's standing in front of me in that short skirt with those ponytails messed up and her lace bra pushed below her sexy tits, nipples pointing at me.

"Damn, girl, you are so fine." I slide out and move her around, leaning her forward into the cab so her naked ass peeps up at me from under that skirt.

I slide my fingers up the back of her legs, lifting the white fabric over her lower back so I can have the full view of her bare pussy between her thighs. At the sight of it, I groan, dropping to my knees and putting my face between her legs, dragging my tongue all over it.

Her moan is so loud it echoes in the cab, but I'm not about to stop. I'm going to show her how happy she can be right here, then we'll talk about what's next.

CHAPTER 33

Blake

GRIPPING THE SIDES OF THE SEAT, MY EYES CLOSE AND I COME SO hard, my knees buckle. I'm pretty sure I leave my body. A cool rush of air fans my ass as Hutch's lips press against my bare skin, moving higher to kiss my lower back before he straightens and slides his thick cock so deep, I rise onto my tiptoes.

Spasms grip my core, and he groans low. "That's my girl."

His arm is around my shoulders, and he lifts my back to his chest, thrusting hard and fast as his mouth covers my neck with kisses, tracing up behind my ear and into my hair.

"I've wanted to fuck you all night." His voice is hot, and his sexy words are making me come again. "You are so fucking gorgeous."

He's close, and my eyes squeeze shut as his hand slides over my belly, between my thighs. I'm so sensitive, I jump when he touches my clit, letting out a loud whimper, and he breaks hard, groaning in my ear.

"So good," he moans low, holding me steady as he pulses again and again.

He exhales heavily, lowering his face to my shoulder as he finishes, and I turn my head to kiss his temple, his cheek, any place I can find his skin.

The touch of my lips makes him lift his head and kiss me deeply, sliding his tongue to mine and sucking my lips with his.

He slides out and turns me, lifting my butt onto the seat and hugging me close as his lips move to my neck and up to my ear. "I've never been this way. You make me crazy."

His words tickle in my stomach, and I wrap my arms around him, holding him tightly. He's right. We're special together. It's been that way from the start, and it wasn't just the danger. It wasn't my anger or even his pent-up need.

Only now, real choices have to be made. We're on the other side of the storm, in Hamiltown, and it's not only us we have to consider.

How would he feel about being with me, knowing I'll always have my sister to protect? I know he thinks she's trouble. I know he thinks she's messed up and makes poor choices. He only tolerates her around Pepper because I asked him to, and Pepper is so important to him.

His breathing slows, and he slides large hands up and down my sides. He's so warm and strong and amazing and beautiful. He's a work of art, and I don't want to think about the obstacles when we're together. I only want to be lost in his sexy gaze. I want to bask in his admiration, letting it wash over me and give me strength.

"I might have to get you an entire wardrobe of those skirts." He chuckles, kissing the tip of my nose. "And I might never fuck you in a bed again."

"You know I love this place." I trace my fingers in the soft, dark waves around his ears. "It's our happy place."

He lifts his chin looking around the dark patch of woods.

"I'll do some research. Maybe I can buy the land and make it private property."

My nose wrinkles, and I lean forward to kiss his full lips. "We can't have horny teenagers interrupting us."

"We're the only horny people allowed."

"It can be on the sign. Posted, no horny people allowed except us."

He laughs for real, and I bite my bottom lip. I love the sound of his laughter. It's such a rare thing, at least it has been for the time we've been together. Maybe I can change that.

Maybe I'm presuming too much.

Only it doesn't feel like I am.

"I'd like for you to spend the night with me." He leans down to kiss my cheek. "But Pepper has school tomorrow, and when you're in my bed, I forget to get up and see her off. She's been giving me shit for it."

"Oh, no," I cover my laugh with my hand. "Does she know we're sleeping together?"

"I don't think so. She only knows I've been falling down on my job. The last time you weren't even in my bed when I woke up."

His brow lowers like he's pissed, and I reach up to trace my fingers over the line in his forehead. "I'm pretty sure I was trying to help you solve a mystery."

"Only mystery left is where are we going to dinner tonight? Got any favorite places?"

"As a matter of fact, I do! I want to go back to Slim Harold's and learn to do that shag dance."

He reaches across, picking up our shirts from the passenger's seat. "In that case, I'd better get you to bed. You'll need your rest if you're planning to dance all night."

We hold hands the whole drive back, and I sit sideways in my seat, watching the lights illuminate the line of his perfect nose, his square chin, scruffy beard. When we reach Uncle

Hugh's, I unfasten my seatbelt and lean across to kiss him one more time before we say goodnight.

Placing my hand on his cheek, I look into his eyes. Such intense, focused, beautiful eyes, they steal my breath.

Still I manage to say what I've needed to say for so many days, "Thank you."

My voice tightens, and I try to move away quickly. I don't want to cry, but he's too fast. He catches my arms, pulling me back to him and making me meet his gaze once more.

Again, it's too intense, too focused and beautiful. His brow is lowered, and he holds my chin as he speaks.

"You never have to thank me for protecting you. I want to be that for you. Your uncle hired me, but I would never have accepted money. Even if you'd sent me away, I would've made sure you were safe. I… I hope you believe that."

Butterfly wings flood my stomach, and I nod, afraid to speak. He kisses my lips so softly before releasing me, and I drop my chin scooting out of his truck quickly. I need to sleep. I need to collect my thoughts and clear my head, and I need to talk to Hana. And my uncle.

"What exactly are you worried about, Blake?" Uncle Hugh sits across from me in his study as we share a morning coffee.

He looks at me like something I've never had—a doting parent who is actually interested in my problems and in helping me solve them. Jesus, we should've moved here years ago.

My legs are bent under me, and I barely slept last night from turning over everything in my mind. "I was thinking, first of all, you're so kind to let Hana and me stay here with you. I can look for a permanent place for us to stay in town if we're under your feet or in your way—"

"You'll do no such thing." He cuts me off, and for the first time in my life he seems upset. "This is your family home. It belonged to my father, your great, great grandfather, and you have as much right to be here as I do."

"I'm sorry, I wasn't trying to offend you." I shift in my seat. "I was only worried you've lived alone so long, maybe you were accustomed to things being a certain way, and we might disrupt that."

"I like having my family in the house. It's part of the reason I sent Hutch to New York to get you. I had hoped you'd consider staying here, making it your permanent home."

"That kind of brings me to the other thing I wanted to talk to you about." Looking down into my cup, I want to say this in a way that doesn't sound wrong. "I'd love to stay here. Only, what would I do in Hamiltown? It's a lovely place, but I can't just sit around and not be useful. I'll go bananas."

His brow relaxes, and he stands, rounding the desk to sit across from me in a matching wingback chair. "Tell me what interests you. We have so many options, you'd be surprised. I'm thinking about writing a memoir of my life and our family history here. I could use a research assistant if you're interested in that sort of thing."

Pressing my lips together, I try to think of the nicest way in the world to say I'm not really interested in research.

He reads my expression at once. "Or if you prefer retail, I'm certain Carmen would love to have your help at the store. She goes on buying trips to Atlanta several times a year, and I bet you have excellent taste."

Again, he sees the lack of enthusiasm in my failure to meet his gaze. No one ever believes I hate shopping.

"Ah, wait a minute!" He holds up a finger. "What was your major in college? Psychology?"

Chewing my lip, I nod. "But I don't have any clinical experience. I only got my bachelor's degree, so I don't know what I could do with it."

"Dirk is very into criminal psychology. He'll be teaching a course at the college this fall. Granted it's only a community college, but a lot of kids start there on their way to vocational training or larger universities."

I nod, unsure where he's going with this. "I don't think I'm qualified to teach."

"Probably not, but he could make you his assistant or even connect you with someone who could find a place for you." Leaning forward, he takes my hand in his. "We won't stop until we find something you like. If you want to stay here, you're going to stay."

"I do want to stay…" My mind drifts to Hutch, and I want to say I want to stay with him. "The last thing I want to do is be a burden or sit around doing nothing, like I expect someone to entertain me or…"

Marry me. The words flit across my brain, and just as fast, I shake them away. It's too soon and far too presumptive. I have to make my own way, and if more happens, so be it.

My uncle is on his feet, holding out his hand and escorting me to the kitchen. "Relax your mind. I'll be sure you get what you want, I promise. I got you this far, didn't I?" He gives me a mischievous wink, and I wonder if he can read my mind. "Now I have to make some calls."

He leaves, and my shoulders fall. Glancing at the clock, I realize I've got a little more time before I can even start to get ready for our date.

Norris is in the kitchen when I drop off my mug, scurrying around and preparing for the next grocery run. Down the steps to the basement, I notice the red light is on outside Hana's darkroom.

It was so odd to find a darkroom in the basement when we arrived. I don't remember there being one when we were children, but maybe I simply wasn't interested and didn't notice.

Arching my eyebrow, I glance overhead and wonder if it's

possible our uncle had it installed just for her. More incentive to keep us here. Shaking my head, I exhale a laugh. That tricky old man.

Tapping lightly on the door, I wait for her to give me the okay before entering. As soon as I step inside, my breath catches at all the oversized prints hanging on lines strung around the open space.

"Hana!" I step closer, amazed at the beauty of her work. Walking down the line, I can't believe my eyes. They're all different angles and unique saturations—I've never seen anything like it. "These are incredible."

I stop at a portrait-sized, black-and-white photo of three little outfielders with their gloves up, pretending to catch huge, sprinkled donuts. Their faces are delighted, and in their uniforms and pigtails, she could sell this so easily.

Hanging beside it is a series of images of me and Training Day. The first is black and white, but the white is so strong. The next is more of a halo around my face, cheek to cheek with the horse. It's like we're communicating, which I guess we sort of were.

The emotion she captured is palpable. My heart was so heavy that day, and the only thing that gave me comfort was the quiet animal—until Hutch appeared.

"These could easily be in a gallery." I look over to where her hair is tied up and wrapped in a red handkerchief. "Why haven't you shown them to anyone?"

She's in denim overalls and a white tank with yellow rubber gloves that go all the way to her elbows. "I showed some of them to Hutch."

"You did?"

"Mm-hm." Her voice is quiet as she moves a sheet of photo paper back and forth in a tray, and she tilts her head like she's surprised I didn't know.

I am surprised. "What did he say?"

"He said I have a unique talent and a good eye."

"That's the understatement of the century." I walk over and watch as the print she's developing slowly grows more distinct.

The image that appears is of Training Day's large black eyes and my lighter ones gazing out from a field of white. It's startling and breathtaking and somehow mystical.

"How did you do that?" I speak in a whisper.

Her lips twist as she holds up the dripping page, inspecting it a moment before carrying it to the clothesline. "It's just different exposure techniques. It's not hard, but you have to know what you're doing."

"Obviously, you know what you're doing."

"These are all finished." She flips on the lights. "I'll let them dry, and we can box up the ones of the players and give them to Coach Miller."

"You should keep some to show, I mean if you'd like to do a show."

Nodding, she starts for the door. "I will, but I always give the team their pictures. I'll get releases if I decide to do anything more with them."

I follow her up the stairs and through the kitchen, where she takes a piece of toast off a tray and carries it out to the side porch. The breeze is blowing, and it's getting warmer every day.

She sits in one of the rocking chairs, looking up at me, and as always, she seems to know what I'm thinking before I say a word.

"I don't want to go back to New York," she says before taking a bite of toast. "At least not to live. I could go there to visit or to show my work or something like that, but I never want to live there again."

Nodding, I lean against the rail across from her. "I talked to Uncle Hugh, and he wants us to stay here with him."

"How long?"

"Forever if you ask him." I exhale a little laugh. "He's

bending over backwards to find something to make me happy. I see you're clearly following your muse."

"I thought he'd already found something to make you happy. " She rocks slowly, her dark blue eyes studying my face.

My chin drops, and I'm suddenly self-conscious. "I don't know what you mean."

"Don't you?"

When I look up at her again, heat rises in my cheeks. "Hugh is old, and like most old people he loves playing match-maker. That doesn't mean he's right or the people he's trying to match up are going to follow his wishes or feel the way he wants them to feel." I'm saying too much, too fast. "How could he even know what anyone wants?"

My sister stands and puts her hand on my arm. "You've always been the smart one, the strong one, while I was the fuck-up. Take it from the fuck-up. He knows."

She leaves me on the porch with my stomach in knots. I want to scream, *I know! I want him to be right!* But I don't.

Pushing off the rail, I decide I'm not acting like myself at all. I am a controlled, strong woman, not a silly girl who obsesses over crushes. I'm going to follow the plan with Uncle Hugh, see what's out there for me to do in this teeny little town, and live my life.

And I need to start getting ready right now, because if I'm going to look as good as I want to look tonight, I need to shave my legs three times and curl my hair, and I have three different dresses I love—maybe I can get Hana to take pictures and we can vote on which makes me look hottest.

Either way, I have a lot to do and only... four hours to do it.

CHAPTER 34

Hutch

"I DON'T LIKE THIS BAD HABIT YOU'VE STARTED, WAKING ME UP AT this hour." My brother is scrounging around in his kitchen, grumpy because it's noon.

I shake my head. "I take it you pulled another all-nighter. What's the latest on Ivan X?" He straightens, holding a jar of instant coffee, and I recoil. "You're not drinking that shit, are you? Get dressed. I'll drive you to Steamy Beans."

Dirk sets down the coffee crystals, and he rakes his fingers through his wild brown hair before pulling on a cap. "Where's my shirt?"

Rush hour has ended for the coffee shop in town, and it's my brother and me and one other table having cinnamon in-fused coffee and scones.

"He's a sneaky bastard." Dirk takes a big bite of raspberry scone. "He's covering his tracks way better than he did with that blackmail scheme he pulled on Blake. Either he got wise or he was trying to get caught."

"Why would he try to get caught?"

"You're right. He's an idiot, but he's learning." Dirk leans back in his chair watching me. "Speaking of learning, I learned Uncle Hugh is looking for something for Blake to do in Hamiltown. Seems she wants to stick around, but she wants to have a reason."

My chest tightens, and I sit a little straighter. "What kind of reason?"

"Oh, I don't know, something that won't make it seem like she's waiting for a guy we all know to pop the fucking question. What the hell are you waiting on, man? You two couldn't be more made for each other."

"We've been together for two… three weeks? I can't propose—"

"You've known Blake your whole life. You had her sent to the nuns when you thought she was partying too much in high school."

"That's not why I did that—"

"Don't forget, you've been jerking off to her magazine spread for three years."

Anger flares in my chest, and he holds up his hands.

"I'm not saying *I've* been jerking off to her, but that was a hot pictorial." He lifts his mug. "What was she even selling? I only saw one thing." He takes a sip of coffee and holds up his fingers. "Sorry, two things."

"Now I'm going to kick your ass."

"See?" He points a finger at me, winking "There it is. She's your woman. You wouldn't want to rip my head off right now if she weren't." He shakes his head taking another bite of scone. "I'm only making a point, bro, shit. Breathe."

I do inhale, then exhale slowly. "The truth is, I've been thinking about it."

"So what's stopping you?"

"Pepper."

Our eyes meet, and he frowns. "You think she doesn't like Pep?"

"No, she likes her. I know she likes her, but there's a big difference in liking a kid and wanting to be her…" Shifting in my chair, I can't think of another way to say it. "Her mom."

"First, she'll never be Pepper's mom. Judy was Pepper's mom." I give him a look like, *No shit, Sherlock*, and he continues. "I get it. But I mean, I help you with the Pep. It's not like it's all on you."

"You're a good uncle. I appreciate it." I nod. "But when the shit hits the fan, Pepper's my responsibility. We're a package deal, and it's a lot to ask somebody, especially somebody like Blake. She's special."

"So fucking ask her. How else will you ever know?"

He's right, but I have another reason for waiting. "If she's not interested, our relationship will change. I'd like to enjoy spending time with her a little longer before I drive her away."

"You're not going to drive her away." Dirk leans forward. "I'm no expert in women by a long shot, but from what I've seen, Blake's not going anywhere. I'd bet my motorcycle on it. Now get off your ass and get that girl a ring."

Leaning back, it's the same thing Carmen said—almost. Whatever, there's only one way to know. I'm just not sure I'm ready if the answer is no.

"I'm thinking about giving her Mom's ring. If that's okay with you?"

He nods, finishing off his scone. "I like it. Hugh's always been like family. Blake is his niece. It's like she was meant to have it."

"Thanks, bro." I stand, leaving cash for the bill. "I've got some shit to do, need a ride back to your place?"

"Nah, I'm headed over to the office."

I'm headed back to the house, all the way back to the small, fireproof box I keep in the back of my closet. Taking it out, I move the papers aside, Pepper's birth certificate, my passport, and a small, velvet pouch.

Inside is the one thing I have left of my mom's, a ring she took off after we came back here and gave to me. She told me to only give it to someone I would be faithful to, who I'd treasure as deeply as my own soul.

It was the kind of love she dreamed of having, and I understood what she meant. I've been thinking about it for a while now, and I slip the small pouch in my wallet.

Sitting in my truck in Hugh's circle driveway, I've never felt more awkward. I'm in jeans and a button-down oxford, and in twenty years, I've never hesitated before marching up to that door. Hugh's house has always been my second home.

I quickly filter through all that's happened in the last month, hell, all that's happened in the last few years. This old man is like that guy in *The Wizard of Oz*, hiding behind the curtain, turning knobs and pulling levers.

He's orchestrated everything that's happened, from sending me to check on her to making me promise to keep her safe then getting out of Dodge. Dropping my chin, I exhale a chuckle. Damn, him. He's going to gloat so hard when he finds out what I'm planning to do tonight.

I grasp the door handle, ready to step out and get things moving, when the front door opens, and my breath stills in my throat. Blake steps out on the landing looking like something out of my hottest wet dream.

Her dark hair is shiny and loose over her shoulders, and she's wearing a red dress that hugs her curves like it was sewn on her. Her lips are pale pink, and her eyes are round and blinking quickly like she's as nervous as I feel—and as fed up with all this bullshit as I am.

Grabbing the reins, I get out and go to her, reaching for her waist and pulling her firmly into my arms like she belongs to me, because fuck it, she does.

I lean down and kiss the side of her jaw so I don't mess up her pretty lipstick. I can tell she spent some time on her look tonight, and she's rocking it.

"You are the most beautiful thing I've ever seen." Her body relaxes in my arms, and my certainty is complete. "You sure you want to go to Slim Harold's? I should take you someplace nicer. You're seriously incredible in this dress."

"You like it?" She looks down then up again, meeting my eyes with sparkles in hers. "I wanted a short skirt, but not too short for when you teach me to shag."

Hell, her sassy voice has my dick rising to life, especially when I remember her sweet little ass last night in that cheer-leader skirt. "Are you wearing underwear?"

Her head tilts, and she leans closer. "I'm wearing a thong. I didn't want to take any chances if I fell."

"I won't let you fall, baby." I pull her to me again, kissing her cheek a little closer to her lips this time. "Just hold onto me."

Slim Harold's is packed for a Friday night, and it's mostly the old-timers out on the floor doing their classic dance to every song that comes on the jukebox.

Blake is at a high-top table across from me. She's having the house specialty—thick-cut bologna sandwiches with fried corn on the cob. I literally can't believe she's eating this, con-sidering the cuisine I'm sure she grew up having.

I'm having a burger and fries, wishing we were at some-place a bit classier, but this is what she wanted.

She's turned in her chair, watching them with fascination.

"It's like a twist, but with a little jitterbug and a Charleston mixed in."

"I think they made it up."

"Of course they did! That's what makes it special." She laughs looking back at me, and her eyes are dancing.

I love that she's having fun here. We're in this crowded, hometown bar and grill, sharing this moment. I reach across the table, and she puts her hand in mine.

"Hey…" I'm not sure how to start this gracefully. "I've been thinking about us and where we stand now. I guess we have a few things to talk about."

She nods, shifting her entire body to face me. Her eyes are serious, like she's been thinking about it, too. "Okay," is all she says.

Clearing my throat, I just fucking say it. "I'd like us to be more, but there's something we have to discuss." She nods, and I continue. "Pepper is a part of my life—a permanent part— and I need to know how you feel about that, about me being responsible for her. I'm like her dad."

She blinks fast looking down like I've said something she didn't expect. My stomach sinks, and I feel like maybe we all got it wrong. It wouldn't be the first time I was out in left field with her. A spear of pain slices through my stomach, and *damn*, I don't want to end this with her yet, not yet.

Before I can start to backpedal, her pretty eyes meet mine again. "Hana is a real part of my life, a permanent one. How do you feel about that? I'm not her mom, but we've never had good parents."

My lips part, and shit, I was not expecting her to say that. Of course I knew Hana was a big part of her life, but it never occurred to me she might be as worried about her sister as I am about Pepper.

Sliding my thumb across her fingers, I lift her hands to my

lips, kissing her knuckles. For a moment I study her slim fingers, then I just fucking say it.

"I love you, Blake." Lifting my eyes, I'm surprised to see her blinking fast, like she might cry. *What the hell?* "Is that okay?"

I start to apologize if I said too much, but she's nodding before I finish my sentence.

Sliding out of my seat, I go to where she's perched on the tall chair and put my arms around her waist. She leans closer, resting her chin on my shoulder, and it's kind of perfect. The music is loud, and the crowd is having a good time dancing and enjoying the night. But in each other's arms, it's just the two of us.

"Your uncle said something to me the other day, and I get it now." She lifts her head to meet my eyes. "He said, we all take care of each other. It's what families do. There are always hazards in life, shit's always getting fucked up, but you have me, and I have you… and we have Dirk and Hugh and Lurlene and Carmen and hell, we even have Hana and Scar and Pepper."

Blake snorts a little laugh through her nose, dropping her chin. "That's a big group."

Reaching out I cup her chin with my finger and lift her face to mine. "Last night you thanked me for helping you, but I've always wanted to be your hero, Blake. Even when you hated me, I wanted to be there for you." I hesitate, and my brow furrows. "You're my lady."

She blinks quickly, her gorgeous face softening with a smile, and she slides her hand over my cheek, leaning closer to speak in my ear. "I love you, Hutch Winston."

Damn, if a little earthquake doesn't move through my chest.

"Come here." I lift her off the stool so she's standing in front of me, her cute head only reaching the center of my chest.

Lowering to one knee, I look up at her pretty face, watching her eyes go wide.

"Stop the music!" Carmen's voice rings through the crowd. "Something about to happen!"

The jukebox dies—I guess somebody unplugged it—and I notice the tone of the crowd has shifted. People are turning to see what's happening.

It's not really a celebrity event, but most of these people know me pretty well. They call at all hours of the night snitching on each other. It's one of those situations where they'll all be talking about us tomorrow.

Reaching into my pocket, I fish out the small pouch, fumbling with the strings holding it closed. The ring is a modest, two-carat, pear-shaped stone with little yellow diamonds around it like a starburst.

Holding Blake's hand, I decide I want to kiss it as much as anything, so I do. I press my lips to the top of her knuckles, and before I'm even done, she's fallen to her knees in front of me, sliding her hand through my hair and pressing her lips to my cheek.

"Are we really doing this?" she asks, meeting my eyes like she trusts me to know the right answer all the time. *God, I hope I never let her down.*

"Yeah, baby." I show her the ring. "My mom told me to give this ring to the person I'd always be faithful to, to the person I couldn't live without, to the person I'd love as deeply as my own soul. That person is you, Blake. Will you be my wife?"

She's nodding before I even finish my sentence, and I slide the slim band on her finger. "I love you so much. I'd love to be your wife."

I kiss her lips, but more than that, I pull her body to mine, wrapping her in my arms as the room explodes with cheering and clapping and the whole damn town acts like it's the Fourth of July.

Her arms are around my neck, and I feel her breathing fast. I feel her body shaking like she's crying, and I just want to hold her. I want to take her home and hold her in my arms all night, kiss her lips, smooth my hands in her hair, and feel her skin against mine.

"Let's dance!" she cries instead, hopping to her feet and pulling my hands so hard, I have to laugh.

So much for my sentimental shit, but we've got plenty of time for that.

"You want to learn to shag?" I'm ready to start our first lesson when Carmen pushes in between us.

"I knew it! I knew it at the donut shop! This is the biggest news to hit this town since…" She looks around, thinking. "Since ever!"

She's hugging my fiancée, and I'm leaning back with my arms crossed feeling pretty proud of myself. Hugh was right—this is a good plan.

Somebody restarts the jukebox, and up first is an old Christina song, the one about a genie in a bottle, and my beautiful sex kitten shimmies out onto the floor curling her fingers at me like she wants me to join her.

Old timers close in around her in pairs, doing their dance to whatever rhythm they can find, but Blake isn't paying attention to them. Her eyes are hot, and she does a little hip-shaking dance, when I reach her, she turns, moving that sexy little ass against my dick. Like I need a reason to crave her more.

I'm behind her, moving my hips with hers, and she leans back against my chest, pressing her lips to my neck. I turn her around, and when our eyes meet, it's pure fire.

She smiles, rising onto her tiptoes. "I can't wait to be your wife."

She's so hot, I'm ready to throw her over my shoulder. "Let's go home. I'll teach you that old dance tomorrow."

Our fingers lace, and I take my credit card out, leaving it on the table. We'll work out the bill tomorrow as well. So much time has gotten away from us, I don't want to lose another minute.

Her lips are at my ear, kissing my neck, whispering hot words to me the entire drive back to the house. We slip in the back way, and I'm thankful Pepper's spending night with a friend, because we're about to get loud.

I take her to the place where it all started, my bedroom. She's in my arms, in my bed, and I'm tracing my lips over every inch of skin I can find, rocking our bodies to the heights of ecstasy.

We're made for each other, and as I hold her in my arms, drifting to sleep, I know I'll always be her knight. I wasn't able to be a shiny, white one like in the fairytales. I'm flawed and not perfect, as much as I want to be.

What I am is a man who loves her, who's willing to put down his life for her. I'll do whatever it takes to keep her safe, and what's crazy is she wants to do the same for me.

Holding her sweet face against my chest, I stroke her soft hair as I press my lips against her forehead. We've faced our demons, and we've come out on top.

We've always been fearless, but before we were two halves of a perfect whole. Now we're titanium, creating something new and unstoppable. That's how it's going to be, the two of us, and our family, all of them, forever.

EPILOGUE
Blake

"**O**H EM GEE, CHECK IT OUT!" CARMEN IS LYING ON THE FLOOR of my bedroom, swiping through wedding dresses on my oversized iPad pro. "This is the one—it even has a cute little cheerleader style skirt. When you guys disappear from the reception, everyone will know why."

"Let me see." I temporarily leave my own preparations to see what she's found. "That's hot. But would it be appropriate for the groom to be sporting a woody in front of all our friends and family?"

"Who knew Mr. Tall, Dark, and Stubborn was so into cheerleaders?"

"Have you ever met a guy who wasn't into cheerleaders?" I swipe a little more, pausing on a short, white dress with a deep, V-neck and flowing sleeves. "Oh, I love this one. This might be the one."

"Yes! With your hair all gathered up in a messy bun with tendrils and a long, white veil." Carmen falls back, holding her chest. "It'll be breathtaking. We should do it out at the beach, barefoot. The breeze blowing, the waves crashing—"

"We've got plenty of time to plan. The wedding is six months away. Hana's birthday is this weekend. Would you focus?"

"Okay." She sits up, putting the iPad on my bed and immediately picking up a book I forgot to put away. "Don't tell me you played it?"

Her lips press together, and she's on the verge of bursting into laughter. It's the board book with a giant hole in the center, and the title *Penis Pokey* in a bright red banner across the top.

My face flames red, and I grab it out of her hands. "What's that doing out? Pepper might find it."

"Oh, no, you're not getting off that easy. Did you play it? I want all the details."

I give the hall a quick glance before closing the door and turning back with a snort. "Nobody got off easy. It was awful. He's too big for the hole!"

Her eyes widen comically, and she squeals, pointing to the book. "Bigger than that? Holy shit."

"I mean, not at first, but once we got going…" Covering my face with my hands, I shriek, "It got stuck, and we couldn't get it off. It's a freaking board book."

"What did you do?" She bounces onto her knees.

Leaning back, I give her a smug grin. "I mean, I couldn't leave him like that. I had to help him finish with my mouth."

"Ew!" She throws the book at me, and I catch it fast, laughing more.

"It's not dirty. I swallowed!"

"I swear to God, you are too good for him." She shakes her head, going to the desk, where I have my plans for Hana's party on my laptop. "Hutch Winston was the most uptight, controlled, never crack a smile… hard ass. You're shaking that up for sure."

Sliding the book in my drawer, I remember that first night I walked in to find him in the shower moaning my name. "He shook me up pretty good, too. He's everything I've ever wanted."

"Now you're just gloating." She waves me away. "Let's get back to Hana's birthday before I go home and have a pity party."

"We'll find you a man, don't worry." I pat her back. "Maybe he'll be shagging at the party."

"Maybe I'll shag *him* at the party." She cocks an eyebrow, and I wave her away.

"Not until after we cut the cake. Now, what do you think about this design?"

I show her a top hat cake with sparklers on top and tiny champagne bottles lining the sides.

"These are so cute." She leans closer. "I've never seen bedazzled champagne bottles."

"This service will come and decorate the main house with iridescent beaded curtains and black lights. They'll even use these iridescent balloons, so the whole thing will be like bubbles and celebration. I want to have her name and *Happy Birthday* spelled out in pink roses. They're her favorite, and I love these camera party favors. Read the tags."

Carmen lifts the pink card attached to the camera. *"Help me remember tonight.* I love it. This is going to be the talk of Hamiltown. Everybody and their sister are going to be copying what you've done here."

"I hope she likes it." Leaning back, I pick up my phone. "Hana's had enough sadness in her life, and I don't know if she even remembers half her birthdays. I want this one to be memorable—in the best way."

"What are you getting her?"

My chest squeezes, and I grab Carmen's hands, pulling her to the bed to sit across from me. "It's a big surprise. Can you keep a secret?"

"Nope." She shakes her head, frowning. "But tell me, and I'll avoid Hana like the plague until her birthday."

That makes me snort, but I can't keep a secret either. "I have a friend, Erin, she's a curator at the Milo gallery in New York. I sent her some of Hana's photographs, and she's going to arrange for her to have a show there pretty much whenever she chooses. Erin thinks she can get a lot of buzz going for it, especially with our family connections and all."

I stop to breathe, and I feel the flush in my cheeks. Carmen's eyes are wide, and she chews her lip. "That's a good thing, right?"

"Yes!" I cry. "It's a great thing. It's her introduction to the art world."

"I'm sorry!" Carmen covers her eyes. "I don't know anything about the art world. I don't know how it works."

"It's a really good thing. It usually takes a long time for artists to get a show, and then they have to have built some kind of buzz or know somebody…"

"Sounds like Hana knows the perfect somebody." Carmen pets my arm. "Her awesome big sister!"

"Stop it." I give her a little nudge with my shoulder. "What did you get her?"

"I found the cutest little camera bag. I know she doesn't need it, but I only know one thing she really wants. Besides your thing, of course."

My brow furrows, and I feel like I missed something. "What?"

"Seriously? You don't know the one thing your sister wants for her birthday?"

Shaking my head, I'm at a loss until Carmen levels her dark

brown eyes on mine. "I'll give you a hint. He's six-foot-four, solid muscle, scary as fuck, so fucking hot it's scary."

"Oh," I exhale a nervous laugh. "Hutch said he would tell Scar about the party. Then he told me Scar's not much for parties. I don't know if that means he's not coming or if he'll come and scowl the whole time."

"Shocker," Carmen deadpans. "I'm certain he'll be there, though. Your little sister has that beast wrapped around her pixie finger."

"I guess it's okay. He's just—he's Hutch's age, and Hutch is five years older than me."

"She's legal now, friend. The little bird is going to fly."

"Trust me, I know." Picking up my phone, I tap in the number for the party service. "She's been flying a long time."

The oversized dogtrot between the main house and the carriage house is lined in an array of iridescent streamers, balloons, black lights, and sparklers, and party music drifts outside on the breeze. Uncle Hugh is inside with Carmen and her mother and the entire softball team.

Several girls from town who've posed for Hana are here, and I'm outside in the breezeway, waiting for my sister to come down from the main house when Hutch's warm voice greets me from behind.

"I think you get sexier every time I see you." Warm hands span my waist, and I turn as a swirl of butterflies fills my stomach.

"Hey, handsome, how was your day?" Sliding my arms around his neck, I meet his lips with mine, kissing him briefly before gazing up at his gorgeous face.

"Sheesh—I'm going inside." Pepper dashes through the door at the end of the alley, through an arch of pale pink roses and past by a wall of more pale pink roses reading *Happy Birthday, Hana.*

My nose wrinkles and I return to kiss my fiancé once more. "I might've gone a little overboard with the roses."

"It does look a little like the Rose Bowl parade." He chuckles, kissing me back. "But it's her favorite flower."

"True." Sliding my hands down his arms, I lace our fingers. "Maybe she can use them in her work. She's been taking pictures nonstop since I gave her my gift. I think it might have freaked her out a little bit."

"I have an idea. She could take some pictures of you in that white cheerleader skirt, nothing else, these roses." He squints one eye and puckers his lips in a way that makes my core squeeze. "Hot."

Rising onto my toes, I kiss him again. "We don't need Hana to create that scene. I can steal some of these tonight."

"How long did you say we have to stay at this party?"

My nose wrinkles, and I laugh. "I told Carmen she has to stay until the cake is cut."

"Let's get cutting."

I'm about to tell him to stop when the heavy thump of boots on the wood floor interrupts us. "There's a bunch of little girls inside."

Turning, I take a step away, pressing my back to Hutch's chest. "Scar, hey, um, yeah, the softball girls wanted to come. They've all gotten really close from Hana taking their pictures at the games and stuff. They won't stay long."

"I won't stay long." He blinks down at me with those icy, wolf eyes. "Where's Hana?"

"Is somebody looking for me?" My sister's voice is high and clear.

She skips up in an ivory Chanel shorts set. The shorts are all the way up her slim thighs, and she's wearing a matching cardigan in the same color over her matching tube top. Her long, spiral curls fall behind her shoulders, and her cheeks are pink and full. She looks really good, and healthy, and I see the smolder in Scar's eyes when he looks down at her.

She's only gotten stronger as the months have passed in Hamiltown. "I thought you were still in New York." Hana walks straight to him, holding out her hand.

He takes it in both his large ones before leaning down to kiss her cheek. "Happy birthday, baby girl."

My stomach tightens, and I pull Hutch's arms around my shoulders. He keeps telling me Scar won't hurt her, and I can only trust him.

For Hana's part, she's completely unfazed by his size or appearance. "I don't think you heard. I'm twenty-one now. I'm not a baby anymore."

Scar's brow relaxes, and he almost smiles. "You've still got a lot of living to do."

She slides both her hands in the crook of his arm, and a hint of sadness touches her voice. "I've done a lot of living already." It's gone just as fast, and she smiles, shouting, "Take me to the party—I want a glass of champagne. I can finally, *legally* have a drink!"

"Finally," I laugh, slipping my hand in her arm and pulling her to me for a brief kiss. "Happy birthday, sis. I'm so proud of you."

She releases the big guy and puts her arm around my shoulder, pressing her head to mine. "This is so beautiful. Thank you for everything."

Inside the little players are running around eating cupcakes and batting balloons at each other. The music is a mix of dance music and DJ bangers, and after ten minutes, Hana runs back to the house to get her camera.

We're all drinking champagne, watching the kids play, and Hana takes pictures of her guests in an array of poses—with the flowers, with the cake, with the balloons, outside and inside.

Hutch grabs my hand when a Buddy Holly song comes on, and he leads me through my beginner shag moves.

"You're getting it!" Carmen cries, and I grab her in a laugh.

"I would never have expected you could do that." She laughs up at Hutch, who only shrugs.

"My mom loved that dance. She expected Dirk and me to dance with her on Saturday nights in the kitchen."

The thought of it warms my heart, and I think about dancing in the kitchen with him. "Where is Dirk?"

I look around, and Scar answers. "He asked me to tell Hana happy birthday for him. He's sorry he couldn't make it. He's following a lead, and I'm actually going back to help him."

My sister's pale brow furrows, and she goes to where he's standing. "You're leaving?"

He touches her chin with his thumb. "You look really pretty tonight."

"Can't you stay a little while longer?" her voice is soft, and he shakes his head.

"I have to keep my promise to you. I'll see you soon." His eyes flicker to her lips, and her tongue touches her bottom one.

One more moment of hesitation, and he turns, leaving us all to start breathing again.

"Phew, happy birthday to you," Carmen mutters, taking Hana's arm. "Let's get another champagne. I'm all heated up."

Another hour, and we cut the cake. It's time for the little girls to go home, but the party's only getting started. Hutch and I use Pepper as an excuse to get away, and I grab a few bunches of pale pink roses, slipping them into my bag on the way out.

With Pepper tucked in her bed and Hutch and me down the stairs and on the other side of the house, I change quickly out of the beige party dress I was wearing and into that white cheerleader skirt I keep at his place now.

Arranging the roses while he brushes his teeth, I'm completely topless when he emerges from the bathroom in those gray sweats I love that leave nothing to the imagination. For example, I can see how much he likes what he sees right away.

"Hang on." He takes out his phone and snaps a picture of me lying on my stomach with my back arched to show cleavage and my feet bent behind me.

"How about this?" I roll onto my back, lifting two of the roses and holding them over my breasts so they just cover the areolas.

"Damn." He walks closer, taking another photo, and I roll onto my stomach again, reaching down to slide the hem of my skirt higher, revealing my lack of underwear.

"Your favorite."

"Hell, yeah." He tosses the phone aside, grabbing my calf and pulling me down to the side of the bed.

My shriek turns to a moan when he buries his face in the back of my legs, dragging his tongue from my clit to my core. Just as fast, he flips me over and spreads my thighs, running his eyes slowly from my pussy up to my breasts then to my eyes, where he gives me a little grin and shakes his head.

"I'm about to make you feel so good."

A bubble bursts in my stomach, making me laugh and I squirm in anticipation. "I know you will."

His mouth covers me, and my back arches as my eyes close in a loud moan. We're just getting started, and it is so good. He takes me from the front and from behind, against the wall and over the bathroom sink in front of the mirror, which by the way, is so damn hot. I love watching his muscles flex and his tattoos ripple as the sweat traces down his face, and when he comes, he takes me to the moon.

Lying in his oversized bed with his muscled arm around

my waist and his lips at my temple, I think about the future and the beautiful things that lie ahead for us.

Hutch likes to remind me I'm not alone anymore. Together, we're forming a big, new family where we all look out for each other.

My uncle said Hutch has always been like a son to him, and now he's becoming his nephew. Our families truly are joined.

It's a new experience to be surrounded by so much love. It's a new experience not to have to be afraid or to look over my shoulder. I spent the first part of my life having to be fearless, because I was alone. Now I have someone, and he's such an amazing someone to have.

I'm still strong, but with my gorgeous knight at my side and my new family, I feel powerful enough to face any obstacles. We still have bad guys to find and questions to answer, but I'm confident in the end, we're going to win.

Thank you for reading *Fearless*!

Up next is **Filthy**, Hana & Scar's angsty, spicy-hot romance. Also available on Audio.

Keep turning for a sneak peek…

FILTHY

Good girls are saved by princes, but my savior is a monster.

After my father died and my family splintered, I became a target, a pawn in a game I didn't know I was playing.
Then he appeared—dark, dangerous, tormented, and always just within reach.
He makes me come alive. He makes me remember.
He makes me feel something I lost years ago: *Safe*.
And he thinks he can keep me at arm's length.

Once upon a time I was a hero, until the sins of my father caught up with me, and I was forced into darkness.
I should've died in that fire. Instead, I served evil men, until I risked it all by walking away.
Now I'm a wanted man. At any time, I could be taken down for what I owe.
What I don't expect to find in my hiding place is her—broken, beautiful, so damn tempting.
I was hired to keep her safe. I shouldn't touch her with my filthy hands.
But every day it gets harder, then she starts sneaking into my bed.

Together, we're filthy, but together, we can find our way through the flames.

(FILTHY is a stand-alone, bodyguard, romantic suspense novel. It contains a fierce, wounded alpha-protector and the damaged young woman he's hired to save. No cheating. No cliffhangers.)

PROLOGUE

Oskar

Seven years ago

WIND WHIPS THROUGH THE CAB OF OUR MILITARY-ISSUE RANGE Rover, and we're traveling home in peace, no assignments left to complete.

My elbow is propped on the open window, and the unusually warm breeze twists loose strands of my hair around my eyes, hidden behind aviator sunglasses.

My partner Hutchence Winston, or Hutch as everyone calls him, is light. He's finished, retiring from active duty after four years in country.

I don't share his status, and my mood is not as light.

"Varna's a far cry from what you expected when you got here four years ago." Glancing at him, I consider all we've seen in our time together. I consider how it will be when he's gone, and my stomach pinches with sadness. "No black and white ice deserts or peasants standing in bread lines."

"Was I that much of a stereotype?" Hutch laughs, gripping

the steering wheel as the vehicle takes a hard bounce over the rough terrain into Bucharest.

"You were just another American."

Hutch is a typical, bold Marine. He's big, although not as tall as me. He's stubborn and a natural leader, but unlike the other Marines I've encountered, he doesn't act like he knows everything or like Langley is the center of the universe.

We're actually good friends.

"This country is beautiful… when it's not trying to freeze you to death. Which isn't often enough for my taste." He glances from the road to me. "Sure you don't want to come back with me? You are an American, after all."

An old bitterness twists in my chest at his words. "Only on paper, my friend. America is a stranger to me now."

"Only a stranger if you don't have friends, and you have them."

Lifting my chin, I look away, out the window. I have no reason to be loyal to this place. Without explanation, my father dumped me here at the age of six, to be raised by strangers who were promised a pension to keep me alive. I grew up no better than a foster child with a resentful family waiting for their monthly check.

I was hidden away from my family, my friends, until I was nothing.

Alone, I taught myself to hunt, to shoot, to use tools and build things by hand. I learned geography and where the moneyed class went for holidays. I studied and went to college, and as soon as I was old enough, I joined the military and eventually found myself working with the Americans, tracking down terrorists and flushing out spies.

"That paper is all you need." Hutch pulls me back to the present. "I could use you in the States. You're the best tracker I know, and one of the few people I'd trust with my life."

I feel the same about him, but I don't say it out loud. He

doesn't need to know my reasons for staying, about the letter burning a hole in my pocket.

"It's not so easy to drop everything and leave for a whole different country."

The letter arrived last night via special courier. It was hand-written on expensive stationery bearing a Muscovite stamp. I read it quickly, then stuffed it in my pocket as I tried to make sense of the words. None of it made sense.

It was from a man named Simon Petrovich, and it said my time had come. I had to take my place in line, pay my dues. It said I couldn't run from who I am.

Who am I?

Dipping my chin, I look out at the barren terrain. "I have unfinished business."

Hutch doesn't miss a beat, letting out a low chuckle before turning the wheel onto a narrow, country road. "Any chance that business has long hair and soft curves?"

He's joking, and I'm about to reply when my eye catches on a column of smoke off the road up ahead. Dread pits my stomach as we get closer, and I see a crowd gathered in the parking lot surrounding a one-story building.

"What's that?" The closer we get, the less I have to ask.

"Krasivoy Kafe?" Hutch downshifts, reading the sign, and we turn into the parking lot.

Hopping out fast, we join the crowd surrounding the white-planked structure. Black smoke pours out of the large, glass windows, and the heat forces us all to step back.

Firetrucks are nowhere to be seen, and the restaurant is going up like a box of tinder.

"What happened?" I shout in Russian as we locate a paunchy man with a tag indicating he's a manager. His hair is slicked with sweat and his white, button-down shirt stretches over his swollen belly.

"We got as many out as we could," he shouts in Russian, face lined.

A woman in a black trench coat with long pearl earrings runs to where Hutch and I stand, frantically pulling my arm. "My daughter is trapped inside! Please, you have to save her!"

My chest tightens, and I look to Hutch. He's waiting for me to translate.

"Kitchen fire?" I ask in Russian.

The man turns his wide eyes on me, like I asked him why grass is green. "What else?"

"Please," The woman jerks my arm again. "She went to the bathroom, and they dragged me out…"

I can't believe anyone could still be alive, but I don't see flames—only thick smoke. A small cry meets my ears, and my jaw clenches.

"Oh my God!" the woman screams. "My father has money, connections…"

"The firemen are on their way." The man's black eyes meet mine.

"It will be too late!" she screams

"God will save her little soul," the man says.

Fuck. My shirt is over my head while he's still speaking, and Hutch is right behind me. "What the fuck are you doing?"

"A little girl is trapped inside." I'm not a hero. I've never been the type of guy to run into a burning building, but that little voice will haunt me forever if I do nothing.

"Oskar, stop." Hutch is right beside me. "You're not prepared for this."

"You should know, Marine, we're never prepared for hell." I twist my long hair in a bun, tucking it under a beanie, then I dunk my shirt in a nearby bucket of water and squeeze it over my head.

"Cover your face." Hutch shoves his canvas jacket over

my torso. "Bring her to me here. If you get disoriented, listen for my voice."

Diving through the window, I'm immediately disoriented. Thick black smoke steals my breath and my vision. I drop to my knees, coughing as I crawl across the open dining area.

Fire roars from the kitchen like a freight train overhead, and I follow the path to the back where the bathrooms would be.

It's closer to the kitchen, and the heat is overwhelming. Panic constricts my lungs.

Pausing to center my mind, I close my eyes and force calm, remember my training, my instincts… and listen. A whimpering cry is to my left, and I dash in that direction, pulling up short as a flaming board slams to the ground in front of me.

With a lunge, I reach him. A little boy is huddled in a corner.

"Come here," I say in Russian, but I don't wait for his cooperation. Bending to scoop him up, pain flashes through my shin. "Shit! Don't kick me!"

He's in my arms, but at my full height, the smoke is disorienting.

"Hutch?" I yell.

Faintly, through the darkness, I hear my name and run for it. When I reach my partner, he takes the boy as I dive through the opening.

"No little girl." I drop to my knees, gulping at fresh air. "I didn't make it to the bathroom. It's too hot–I'm afraid it's too late."

"Please!" The woman's face distorts as tears streak her cheeks. "My father has so much money. He will give you all the money you want."

"What good is money if you're dead?" The manager shouts at her.

The woman's eyes go wild, and she lunges forward as if

she'll run into the building. Hutch catches her around the waist, and she crumples in his arms, crying "No…"

My chest burns hotter than the fire at her display of grief. I don't know if the cry I heard was the little boy or her daughter. I only know I have to try one more time.

Turning on my heel, I charge again into the burning darkness. It's more of the same–heat, blindness, impossible to breathe–only now I feel light-headed from smoke inhalation.

I can't pass out. I have to hold on a little longer.

The roar of burning is sliced by a loud groan overhead. The beams holding up the roof are almost burned through, and the clock is ticking. I'm on a fool's errand. A child in here this long would have certainly inhaled too much smoke or succumbed to the heat.

Giving the room one final sweep, I hear Hutch screaming for me to get out when my eyes land on hers across the dining room. Oversized dark eyes, pale, ashy hair. She's so tiny, crouched in the corner, watching me as if from another plane of existence.

She doesn't seem traumatized or overcome. She seems to be waiting for me to save her, wondering why it took me so long.

Another loud groan echoes overhead, and holding my forearm over my nose and mouth, I look up to see the rafters wavering precariously. It's going to fall on us. A load-bearing beam crumbles like a broken toothpick.

I'm out of time.

Closing the space, I scoop her up and hold her close as I pump my legs, running hard, frantic to get to safety before it's too late. Her small head tucks beneath my chin, and her little hand clings to my arm.

My heart pounds in my chest. I'm not going to make it.

I *have* to make it. I can't let her die.

Hutch's green eyes stand out in the black soot covering his

face. They're twisted in horror as another loud groan turns into a long rip. The roof is coming down. I have no choice but to throw her. Tiny nails scratch my skin as I rip her from my chest.

It's a sensation I'll never forget, her cry a sound that will echo in my mind.

"Oskar!" Hutch's shout is the last word I remember.

Flashes of light, of pain, so much pain.

Crying, roaring, screaming.

Then black.

I'm on my stomach in a hospital bed with bandages over my eyes. Hutch's voice is at my side, but it's several days before I register what he said to me.

"I can't stay any longer, friend." He sounds so troubled. "I've got to get back to my family. Come find me when you're well. I'll have a place for you."

But the little girl… *What happened to the little girl?*

It's mist and shadows. The pain medication keeps me in a dreamlike state, and I count time by the nurses tending to me. One speaks in Russian, saying my first round of skin grafts was very successful. She places a device in my hand and says to press the white button if the pain becomes too great.

Her tone is light, and she says I'm a hero. She says everyone in the city is talking about me.

"The little girl–" My voice is thick from lack of use. "Is she alive?"

"Her family came to thank you, to give you money. Your American friend spoke to them. He told them you were not able to see anyone."

She's moving things around, rustling papers. She keeps talking, saying my picture is all over the Internet, on the news, in magazines. *No, fuck no,* I think before a wall of pain hits me so hard, I press the button, passing out as the meds drench my system.

The bandages are off my eyes now, and someone has placed a mirror below me tilted toward the window. I assume so I'll have a view of the sky and trees. I want to see my face, my body, but I'm unable to move in this bed. At least the pain has subsided, and I no longer hold the device with the small, white button.

"You're very lucky." A man speaks in Russian at my bedside as if conjured from nothing. "Your face and hands were spared. You're unscarred from the waist down."

A long stretch of silence follows, and I feel I should say something. "Thank you."

"I'm signing your release order. Your skin grafts are nearly healed, and you will continue to improve with time."

Release order. I'm able to leave, but where do I go? The last thing I remember is the letter, but I'm sure whatever it was about has expired or been forgotten.

"Your bill is paid in full, and your relative brought you clothes." He places a yellow sheet on a nearby chair. "When you're ready, you're free to go."

My brow furrows—what relative?

He leaves, and I realize I can get out of the bed. Placing my hands on the sides of the mattress, I'm stiff and sore, and bandages cover my torso and arms.

Stepping to the mirror over the sink, I recoil at my reflection. My beard is unkempt, and my hair is dirty and matted. My eyes are white-blue, stark against the darkness of my skin, and at the tops of the bandages I see the destruction. Melted bits of skin not quite covered with gauze. I look like I've been to hell and met the devil.

Only I was wrong, the devil is here to meet me.

My door opens, and a short man with flat blue eyes and

light brown hair enters the room. He isn't smiling. His face is unlined, as if he's never smiled a day in his life.

I tower over him, and in these bandages, my crazy beard in need of a trim, and my wild hair, I imagine I look like a demon.

"Get dressed." He speaks English with a slight accent. "You'll stay in Minsk until you're well enough to assume your post in New York."

"You're supposed to be my relative?"

Dead eyes blink up to me, and he nods briefly. "Simon Petrovich." He produces a document that looks suspiciously like a birth certificate. "Your father gave you to me long ago when he could no longer pay his debts. You're in my service now."

"Why am I meeting you for the first time today?"

"It was supposed to be six weeks ago. This pointless act is costing me time."

Pointless act. "I'm not going with you. I don't know you, and I owe you nothing."

His voice lowers to a growl. "If it weren't for me, you'd be dead along with your entire family. Now you'll get your strength back and go to my brother in New York. He needs a bodyguard, and you'll do nicely."

Hesitating, I turn the paper over and back. "My last name is Lourde, not Petrovich. You are not related to me. If you provided for me financially, I thank you, but this is not legally binding."

Another cold smile stretches Simon's lips. "You look at me and think, I am not afraid of this man. I have rights. I am a hero. I am somebody."

"I don't think I'm a hero."

"You are nobody. You are a freak and a monster, and you will follow my orders or I will have you arrested for war crimes and executed."

"War crimes?"

"You aided the Americans in the destruction of several hospitals on the border of Belarus. Innocent civilians were killed, your countrymen."

"I did no such thing–"

"Your arguments are pointless. You will take your place in my service or you will not take another breath." Turning his wrist over, he glances at his watch. "I'll see you in the car."

He leaves me to finish pulling on the soft-knit pants and long-sleeved shirt. The fabric is clearly expensive, and the weave is loose to cover my bandages. From everything Simon has said, he's clearly very wealthy, which means he's dangerous.

I'm too weak to fight, and Russian thugs can be problematic. For now, I'll go to Minsk and get stronger, then I'll see what this bodyguard duty entails. I'm not afraid to walk away, but I want to have a fighting chance before I gamble my life.

Get FILTHY today, and fall in love with this wounded alpha-protector and the damaged, beautiful girl who saves him.

★Also available on Audio.

BOOKS BY TIA LOUISE

ROMANCE IN KINDLE UNLIMITED

THE BRADFORD BOYS
The Way We Touch, 2024*
The Way We Play, Oct. 2024*
The Way We Score, Jan. 2025*
The Way We Run, 2025*
The Way We Win, 2025*
(*Available on Audiobook.)

THE BE STILL SERIES
A Little Taste, 2023*
A Little Twist, 2023*
A Little Luck, 2023*
A Little Naughty, 2024*
(*Available on Audiobook.)

THE HAMILTOWN HEAT SERIES
Fearless, 2022*
Filthy, 2022*
For Your Eyes Only, 2022
Forbidden, 2023*
(*Available on Audiobook.)

THE TAKING CHANCES SERIES

*This Much is True**
*Twist of Fate**
*Trouble**
(*Available on Audiobook.)

FIGHT FOR LOVE SERIES

*Wait for Me**
*Boss of Me**
*Here with Me**
*Reckless Kiss**
(*Available on Audiobook.)

BELIEVE IN LOVE SERIES

Make You Mine
*Make Me Yours**
*Stay**
(*Available on Audiobook.)

SOUTHERN HEAT SERIES

When We Touch
When We Kiss

THE ONE TO HOLD SERIES

*One to Hold (#1—Derek & Melissa)**
*One to Keep (#2—Patrick & Elaine)**
*One to Protect (#3—Derek & Melissa)**
One to Love (#4—Kenny & Slayde)
One to Leave (#5—Stuart & Mariska)
*One to Save (#6—Derek & Melissa)**
*One to Chase (#7—Marcus & Amy)**
One to Take (#8—Stuart & Mariska)
(*Available on Audiobook.)

THE DIRTY PLAYERS SERIES
*PRINCE (#1)**
*PLAYER (#2)**
DEALER (#3)
THIEF (#4)
(*Available on Audiobook.)

THE BRIGHT LIGHTS SERIES
Under the Lights (#1)
Under the Stars (#2)
Hit Girl (#3)

COLLABORATIONS
*The Last Guy**
The Right Stud
*Tangled Up**
(*Available on Audiobook.)

PARANORMAL ROMANCES
One Immortal (vampires)
One Insatiable (shifters)

GET THREE FREE STORIES!
Sign up for my New Release newsletter and never miss a sale
or new release by me!

ACKNOWLEDGMENTS

In case you were wondering, yes, launching a brand-new world is daunting and very scary. Thank God I'm surrounded by a group of hugely supportive people cheering me on and anxiously awaiting this new adventure. I don't know how I'd do it without you! (That includes _you_, dear reader!)

As for the team behind the scenes, I am so grateful for my husband "Mr. TL" for his encouragement, brainstorming support, and insightful critiques. You're my rock.

Thanks to my beautiful daughters who aren't so little anymore, but still believe in me and support me from afar. I love you ladies!

Thanks so much to my alpha readers Renee McCleary, Maria Black, and Ilona Townsel for your encouragement and feedback in the early stages. You guys are invaluable to me.

Huge thanks to my awesome betas, Jennifer Christy, Amy Reierson, Courtney Anderson, Amanda Shepard, and Britni Van for your enthusiasm and fantastic notes!

Thanks to Lori Jackson for the gorgeous cover design, to Wander Aguiar for the ideal, sexy Hutch, and to Stacy Blake for the perfect paperbacks!

Thanks to my dear Starfish, to my Mermaids, and to my Veeps for keeping me sane and motivated while I'm in the writing cave.

I can't begin to put into words how much I appreciate the love and support of all the book bloggers/tokers/gramers, of my author-buds, and of my readers, friends, and family. I love you guys!

I hope you all devour this new adventure and come back begging for MORE! I confess, I'm a little obsessed with these guys.

Stay sexy,

<3 Tia

ABOUT THE AUTHOR

Tia Louise is the *USA TODAY* best-selling, award-winning author of super-hot and sexy romances. She'll steal your heart, make you laugh, melt your kindle… and have you begging for more!

Signed Copies of all books online at:
http://smarturl.it/SignedPBs

Connect with Tia:

www.TiaLouise.com
Instagram (@AuthorTLouise)
TikTok (@TheTiaLouise)
On Facebook?

Be a Mermaid! Join Tia's Reader Group at
"Tia's Books, Babes & Mermaids"!

allnightreads@gmail.com